D1395675

# No
# Ordinary
## *Love*

## Sonia Mael

PARTRIDGE

**To order additional copies of this book, contact**
Toll Free 800 101 2657 (Singapore)
Toll Free 1 800 81 7340 (Malaysia)
orders.singapore@partridgepublishing.com

www.partridgepublishing.com/singapore

*Love, in all its manifestations,*
*is an integral part of life.*

—*Sonia Mael*

# CONTENTS

# PROLOGUE

HE HURLED THE vase vehemently across the room. It landed on the floor with a crash and splintered into tiny smithereens. She looked at him in alarm, her eyes wide with shock and disbelief.

"Josh!" she cried, appalled at such unprecedented behaviour.

Josh's face turned deathly white. Heavily he lowered himself onto the nearest chair, weak at the knees, and covered his ashen face with shaky hands.

"Oh, my love," he moaned, his voice laced with desperation and regret, "I've become like him."

They had returned from a birthday bash of one of their friends. She had enjoyed herself tremendously, her face flushed with exertion, having changed dance partners often as the music blared throughout the night, not realizing that Josh was standing on the side animatedly talking to his friends, while from the corners of his eyes he was watching her, his heart consumed with jealousy.

"Become like whom, darling?" she questioned, going down on her knees in front of him, her hands stroking his arms with immense tenderness.

"Like whom, Josh?" she repeated insistently when he didn't answer her immediately.

He removed his hands from his face and looked down at her with eyes that betrayed his own shock at the horrendous implication of his action, pupils dilated, lips trembling. Obviously, he too was sickened by his own behaviour.

"My father," he answered, his voice so soft she could barely hear him.

"Why?" she queried. "What did he do?"

"He was a perverted son of a bitch," he replied with vehemence, to her consternation. Josh had never uttered any profanity in the months they had been together. He had always been gentle, considerate and tender to her. His voice rose an octave. "What didn't he do! My mother bore the brunt of his anger and jealousy all her life."

To her dismay, she began to realize that Josh didn't fancy seeing her dancing with other men and had allowed his jealousy to get the better of him.

"I'm sorry, Josh. Your behaviour was most unnerving. I didn't think you would have been annoyed at such innocent fun," she replied, feeling a faint disquiet at his unreasonable attitude.

"I shouldn't be, Kat," he replied, now concerned that *she* would be aggravated by his display of bad temper. He took her hands in his and made an attempt at an apology, his eyes silent mirrors that reflected the depth of his misery and compunction.

"Please forgive me, Kat. It just assailed me all of a sudden. Before I realized it, I had given way to my frustrations and anger that had been simmering while we were at the party."

She realized that he too was dismayed by his own shocking response. "Josh, we need to talk about this. Come and sit by the window while I make us a drink," she coaxed him.

That night, for the first time since they had discovered their love for one another, Josh bared his soul to her. If previously he had been uncommunicative and withdrawn about his background, his family and his younger days, now everything was thrown open, with no holds barred. Little by little, he related the pain and anguish that he had suffered since he was a little boy, for a long time buried deeply in his subconscious, which he was too ashamed to confide in anyone. Only with her gentle ministrations and by looking at her tender eyes was he able to dislodge those banked-down, horrific memories of his distant past, desolation in the depths of his eyes, his voice hoarse with the pain of remembrance.

"We lived in the working class area of Croydon. My father was a truck driver who travelled a great deal on his job," he began. "Our life was peaceful and normal while he was away, but when he came home, it was hell." He drew a long and painful breath, which ended in a sob. "He would celebrate his off days with visits to the pub, and when he became inebriated, he was a total monster. Every little mistake annoyed him, a word or a gesture would make him angry, and Mom would be the recipient. Any slight, real or imagined, would arouse his ire and bubble over into violence." He sighed as he returned the pressure of her hands for she felt his pain. "I tried to help Mom once, and he smacked me so hard that I was knocked down and my head hit the dining table." He laughed mirthlessly. "He was so contrite that night that he stopped drinking for two days."

He frowned as he recalled, "The thing is, once he realized his mistake, he would be filled with self-reproach and remorse. He would apologize profusely, but given a day or two, the cycle would begin again."

"You didn't lodge a police report?" she prodded quietly.

"Mom didn't want to, and she forbade me from doing it," he answered. "She didn't want to be ridiculed by the neighbours. She always thought it was her failure as a wife that made him abusive towards her."

"How old were you then?" she enquired gently.

"Eight. I remember it well. It was a day after my birthday and Dad had taken us out to celebrate at the zoo." A little smile tugged at his lips. "I had a wonderful time. That was one of the rare family days we had without rancour. Dad's disease became worse as he grew older, and Mom put up with his anger, which would be triggered by the most insignificant thing."

"Your Mom didn't do anything about it? Tell her family, for instance?" She was perplexed as to why Josh's mother didn't reach out for help. She had little to no direct exposure to such domestic problems, and it confounded her a great deal.

"No. Sadly, my grandpa died when I was two. My grandma lived far away, and Mom didn't want to burden her with her problems."

"Oh, Josh. I'm so sorry you had such an unhappy childhood." Her thoughts reverted to her own happy childhood, surrounded by a doting family: an adoring father who treated her with utmost love, a gentle and loving mother who never raised her voice at her, a kind and generous grandmother who was the epitome of wisdom itself, plus a multitude of like-minded relatives.

"Contrary to what you're thinking, I was loved, Kat. Mom lavished her love on me, being an only child. Only I couldn't accept the fact that she willingly put up with my father's abuse. Despite the violence and sometimes degrading verbal abuse, she still insisted that he couldn't help himself and that he loved her. Because of that, she continuously forgave him." His face became tight with anger and frustration.

"When Dad beat her, assaulted her or slapped her, she always told me that it was her fault," he reiterated with a degree of frustration and rage. "The verbal abuse was legendry," he added.

Her sadness at the picture he'd elicited as a little boy drew out the maternal instincts in her. She put her arms around him and hugged him, tears welling up in her eyes, feeling the pain he was going through as if it were hers too.

He returned her embrace in gratitude and desperation. *It feels good to be able to unburden something you've hidden from the one you love, someone who understands your pain,* he thought gratefully.

"Are you still in touch with your parents?" She was shocked to realize how little she knew of his background, much less about his parents.

"No. I ran away from home at fifteen to stay with my grandmother … until she died of cancer when I was seventeen. I did odd jobs to continue studying. I wanted to escape from poverty. I wanted to be an architect, and nothing was going to stop me. Grandma left me some money that she had been saving up, and that helped to tide me over until I obtained financial assistance from the university." He released her and walked to the window, his eyes looking out into the far distance, his mind in turmoil.

"And *your* mom?" she insisted, her eyes following him.

"For a long time, I was angry with her," he said wistfully, turning back to look at her. "I asked her—no, begged her—to go away with me to Newcastle where Grandma was, to start a new life, but she consistently refused. She said Dad needed her. The sad thing is, now that I understand the situation better, Mom, like many battered women, could not accept the fact that she may not be at fault and that the sickness lies with the abuser." There was a lingering pain in his voice. "My mom died of a heart attack when I was in my first year at Newcastle U," he said sadly, "but I had renewed my contact with her by then. I visited her often, though I always made sure my dad was away at the time of my visits."

For a long while, he remained silent. Then, as if he had finally made up his mind to come clean with her, he said in a strangled voice, his eyes looking pleadingly at her, "Kat, I'm afraid I may have inherited my father's malady, though unlike him, there's not a drop of liquor in my blood. A long time ago, I made a conscious choice to be a teetotaller." He paused for a pregnant second. "I don't want to hurt you. So far I've not been tested." Panic and desperation laced his every word. "I've never loved anyone the way I love you, so my temper had always been held in check. I'm so afraid that one day it will rear its ugly head and I won't be able to control myself." He continued thoughtfully. "You know what they say about the apple falling not far from the tree?"

He held out his hands to her, his eyes silently begging her to understand and help him. She went to him willingly, and with extreme gentleness, she whispered soothingly in a voice that was soft and comforting, "You're nothing like him, Josh. You're the gentlest, most caring man I have ever met. That's one of the reasons I fell in love with you. We'll fight this together," she promised.

For a while, he believed that she could be right about him. He felt comforted and confident that his love for her was strong enough to overcome the mercurial temper that he might have inherited. As they wiped the tears from each other's eyes, they discussed their plans for each other and how they would spend the Christmas holidays together with her parents, who planned to visit. They helped each other pick up the shards of broken glass on the floor, while he begged her for forgiveness. The emotional stress of the evening took its toll, but they continued talking long into the night, and as with lovers everywhere, they renewed their pledge to one another, convinced that their love would be strong enough to withstand the test of time.

Many times in the near future, Josh would be assailed by similar attacks of jealousy which he consciously fought to overcome, with all the willpower he could muster, knowing deep in his heart that she was the best thing that could ever happen to him, that she was sweet and honourable. Most times, he was able to fight the evil that spawned that emotion, but there were other instances when he would have given way to his baser instincts and hurt her with cruel words which were at the tip of his tongue. Thankfully, those instances were few and far between and he succeeded in suppressing them; Katarina was none the wiser. His love for her was deep and strong, and his need for her was more so. Even so, he looked ahead into their future with great trepidation.

# CHAPTER 1

"MMM, THIS *PULUT udang* tastes delicious, *Mak*, as usual," Malek complimented his mother as he bit into another mouthful of the *kueh*, a roll of glutinous rice flavoured with spicy coconut and prawn *sambal* that his mother had prepared for his afternoon tea. He was lolling in his favourite settee, a copy of the novel *War and Peace* in his hand, enjoying the cool afternoon breeze wafting gently through the open veranda.

Having lost her husband when her son was in his early teens, she had lavished her love on Malek and spoilt him with her excellent culinary skills. She had ensured that he completed his education up to Senior Cambridge level, even though they were in dire financial straits and she had to supplement her income by selling *kuehs* through the many Indian vendors to whom she paid 20 per cent of the proceeds. She and her son had not only survived but also flourished, and Malek had been a diligent helper in the kitchen.

Now thirty, Malek held a good job at the land office and had risen in the ranks quite quickly, for he was an intelligent and hard worker. There was also the possibility that he would be appointed chief clerk in the near future, the highest position he could hold with his qualifications.

His mother had not uttered a word for several minutes, quite unlike her normal effervescent nature. He studied her serious features and thought, *Uh-oh. Here we go again.*

True enough. She soon launched into her favourite diatribe. "Lek," she began, her eyes scrutinizing his features, which were now in a defensive mode. Her son always reminded her of her late husband when he assumed that stance, but that did not deter her. "I'll be fifty-two next month. I'm not getting any younger."

"*Mak*," he interrupted.

She shushed him by raising her forefinger peremptorily. "I want you to listen and listen well."

As always, that tone drew his attention. Although gentle by nature, she'd nag him whenever she needed to.

"I have introduced four beautiful, young, eligible women in the past two years." Her voice was firm as she displayed four fingers to emphasize her point. "But none of them met with your approval." She took a deep breath. "You couldn't find one yourself." She shook her head in disbelief. "I want you to settle down within the next three months." *There,* she thought, *I have given him my ultimatum.*

"*Maa-aak,*" he protested, "that's a very tall order. Where will I find a suitable candidate within such a short time?"

"That's because you have not been looking," she answered tersely. She recalled with a certain amount of bitterness the reason he had not been looking. Her son was a handsome, respectable young man who would make any in-law proud, but for his pedigree. His father was a "nobody".

When he was twenty-two, Malek fell in love with the daughter of a senior government servant, but her father furiously put an end to the blossoming relationship, as Malek had nothing to his name. Malek's father had been a *peon* in his office. Malek had closed his heart to any woman since. He recalled that episode with bitterness. He dragged his thoughts back to his mother.

"… found a suitable girl for you," he heard her say. "She's eighteen, and she just started working as an assistant nurse at the hospital. Her name is Suraya," she continued imperturbably, not wanting to hear him protest. "She is an only child—like you. She's a good daughter, very pretty. And I've asked Pak Su to match you both. According to your uncle's calculations, you're a well-matched couple," she finished in one breath.

He gaped at her in wonder and frustration. "Might I be given permission to take a look at this paragon of beauty who's going to be my future wife?" he queried, his aggrieved tone laced with sarcasm.

"Certainly," she replied sweetly, ignoring his annoyance. "We have been invited to tea at their house tomorrow."

"And I suppose you have accepted it on my behalf?" he asked, defeated. He would always lose in a battle of wills with his mother, whom he respected more than anyone else.. She would fight for him tooth and nail if need be, yet she would respect his wishes if he was willing to stand up to her. In this instance, he didn't feel the need to antagonize her, so he acquiesced, albeit ungraciously.

The matchmaking was a total success. At the appointed hour, Malek and his mother presented themselves at Suraya's house. As Suraya self-consciously walked into the sitting room carrying a tray with tea and condiments, Malek's eyes fixated on her. He had never met anyone with such grace and beauty, and he was at a loss for words.

Malek assessed her to be around five feet six inches tall. She had the features of mixed Arab and Malay ancestry: straight, pert nose; long, curly black hair cascading down her back; eyes like black onyx, demurely hidden under long, thick lashes; kissable lips like cherries; and to top it all, a seductive hourglass figure. She had little idea of the thoughts racing in his mind as she carried the tray of *kuehs* she and her mother had prepared earlier for her would-be suitor. As expected of her, she modestly cast her eyes to the floor as she entered.

Suraya was a girl of her time, properly brought up without a whiff of scandal or gossip to her name; she was a true *gadis pingitan*. Even so, she had always been aware of that handsome eligible bachelor, though never for a moment did she have any idea that she would be the lucky one to pluck him out of his self-imposed bachelorhood. She had dreamed of him often, how tall and well built he was, having been the college rugby captain, and how his smile softened the stern edges of his mouth and eyes, for he seldom smiled. And his voice ... Ah, the warmth and modulated depth of his voice could melt the ice caps of the Himalayas.

Theirs was a union encrypted in heaven, Malek often told her, for they were so much in sync with each other in their thoughts and the choices that they made throughout their twenty-two years of life together. They made a striking couple, and both were thankful that Malek's mother had skilfully commandeered their first meeting.

Their wedding was a joyous affair. Because each was their only child, their families decided to give their all. A huge celebration was planned, attended by their friends and relatives from near and far. The war that was raging in Europe was a distant event that hardly touched their conscious thoughts.

Soon, however, the newly-weds' joyous union became tinged with apprehension as rumours began to spread that the Japanese were on a mission to conquer Malaya. The defence tactic of the British government, spearheaded by Winston Churchill, later proved to be erroneous, but it would indirectly assist in the victory of the Japanese in Malaya. The British had firmly believed that the Japanese would attempt an amphibious operation, directly hitting the British naval base in the East at Singapore, which was then strongly fortified. However, the greater strength of the British Army and Royal Navy was concentrated in Egypt to protect the Suez Canal from Hitler's anticipated onslaught.

The British were not aware that Japanese spies had been deployed to Malaya years before to infiltrate the pro-independence movement that had begun to take root against the British administration and to obtain information regarding the allied troops, including their strengths and positions. There were Japanese shopkeepers and planters who went about their business undetected. It therefore came as a shock when on Monday, 2 December 1941, just before midnight, Japanese troops quietly landed at Padang Pak Amat Beach and hundreds of Japanese soldiers swarmed Kota Baru, the capital of Kelantan, to the north-east of the Malay Peninsula. Simultaneously, to the north-west, Japanese soldiers landed at Patani and Songkla in Thailand and started marching towards the Thai-Malayan border into Perlis.

The British were unaware of the Japanese-Thai policy of irredentism. In return for the right of passage through Thailand, the Japanese had agreed to the Thai claim of the right to rule states that had a percentage of people of Thai origin: Kedah 2.96 per cent, Perlis 2.44 per cent, Kelantan 2.13 per cent, and Terengganu 0.02 per cent. The Japanese kept their part of the bargain. In October 1943, these states were handed over to the Thais, but the Japanese retained the power to enlist young Malays from these states in their "volunteer" army.

The British Sixth Brigade, stationed at Kampung Manggol, retreated via Kodiang to Jitra, only six miles from the Thai border, as they were unable to withstand the strength of the Japanese Army. Within fifteen hours, Jitra fell into the hands of the Japanese. That was a sad day for the British Army, which was made up principally of Gurkha and Punjabi soldiers who, at the first clash at Changlon, inadvertently dropped a map of the area that the Japanese used to their advantage.

Then the retreating British soldiers made another blunder; they destroyed the connecting bridge as they retreated, unaware that their own troops were following them. This forced the British Army to abandon their field and machine guns and their three-month supply of food.

Alor Star, the capital of Kedah, was expected to be the next target. An emergency meeting at Malek's office warned of such eventuality, and the staff were advised to remove their families to remote places out of the route of the marauding Japanese Army. The troops in Kelantan had begun to march southwards into Terengganu, and those in Kedah were expected to follow a similar strategy.

Malek hastily picked up his wife at the hospital and then rushed home for his mother. Along the way, he explained briefly about the crisis they were in.

"Where shall we go, *bang*? Will it be safe there too?" Suraya was apprehensive.

"I don't know, *sayang*. The least we can do is get out of harm's way and pray to Allah for our safety," he assured her. "We'll seek refuge at Tok Ayah's *pondok*. It's far enough from the main roads. I don't think they will veer away from the roads," he informed her. "I have a feeling that the Japanese won't antagonize us unless we oppose them openly," he added, as an afterthought.

They then rushed home to pick up his mother. "Hurry, *Mak*. We have to go," he said, trying to bank down the panic in his voice.

"What's going on?" she asked.

"I'll explain later," he said as he helped his wife pack some clothes and provisions to tide them over at least for the first few days. "Come on, Sue." He hurried her along, his eyes keeping a wary eye on his mother.

They were fortunate to hitch a truck ride around the corner of the road, and for the next twenty minutes of the ride, he explained to his mother that the Japanese had started their attack on Malaya and it was best that they stayed out of the way of the advancing army. He did not confide in her or his wife that he and his friends were of the opinion that the British would not be able to protect them or deflect the Japanese attack. The fall of Malaya seemed imminent.

His grandfather's village was three miles away from the road, so for the rest of the way, they had to walk along the narrow footpaths. His grandparents were surprised at their unexpected visit but were joyful to see them. The news of the fall of Jitra had not penetrated the village yet, so as briefly as he could so as not to scare the villagers, who were mostly his grandfather's adherents—mostly seniors above fifty—Malek explained that they would have to stay put and stock up food for a few days. He assured them that they would be safe, as they were not in the path of the advancing army.

His grandfather was a man of religion. At seventy, he was still hale and hearty, lean and strong, his head sparsely scattered with white hair. Despite suffering from Parkinson's disease, he was lucid and mentally focussed. After the death of his first wife, Malek's grandmother, he had started the *pondok* community and remarried. The community became popular with the elderly, who looked up to him as their spiritual leader. In his calm and modulated voice, Haji Ahmad convinced them that Allah would protect them if they were extra careful, more vigilant, and listened to Malek's wise advice.

That night, after a simple meal, Suraya turned to him with fear in her eyes. She had supported him stoically and had said very little throughout the journey or the dinner, unlike her usual talkative self.

"*Bang*," she said softly, her eyes looking out into the darkness, "are we really safe here?"

"I think so, Sue—at least I pray so," he replied, his hands lovingly messaging her tense shoulders with all the tenderness and love he felt for her. "We're far away from the main roads. I don't think the Japanese will stray from those main roads. They want a quick conquest. Once they conquer Alor Star, they'll move southwards. Their main targets would be Penang and Singapore." He nodded thoughtfully. "That's what I believe. We'll be careful and not get in the way," he concluded. He pulled her up gently from the stool she was sitting on. "Come on, *sayang*. Let's go to bed."

Fear of the unknown made their sleep intermittent at best. Throughout the night, from far away, they could hear the drone of what they assumed to be fighter planes. She was grateful that they had each other as she clung to him in fear. A series of explosions woke them up from their restless sleep. The air was filled with an acrid smell. She was terrified, and her nails, like talons, bit into his flesh as her arms tightened around him. He hardly felt any pain, as he too was in a state of shock.

"What is it?" she whispered.

"I don't know," he replied. Gently he released her.

"Don't leave me alone!" she cried. She was shivering in fear.

"I'm not going to," he assured her. "Come with me." In the darkness, he found her hand and pulled her up. "We can't risk lighting the *pelita*," he warned her, "in case the enemy drops a bomb. We also have to go and check on the old folks."

In the darkness, his grandparents and his mother were huddled in the centre of the house. He was glad that they had the presence of mind to stay in the dark. Everyone seemed to be questioning the source of the strange odour, but that night there didn't seem to be an answer.

The next day, Malek couldn't contain his curiosity any longer. Against his wife's and his mother's objections, he took hold of his trusty old bicycle, advised his family to stay indoors for their own safety and made a hasty trip to town. It was a long ride. There were no signs of soldiers, be they Japanese, Gurkhas, or Punjabis, but there was a great deal of destruction along the way. He was accosted with skeletal remains of buildings and shops that had burnt to cinder. He wondered sadly if there were many human casualties. Along the way, he was joined by several other cyclists who suggested that they made their way to the State Mosque, where they would be apprised of the real situation.

Here he met up with many of his old friends and they conversed quietly. It seemed that the British had blown up the Alor Star Air Force Base before their retreat, thus giving rise to the strong acrid smell and the thick, dark smoke that was still billowing into the air.

Rumours were rife that the Sultan had been abducted by his son, Tunku Abdul Rahman, the district officer of Kulim, as His Majesty was being escorted by the British to find safety in Penang. Tunku was of a different mind. He was opposed to the idea of his father abandoning his *rakyat*. In their absence, the Japanese appointed another son of the Sultan, Tunku Muhammad Jewa, as Acting Regent. The latter, who had earlier dismissed the idea of escape in search of refuge, then advised all those who were present at the mosque to remain calm and to carry on with their normal duties.

After having joined the congregation in prayers, he cycled home. Suraya was furious with him. She had been sick with worry, and she harangued and nagged him until he gently pulled her into his arms and put to rest the anger and the fear that his trip had caused. She sobbed with relief that he was safely back with her again. She had imagined all manner of harm that could have befallen him.

Later that night, after *isyak* prayers, everyone attended the dinner at his grandfather's house. It was to be the last *kenduri* for the next three years, as food became scarce and safety could not be guaranteed. Malek took the opportunity to update them with current events.

"Malay diplomacy won the day," Malek announced proudly as he explained how the Japanese had appointed Tunku Muhammad Jewa as the Acting Regent to bring back some semblance of authority to the state of Kedah, which had become chaotic due to the absence of government. Japanese soldiers and locals had taken to looting and robbery.

"Tunku saved us all," he continued. "We can't be sure what the Japanese would have done to the Royal Family otherwise." He paused for breath. "The Regent advised us to carry on as before," he informed his audience.

He happened to look towards the door, and his eyes caught sight of his wife, whom he hadn't seen for some hours, as she had been busy in the kitchen. She was in a bright orange *baju Kedah*, eyes training on him with pride and admiration, lips smiling with love and adoration. His heart missed a beat, and for a moment, he lost his train of thought. His grandfather, who did not miss the byplay of seduction, discreetly and softly coughed, and successfully brought back his grandson to the matter at hand.

"If we value our lives," Malek continued sheepishly, "we have to obey our new masters now."

Malek would later convey to his wife how Japanese justice worked. It seemed that after the conquest of Alor Star, a few Japanese soldiers had ransacked Tunku Mohammad Jewa's residence and stolen some valuables. "Tunku informed the Japanese Major," Malek cackled with amusement. "And you know what the major did?" He delayed the information on purpose, as he caught sight of his wife's eyes, which were as big as saucers. He sipped his coffee slowly, as though savouring its delicious taste, as he stared at her with the benevolence of a lover who secretly mused over his woman's enchanting beauty, his lips upturned in a gentle smile.

"What?" she asked impatiently, tugging at his sleeves.

"Well, I don't want to shock you." He smelled the aroma of his coffee. Then he dropped the bombshell. "The major ordered the culprits to commit *hara-kiri* right in front of Tunku."

Not having heard the term before, she listened with wide-eyed horror as he explained what it meant. In the years ahead, Suraya, indeed the whole population, would be more shocked, as they were to be exposed to more incidents of Japanese cruelty and their unique code of conduct.

Malek would often remind his grandfather's congregation of this. "When you come across Japanese soldiers, bow low," he stated. There were voices of protest. A Malay bowed low only to royalty or in prayers. Malek hastily counteracted. "Do you value your head on your shoulders or do you prefer to have it dangling from a tree as they tie you up by your legs?" The murmurs died down. "Japanese justice is swift and harsh," he warned.

"We must protect our women and children too," he advised them. "I hear that young women are often kidnapped and taken to Japanese bases as *comfort women* for the soldiers."

Not many Malay women were reported to have been such victims, but there were many sad stories of young Chinese women who had been abducted for such a purpose. Despite her husband's advice to the contrary, Suraya had insisted that she continued working, as nurses were sorely needed. He had reluctantly agreed but had insisted that she allowed him to cut her beautiful locks so as not to attract attention to her beauty and desirability. He also wanted her to dress as dowdily as possible to camouflage her natural beauty. He did the honours himself. The pain of seeing his wife without her crowning glory was as sharp as the scissors he was wielding. As a precaution, he asked her to carry a picture of the Emperor at all times, fully aware that the Japanese soldiers revered him above all else.

The speed of the Japanese conquest of Malaya was unheard of before; Jitra fell on Thursday 11 December 1941, Alor Star on Saturday, Gurun on Sunday, Penang the following Friday. Kuala Lumpur was captured on 11 January 1942. A string of conquests of the towns in Selangor, Pahang and Johore followed suit. Thousands of Japanese soldiers travelled in jeeps and bicycles for an average of twenty kilometres per day, for a total of 1,100 kilometres, until they finally captured their main target: Singapore, the "Gibraltar of the Orient", on 15 February 1942, a feat which took them a mere two months.

# CHAPTER 2

THE JAPANESE OCCUPATION was often remembered with sadness, as Japanese cruelty was well documented. Diseases were prevalent; malaria was common. Many people were anaemic. There were frequent beheadings, especially of the Chinese. On occasions, their lives would be terminated at the end of Japanese bayonets or firing squads. Some incidents would have been hilarious if not for their unheard-of cruelty. For instance, a youth was slapped for not bowing to a soldier. He was made to hold a small boulder on top of his head for ten minutes in the hot sun. The word *bagero* would be remembered for a long time, as Japanese officers yelled it in fits of fury. Malays who were suspected of being anti-Japanese became victims too. They were lined up against the wall and shot one by one.

The hardships experienced would be repeatedly narrated to the next generation of children as a warning to be frugal in their lives: how food was severely rationed, how tapioca replaced rice, and how every other item of food was hard to come by. The Japanese currency had little value. After the Japanese had surrendered, bag loads of worthless Japanese "banana money," so called because of the banana tree motifs on the notes, were left for children to play with. On the flip side, the Japanese did try to alleviate the economic difficulties of the Malays by supplying the schoolgoing children with rations of sugar, rice and coconut oil.

The social upheaval had very little effect on the newly married couple. Malek's job at the office changed little, as the Japanese left the day-to-day running of the office to the Malays, while Japanese officers held the more senior posts. Malek had shifted his abode to Bakar Bata to be closer to the hospital where Suraya worked, and he made it a point to accompany her to and from work in order to ensure her safety.

Had it not been for his English friend, George, Malek would never have dreamed of living in that single-storey brick house with two spacious bedrooms in such an area where only the well-off and the well-connected resided. His meagre salary would not have been sufficient to enable him to acquire such a bungalow.

After a week of enforced absence, Malek returned to work on the first Sunday—Friday and Saturday being weekends in Kedah. The land office, like most of the buildings, had not suffered much damage. The interior was as he had left it, except that a Japanese officer had filled the senior post. A roll call in the morning required the staff to stand in line as the Japanese flag was hoisted, accompanied by the singing of the Japanese national anthem *Kimigayo* as they bowed their heads in abeyance, a show of respect to the emperor of the *"Land of the Rising Sun."* The Japanese were overly scrupulous about these matters. Woe betide anyone who displayed a modicum of disrespect!

That morning, as Malek was riffling through his papers, he came across a thick envelope addressed to him in the neat handwriting of his friend George Smith. He was momentarily nonplussed. A cursory glance pointed to George's signature on the cover letter, to which was attached a thick wad of documents. He and George had become good friends, as the latter would sometimes visit the land office for some official business relating to the rubber estate he was managing for a large British company. They had been captains of their respective school rugby teams, and they both loved to play golf. Their common interests cemented their friendship.

Fearing stiff reprimands from his new senior officer, he surreptitiously packed the documents among his personal papers and waited impatiently for the opportunity to study them at home. The previous Monday, on his way home from the mosque, he had stopped by George's house. On finding it locked and untouched by the ruckus the night before, he had left, all the time wondering if George had managed to escape to Penang as most of the English community had done.

As soon as he reached home, he carefully looked through the papers George had left and discovered a bunch of keys as well. The shock of his discovery left him speechless. George had obviously written in a hurry; his normal, exceptionally beautiful script was almost illegible:

*My dear friend,*

*I hope these documents reach you safely. I'm leaving the deed of my house to you. Treat the house as yours, my friend. We don't know how long this war will last or if I'll ever be back in Alor Star again.*

*We're dashing off to Penang before the enemy arrives.*

*Please tell Sue I'm going to miss her nasi lemak and tepung talam.*

*Warmest regards to you both,*

*George*

*PS Please don't forget to say a prayer for me.*

Malek was stunned into immobility. When he recovered his voice, he hollered for his wife, who, not ever having heard such an indescribable sound in her husband's voice, dropped the saucer she was holding and ran out of the kitchen to the veranda, fearing the worst.

"*Bang*? What's wrong!" she shouted back in panic.

Without a word, he handed George's letter to her. "Oh, Sue, I've been remiss as a friend." His tone was low and sad.

Suraya gave the letter a quick glance. Her mouth opened wide, but not a word passed her lips. She sat down heavily beside her husband. Tears rolled down her cheeks. "What could you have done, bang?" she was finally able to utter. "George would not have been safe here. The Japanese would have imprisoned him if they found him—and maybe do worse things to him –but to give the house to you …" She shook her head in disbelief. They held each other as each tried to comfort the other.

For hours, their conversation centred on their generous friend. The tea and cakes Suraya had painstakingly prepared were left untouched, as they recalled with extreme nostalgia, the happy times they had shared with him. He had virtually become part of their family. George had even referred to Malek's mother as *Mak*. Sadly they wondered whether they would ever see him again.

The bicycle became their main mode of transport. He would seat her on the bar that connected the seat to the handle; she would sit sideways with both her legs on her right, and with his arms enfolding her on either side, his hands clutching the front handles, he would happily pedal away for several minutes to and from her place of work. When it rained, she would hold an umbrella open over their heads.

During these times, they would share their dreams and hopes for their future. Always they would wonder if George was safe and if he was able to escape the Japanese dragnet before Penang fell into their hands. They hoped by some miracle that George had been saved.

They were considered lucky because the Japanese left them undisturbed. Stories of young girls being kidnapped to serve as comfort women for Japanese soldiers abounded. Mothers hid their children when they heard that one or two soldiers were on the prowl. Some girls would hide in the ditches or scrubs at the back of the house; some were rolled in *mengkuang* mats and stuffed underneath the beds. Some were dressed as boys, with their hair trimmed. Malek was grateful that his wife had never been disturbed, *probably because of her noble profession*, he thought.

"I'll still adore you," he comforted her as she stared disdainfully at her new image in the mirror. "Even if you're bald."

Sometimes Malek would recount the gossip he heard at the office. "Sue, do you know that our Sultan is back from Kulim?" She shook her head in negation. "Well, he is. The current Regent has relinquished his post to his brother, Tunku Badlishah."

"Hmm, would you have done that if you were in his shoes?" she enquired with laughter.

His laughter echoed hers. "I might not. Power is addictive." He pulled her ear and nudged it with his nose. "Anyway, you'd be too tempting as a regent's wife for me to relinquish the post so easily," he joked.

They were young and in love. It was fun, no matter what hardships they encountered. They were together, and that was what mattered most. Those were the best times of their lives.

As he pedalled along on the bike, she would sing excerpts from her favourite songs; her throaty and husky voice never ceased to fascinate him. *"Bewitched, bothered, and bewildered,"* she would start. *"I'm wild again, beguiled again."*

His well-modulated voice would chime in: *"A simpering, whimpering child again, bewitched, bothered, and bewildered am I."*

Malek had a good singing voice, with a rich timbre and resonant tone that Suraya loved. Being together at the beginning and at the end of the day was a blessing that she would not surrender for anything.

How they yearned for the patter of tiny feet to break the silence and to complement their love for each other. When, after almost two years of marriage, Suraya finally announced that she was pregnant, there was much rejoicing.

Three months into her pregnancy, her mother-in-law arranged for *adat melenggang perut*, a ritual that was customarily carried out to celebrate the arrival of the firstborn. That involved much preparation and an experienced midwife to conduct the ceremony.

The would-be mother would lie on seven layers of *batek lepas* or *songket*, depending on the financial position of the family. The midwife, mumbling words only she knew the meaning of, smoothed the pregnant woman's abdomen with coconut oil before she rolled a young coconut over her abdomen. The position of the coconut as it stopped rolling on the floor determined the sex of the baby. The cloth was then pulled gently from side to side by two women sitting at opposite sides of the expectant mother, one piece at a time, and then it was gently removed. The midwife then said a prayer for the welfare of the mother and the baby.

"It's a girl!" she cried after she completed her *doa*. Her announcement brought tears from Suraya as friends congratulated her with *salaams* and kisses.

The nine months that she carried her baby was a breeze. She considered herself very lucky, as she was never sick, even for a day, and there were no abnormal cravings such as those that she heard from among her friends, who had numerous stories to tell. Malek treated her like a queen to whom he paid homage. There was not a wish he did not try to fulfil or a request that he denied. He was at her disposal, much to her amusement.

***

It was the middle of the month of *Ramadhan*, past midnight, when she woke him up.

"*Bang, bang* …" Her voice was trembling. She shook him desperately. "*Bang*, it's time!"

"It's too early for *sahur*," he protested, eyes tightly closed.

"It's the baby." She raised her voice in panic. "The baby is here!"

"What?" Immediately his attention was captured.

"Please call *Mak*," she said. "My water bag's broken."

He jumped up post-haste and rushed to the guest room, where his mother, accompanied by Suraya's mother, had been putting up once Suraya's pregnancy advanced. The two women had joined his grandfather's commune once the young couple moved to their new house.

The old woman was still in her *telekung* when, upon hearing her son shouting for her, she opened the door and saw him in a state of panic. Malek seldom lost his cool. She promptly discerned the source of his disquiet.

"The baby is coming, *yeah*?" she asked calmly.

"Hurry, *Mak*," he replied, tugging at her arm as she slowly removed her prayer outfit.

"Quickly, *Mak*, *please*! The water bag's broken," he said breathlessly. "Sue's in terrible pain."

"You go find *mak bidan*, Lek," his mother said. "I'll take care of Suraya. Be careful now. Suraya will be all right. It's going to be a long labour since it's the first baby."

Before he left, she pulled him to her. Together they cupped their hands in prayer to calm his nerves and to pray for Suraya and for the baby's safe delivery. She let him go when his pulse normalized.

He had no idea how he was able to find the midwife's house or how she was able to comprehend his garbled explanation as to why she was needed. In his mind, he could only picture the pain and suffering his wife was going through, her eyes tightly shut as she grimaced at every surge and movement the baby made, sweat pouring down her pale cheeks.

When he brought the midwife home, Suraya was still in the throes of pain. He kissed her tenderly as he stroked her hair and caressed her cheeks. He then gave the two women a murderous look as he was pushed out of the room none too gently so they could administer to his wife.

After what seemed to be endless hours of waiting, his mind filled with terrible what-ifs that made him dread every minute that he did not hear any sound from his bedroom, he finally heard the cries of a baby at sunrise. He rushed into the room just as they were removing the afterbirth, by which time the baby had been carefully wrapped in a soft bundle and gently placed in Suraya's arms.

His breath caught in his throat as he neared the bed, and he tried vainly to swallow a sob. Gently he swabbed the remnants of tears and sweat from his wife's weary face, which had now been replaced by a tired smile. He whispered his love to her and with a gentle finger touched the baby's face and tenderly caressed the cheeks in total wonder.

"It's a girl," Suraya whispered.

"*Alhamdulillah*," he whispered back. There were no words he could utter that would express the relief and gratitude he felt with every blessing he had been given.

"We have to give our baby a name now," he said, once he had regained his voice and his composure.

"Katarina!" Suraya announced firmly, her voice hardly above a whisper.

The elderly mother and her son looked at each other. It was a name they were not familiar with, though Malek had been briefed by his wife, who had dreamed of having a baby girl of that name ever since she came across the name in the pictorial love stories that she and her schoolmates had been addicted to at school. From her bed, in a worn-out tone, but loud enough to be convincing, she told them, "Well, it's not a Malay name—or Arabic, for that matter—but I know that in any European language, it means everything that's good and wonderful." She looked at her husband pleadingly. "Don't you want our daughter to be beautiful, smart, intelligent, one of a kind …?"

Her husband burst out laughing. "Enough," he said, putting up his hands as a sign of surrender. He turned to his mother. "We'll just add *Nur* before her name. She will be the *light* of everything that is wonderful. She's certainly the light of my life." He picked up his daughter and kissed her, his eyes moist, his heart bursting with joy.

"There's something else we must do, *Mak*." He turned to his mother. "We want to honour George. Sue and I planned to add George's name. So your granddaughter's full name is Nur Katarina Georgina binti Malek."

"That's a lot of names for a little girl, but I'm proud that she is to be his namesake. Every night I say a prayer for his safety. You haven't heard anything yet, Lek?"

Malek shook his head, the light in his eyes dimmed with concern.

Katarina moved her hands, opened her eyes, and looked straight at her father. For a second, Malek imagined that he was looking into George's eyes, so clear and deep, and he wondered whether George was somehow sending them a message. He shook his head as if to deny such a ludicrous thought. Then the baby emitted a loud wail that brought everybody to attention.

Nur Katarina blossomed under the tender ministrations of her grandmother, who showered everything possible on her. At three months, she was a darling that laughed and gurgled her way into everyone's heart. Her doting grandmother arranged for a *berendoi* ceremony, with all the pomp and extravagance she could think of.

Family and friends converged that Saturday morning. Communal living being the fabric of Malay society, the guests turned up bearing gifts for the baby or food to share after the ceremony.

Friends helped Suraya set up and decorate the special swing made up of *batik lepas* which was tied at both ends to a specially carved piece of wood. The swing was hung from the rafters. A tiny mattress was placed in the centre for the baby—who was draped in a long pink gown embellished with lace and ribbons—to lie in comfort. The scent of fresh flowers, like jasmine, roses and an assortment of other flowers, permeated the air.

As the mother gently pushed the swing back and forth, songs in praise of Allah and the prophets were sung, and in honour of the baby girl, *syaers* in praise of prominent women in Muslim literature were sung too. All the while, the little baby cooed and gurgled as if she understood that the honour was bestowed on her alone.

Katarina was an absolute joy to her father. On returning home from the office, she would be the first thing he would pick up, holding her little body as he drank his tea or read his book, examining her little fingers and toes one by one in total awe. He was a consummate father who would think nothing of changing her diapers, giving her a bath, or singing her to sleep as he gently pushed her swing. It was hard to figure out who enjoyed the experience more, as the baby's shrieks mingled with the hoarse guffaw of the father as it reverberated throughout the house. That little baby was the epicentre of his world.

One evening, Katarina was feeling unwell and creating much disharmony. She had become restless, fretful and fussy, and her temperature had risen slightly. Gently Suraya messaged her little body, which helped to alleviate her discomfort, and the baby began to fall asleep in her arms. Sighing in relief, Suraya laid her gently in her cradle and walked swiftly to the kitchen, where Malek was laying the table. Her mother-in-law had joined Tok Ayah at the *pondok* to celebrate Prophet Muhammad's birthday.

They talked quietly as they prepared a simple meal for the two of them. Suraya was relating to her husband an incident wherein a group of communist guerrillas attacked a Japanese convoy, which resulted in the death of one. The rest managed to escape. She had helped treat a couple of Japanese soldiers who suffered minor injuries.

*"Bang,"* she said, after a moment's lull in their conversation, "there's someone at the door calling out for you."

"That sounds like Azmi," Malek replied. "I wonder what he wants. I'll check. You stay here," he reminded her. They had to be cautious, especially at night. Their house was at the end of the cul-de-sac. It was deathly quiet and lonely at night, when not a soul would dare to venture out into the darkness.

It was not a peaceful period in the history of Malaya. Robberies and kidnappings were common. Suraya had lost a friend to the communist movement, the Malayan Communist Party (MCP), after the Japanese soldiers killed her friend's father and dunked her brother in the river until he drowned. Mei Lin's voice resonated with utter pain and anguish when she recounted the incident to her. It made Suraya extremely sad to think of her dear friend who previously didn't have a wicked bone in her body, but who had been inadvertently thrust into the obscene cruelty borne of hatred and who in turn, responded in kind by joining the guerrillas in the jungle.

In their sitting room, Malek was talking in undertones to his friend Azmi, who had introduced a new friend to him.

"Malek," Azmi began. "We know you're very settled in your job. We never forgot that you were our leader in school, a prefect, and our rugby captain." He paused for breath and watched the effect his short speech had on Malek. "We're actually hoping you'll join us."

Malek had been aware of Azmi's activities and had an inkling of what was expected of him, but he pretended ignorance. "What do you mean, Mi?"

"We're members of Force 136," Azmi stated bluntly. "I'm sure you know that."

Malek nodded. He knew that Force 136 had been set up by the British to act as an underground resistance movement against the Japanese several months before his daughter was born.

"We're going undercover by obtaining intelligence about the Japanese while working with MPAJA," Azmi continued.

The Malayan Peoples' Anti-Japanese Army had been set up by the Malayan Communist Party to fight against the much-hated Japanese, and it had the blessings of the British.

"You guys are very brave, my friend," Malek replied cautiously, not wanting to antagonize them.

"You can do a lot to help us, Malek," Azmi countered hopefully.

Malek shook his head. "Much as I hate the situation we're in, I do not want to put my family's life in jeopardy," Malek explained tactfully.

A sardonic expression flittered across Azmi's face. His lips compressed. He lowered his eyes, a mask descended, and his expression became inscrutable.

Malek hastily added, "I admire what you're doing. I'm a civil servant, Mi. I carry on the work of government, the day-to-day administration of the country, regardless of who's in power. We're the bolts and screws that oil the government machinery, without which there'll be chaos."

He studied his friend's face earnestly and hastened to add, "Don't worry. I'll not betray your trust. The fact that I do not want to join you does not mean that I oppose you." He added with a laugh, "We Malays in general are a misunderstood lot. When we refuse to join the MCP, they say we're lazy and that we're easily contented. One or two of us are perhaps lazy and easily contented. I mean, heck, maybe a thousand of us, but in general, we're a responsible and dependable people." He looked towards his new guest and attempted to convince the latter regarding his stance. "There are many ways of serving our country. You have one way and I choose to do it my way."

At this point, Suraya entered and invited their guests to partake of the dinner that she had quickly prepared while the friends were talking.

Although many suffered in those lean times when food was scarce, their family managed to overcome the shortages exceptionally well. His mother, being the pragmatic person she was, kept the family larder well stocked with her green thumb, planting tapioca, sweet potatoes and several kinds of vegetables, even rearing chickens for their supply of eggs. They never ran out of food, and several times the harvest was so bountiful that they managed to share with family and friends.

As the men sampled Suraya's tasty dishes with relish, their conversation turned to more pleasant subjects, such as their school days and the fun they had as students at the college. After a hearty and delicious meal, they finally parted, their respect for each other undiminished, their friendship intact.

# CHAPTER 3

FOR MALAYA, THE war ended as abruptly as it began. On 6 August 1945, at 7.16 a.m. Malayan time, the Allies dropped the first atomic bomb, nicknamed "Little Boys", at Hiroshima, followed by the second bomb, "Fat Boy", three days later at Nagasaki. The news broadcast over the radio was received with a mixed feeling of horror and relief: *horror* at the anticipation of death and suffering of the thousands of inhabitants of the two cities. After all, the bombs were a new invention, the aftereffects of which were as yet to be verified. And there was *relief* that the Japanese were now attacked on their home ground. Malayans were hopeful that this would put an end to Japanese occupation on their soil.

Sure enough, six days later, Emperor Hirohito, in a radio broadcast to his people, commanded them to accept the Potsdam Proclamation, signed on July 26, which stipulated that the Japanese surrendered unconditionally to the Allies, failing which "prompt and utter destruction" would befall. The emperor's order was not well received by all; some looked upon it as an insult, for they were ready to continue fighting. In Singapore, several hundred Japanese soldiers blew themselves up with a grenade at the Raffles Hotel after a farewell party. Three days later, on 25 August, the emperor issued a decree ordering all Japanese forces to demobilize and cease operations.

For two and a half months, after the Japanese troops withdrew from the Malay Peninsula, Penang and Singapore, there was virtually no government in these states. The Malayan Union, the British attempt at a new system of government, proved extremely unpopular, especially among the Malays, who resented the attempt to strip the sultans of their sovereignty and to grant full citizenship to all immigrants.

This period of unrest and dissatisfaction encouraged the Malayan Communist Party to demonstrate their influence and strength. It was estimated by some that the party was five thousand strong. The communists emerged from their hideouts in the jungle to carry out reprisals against those who were perceived to be their enemies and who had shown their support to the Japanese, their mortal enemy, some of whom were Malays. This planted the seeds of interracial discord that would remain dormant in the society.

The atrocities carried out by the communists were seared in the memories of the locals. Some of the tortures carried out were no less gruesome: one example was when they tied their victim to a tree, blindfolded, while they took turns stabbing him in the heart, and when their vengeance was demonstrated satisfactorily, they scattered pamphlets and victoriously marched back to the jungle. They too, like the Japanese before them, managed to instil fear and hatred among the populace.

Reprisals against the European tin miners and rubber planters were carried out successively. This culminated in the murder of three European planters at Sungai Siput, Perak, in June 1948. Workers and trade unions were encouraged to create trouble. The livelihoods of the ordinary citizens, especially the Chinese (some of whom may not have been their sympathizers) were threatened as the communists forced their way into their lives by making them donate money and food.

On 1 February 1948, the Federation of Malaya was established. The state of emergency was declared on 16 June. For twelve years, the war against communist insurgency influenced the manner in which the Malay states were ruled. One of the first attempts at solving the menace was by declaring an amnesty to encourage them to lay down their arms with a guarantee that no punitive actions would be taken against them. The hardcore communists, who were staunch advocates of the teachings of Mao Tse Tung and who wanted to establish a communist government, scoffed at this.

Malek and Suraya had been following the discourse on communism with interest. Several Malays were attracted to the idea of equality, "*sama rata, sama rasa*", a doctrine of equality promoted by communism, a classless society. These people didn't relish the traditional social strata that existed in the traditional Malay society, with its hierarchy that perpetuated power in the hands of the few of those that inherited it.

***

They savoured the early mornings the most, before the routine of the day started, for they would hardly see each other until the end of the day.

These hours were theirs alone and had been ever since their daughter did not need a change of diapers or her morning feeding. It was their most treasured time. They were speaking in low tones, planning the day ahead, as it was their daughter's sixth birthday. All at once, like a tornado, the subject of their discussion burst into their room, jumped onto their bed, glided between them, and shouted gleefully, with the confidence of a child who knew she was adored and could get away with most anything.

"Wake up, Mummy, Daddy. Wake up! It's my birthday! I'm six today."

Malek shook his head at his daughter's exuberance. He made a mental note to talk to her about privacy. She was the proverbial apple of his eye, but now that she was growing up, she would have to learn that were some boundaries. He looked at his precious daughter fondly as was talking excitedly about her birthday plans with her mother. At six, she was tall for her age. She easily dwarfed her friends of the same age.

The little imp then focussed her attention on him, her little finger tugging gently at his moustache. "Daddy, where's my birthday gift?"

He pretended ignorance. "Does she get a birthday gift this year, Sue? Do you think Gina has been a good and obedient little girl?" Gina was his pet name for her. Katarina always reserved it for her father. "Only Daddy can call me Gina. I'm Katarina to everyone else." She always insisted that to all and sundry.

"Daddy!" she shrieked, promptly wrestling him into huge bouts of laughter.

"Okay, okay," he capitulated. "What did we get her for her birthday, Sue?"

She became tired of her father's teasing. She flounced off the bed and began opening one drawer after another. "Mummy, where is it?" she asked in frustration.

Her father sat up slowly and with fanfare drew out a small jewellery box from underneath his pillow. That drew her attention immediately.

"Ta-da ..." He held it above his chest with a flourish, but before he could utter another word, what felt like a whirlwind, threw itself onto his lap and hugged him with all the force of a forty-pound dynamo.

There were screams and laughter as her father opened the box to display a heart-shaped pendant that could be opened at the side and which displayed a picture of both her parents on one side and of her on the other. With a flourish, Malek clasped the chain around her neck.

She touched the gift with reverence, grabbed her parents with both arms, kissed them wildly wherever she could, and promptly jumped off the bed.

"I'm going to show Grandma. I love it, I love it," she sang, and disappeared within seconds, like the tail end of a whirlwind. Her parents turned to look at each other, both shaking their heads at the antics of their little darling. They had never felt happier than they did at that moment. Their daughter had grown to be a handful, but a loving one at that, and having been blessed with such a lovely gift, they never regretted the fact that they could not have another child, even after years of trying.

***

The outpatient department was exceptionally busy that day. Patients walked in with all manner of ailments apart from the normal cold, flu, and fever. Some were diagnosed with beriberi, some with scurvy, and a host of other complications that were the result of malnutrition and hardships of the war. As there were only two nurses on duty that day, Suraya was kept on her toes for hours without respite, and she was looking forward to the end of the day, when she could go home to her family and celebrate her daughter's birthday. She had baked Katarina's favourite, a rich velvet cake, the night before and had decorated it with icings of elves and goblins that would fire her fertile imagination. She would love it; Suraya was convinced of that.

It was almost five, and the crowd had thinned. All at once, she spied an old woman sitting hunched up on the bench by the door as if she was in abject pain and misery, her head bent on her lap. It immediately brought her into Suraya's focus. There was something uncannily familiar about the old woman, she thought. It was as if she knew her.

Suraya gently touched her on the shoulder. *"Mak Chik sakit di mana?"* she asked solicitously, meaning, "Where does it hurt, Auntie?"

The woman slowly looked up. Suraya was shocked to the bone.

"Mei Lin!" she cried in disbelief. "Are you Mei Lin?"

It couldn't be, she thought. Mei Lin, her classmate, would only be twenty-six, like her. This woman was haggard and emaciated, and she looked almost fifty. She was a shadow of the Mei Lin she once knew.

It had only been seven years since they had parted. She was all skin and bones. Her intelligent round eyes that used to be alive with laughter were lifeless. The skin on her face was dry and wrinkled, and her hands trembled as she lifted them to touch the nurse that accosted her.

"Suraya?" Her voice was weak and so soft that she could hardly be heard.

"Oh, Mei Lin," Suraya interjected sadly. "What happened to you?"

Mei Lin opened her mouth but could say nothing. Droplets of tears trickled down her sunken cheeks.

"Stay here," Suraya ordered, walking away briskly to fetch a glass of water. "Drink this." As she watched her friend sipping the water laboriously, she made up her mind. "You're coming home with me. I'll be done soon." She looked around her; there were two patients left. "In half an hour …" she added.

Back home, there was a lot of activity. Katarina and a few of her cousins were playing in the sitting room, which had been gaily decorated by her two grandmothers with her help. She was decked in her birthday finery, a new dress which her mother had sewn for her, and she proudly displayed her birthday gift around her neck.

She ran out at the sound of her father's car in the driveway, waited patiently until he carefully parked the car under the porch, and then flew into his arms as soon as he alighted.

"Daddy! How do I look?" she yelled dramatically, pirouetting on her toes. "Mummy designed this dress." In return, she received a suffocating hug from her father.

When her father released her, her eyes caught sight of the old woman stepping out of the car. She was taken aback. She stepped back automatically, silently wondering where her parents had picked up the beggar, but her mother had always trained her to be discreet with people other than her family.

"This is my friend, Auntie Mei Lin," her mother said with a smile, but she looked at her with eyes that carried a warning message. She knew it meant that she should tread carefully and be both polite and respectful. She stepped forward and extended both her hands respectfully. After the preliminaries, Mei Lin was introduced to both her grandmothers, who welcomed her warmly.

Mei Lin stared at the little wonder wistfully. She was a beauty, the type of beauty who made one inhale in wonder, a miniature Suraya, with vivid dark eyes and long, curly hair that swished around her shoulders as she danced about. She noticed that Katarina hardly walked but instead traipsed around like a dancer. *What a lovely family Suraya has,* she thought wistfully, wishing not for the first time that she had made some better choices in her life.

Suraya served dinner early for the benefit of her friend, who looked as if she had not eaten for days, immediately after Mei Lin had taken a shower and was given a change of clothes from Suraya's own wardrobe. Still, they were too discreet to question her about her predicament. Mei Lin ate as one who was famished. It was obvious that she had not enjoyed a proper meal in quite a while.

Katarina's birthday party went into full swing as children gathered and sang to her as she cut her birthday cake. When her mother brought it out from the kitchen earlier, she had stared at it in awe.

"Wow, Mummy," she said in wonder, her voice hardly above a whisper, "it's magnificent. I love you, Mummy. You're the best mummy in the whole wide world," she said, giving her mother a giant hug. "Do you mind if I give the first piece to Auntie Mei Lin, Mummy? She looks very unhappy."

Suraya nodded wordlessly. She had no idea what to say to this beautiful daughter of hers; she had been utterly spoilt by her husband but still retained the thoughtfulness and kindliness that she had wanted desperately to inculcate.

Upon receiving the piece of cake, Mei Lin broke down and cried.

Katarina looked at her father and asked, "Daddy, did I do something wrong?"

"No, my darling. It was the sweetest thing that you did. That's why Auntie Mei Lin cried. She was touched by your thoughtfulness." He kissed her and whispered, "I'm proud of you."

Katarina was perplexed. *If Daddy thought it was good, then it's all right,* she thought. She continued to entertain her guests with complete enthusiasm.

Malek was truly proud of his daughter. Between him, his wife, and his mother, he thought they did an excellent job bringing up his little princess, though Suraya had always chastised him for giving in too much to his Gina. In her own gentle way, Suraya would be the one to discipline her, for he never had the heart to deny his little girl anything; but at the same time, he would never contradict his wife.

After the children had had their fill of fun and the little guests had gone home, Katarina had her rounds of good night kisses and finally fell asleep. The adults were then able to settle down for some serious conversation. Malek had not asked too many questions when his wife introduced Mei Lin when he went to pick her up at the hospital. He remembered that she had joined the Malayan Communist Party years before. They had had no contact since. Now he was anxious to know what had made Mei Lin seek his wife and what her status was at that juncture. He did not want to be accused of harbouring a communist in his household. He had said as much to her as soon as they reached home.

"*Bang,*" Suraya replied, "she's asking for amnesty. Do you think you can help her work it out? You have many contacts in the police department. Maybe we can help make it easier for her. She looks as though she has gone through the grinder of life much worse than anybody we know." Her voice was soft and sympathetic.

He looked at his wife with new respect. The first time he saw her, he had been smitten with her outstanding good looks. As their marriage matured, his love for her became limitless, for with her maturity, there developed that deep sense of humanity that was absent in many people he knew. Even though he was twelve years older than she was, he was of the opinion that she was more mature than he was in many ways; her compassion and tolerance gave her that added advantage.

"Of course, Sue," he replied as he helped with her earrings. "We'll do that tomorrow, though you must come with me. I don't want them to have ideas about my relationship with her." He kissed her ear as he clinched the earring in place. "But we must hear her side of the story tonight."

The four adults sat quietly, each wondering about the kind of life Mei Lin had led in the jungles of Malaya. Suraya's mother and her mother in-law who had decided to stay back seemed impatient to follow Mei Lin's story.

"Sue ..." Mei Lin looked gratefully towards Suraya. "I want to thank you, Malek, and Mak Chik for your kindness." She looked towards the them with a faint smile. "God only knows how little kindness there has been in my life."

"Don't mention it, Mei Lin. I wouldn't be able to live with myself if I had ignored your plight." Suraya turned to her husband for confirmation. *"Betul kan, bang?"* she asked.

Her husband nodded silently.

"Anyway, tell us how you managed to live in the jungle for the past seven years," she persisted.

"You know, Sue, why I joined the MCP in nineteen forty-two?" Mei Lin asked.

Suraya nodded.

"I had heard of the Malayan Communist Youth League, MCYL for short. It was an underground movement, as you know. It attracted many Chinese youths who hated the Japanese. Of course, Malays found it repugnant seeing that it propagated communist values." Mei Lin drew a deep breath and smiled slightly.

"I was nineteen, and my heart was full of hatred towards the Japanese," she said, her voice full of contempt. "I had this burning desire to avenge the deaths of my father and brother. I was exhilarated that I was advancing the cause of communism, the ideal form of government, as I was made to believe. Initially, my job was to collect subscriptions from sympathetic villagers, to collect food and to spread communist propaganda as we were taught. We all attended *xuexi* classes, and after a while, I began to teach three times a week, late at night in the jungle camps."

She paused for breath, and as she continued, her tone became tinged with sadness. "I had gone to the jungle against my mother's wishes. She wanted me to take over my father's business ... but what business was there? The Japanese had destroyed everything. Not satisfied with killing him, the Japanese burnt my father's factory down," she recounted bitterly.

"I fell in love with a cadre, and we had a son. We never married in the traditional way, but in our hearts, we were totally married." Her voice broke. "We loved our son, but we were asked to give him up because a baby would interfere with our fight," she sobbed. "They took our son, and I don't know where or who they gave him to. He was only a few days old."

Not one person had a dry eye, as they all felt Mei Lin's sorrow. No one could imagine the strength a mother would need to face up to such a heartbreaking eventuality. Malek took hold of his wife's hand and held it firmly. He understood how she felt.

"And my mother …" Mei Lin sobbed. "My mother is gone too. I don't know if she has ever forgiven me!"

Suraya went over to her and hugged her, tears streaming down her cheeks. "Mei Lin, I'm sure she has," she said in an attempt to comfort her. "I'm a mother. As a mother, I know I could never harden my heart against my child, no matter what she has done."

Mei Lin looked into the distance and continued sadly. "Gradually I became disillusioned with the movement and the manner in which the communist party conducted its affairs. There was an exercise called the 'rectification campaign'," she recalled. "I, like all those involved, was interrogated for days for being an agent of the British. Of course, it was a manufactured lie and I denied it. But they continually insisted that I should admit my wrongs; otherwise, I would be meted out with harsher punishment. I had been kept in a dark and cold drain for days so that I would realize my mistake and repent. As I couldn't stand it anymore, I agreed, and I was forgiven because it seemed that I had realized the error of my ways."

She shook her head in disbelief. "Like a fool, I still carried on as a loyal follower."

She was quiet for a long time. She inhaled a long breath that ended in a sob. "But what they made me do to my love put the end to any remnants of faith I had in their movement. Everyone in the camp accepted the fact that Ah Foo and I were husband and wife, though we didn't go through the ceremonies. He was a diehard fanatic. When his superiors demanded that we give our baby away, he had reluctantly followed orders."

She placed her fingers over her lips to stop it from trembling. "When he and a few cadres were on a raid in Perak, I was called up by my superiors and ordered to admit that my husband had told me that he was a spy for the British. It was a complete lie which I totally denied. It was pointless anyway because when he returned, his hands had been tied behind his back, his red cap removed as a mark that he was a traitor, and he was executed before my very eyes. I denied vehemently. 'I did not betray you,' I screamed, and he nodded as if he understood." She sobbed pitifully.

"I will always remember what a wasted life he led, this man with such ideals, finally to be betrayed by the very leaders he sacrificed everything for."

After a long pause, her sobs subsided and she continued as if in a trance. "I must have fainted, because when I came to, I was lying on the ground and it was deathly quiet. It looked as if the camp had been abandoned. My husband's lifeless body lay on the ground."

Her voice dropped to a heartbreaking whisper. "I dug up a grave and buried him with my own bare hands."

She dabbed her eyes and took a sip of water. Her mouth had gone dry. "I walked out of the jungle as soon as it was light, being very careful to look out for the other members. I was more afraid of them than I was of wild animals."

She closed her eyes tightly, and when she opened them, they were less tortured than before. "Finally, I reached a rubber plantation where a couple of Malay tappers were at work. They were suspicious of me at first, but I guess they could read the truth. They gave me food from their own supply and helped put me on the company truck which dropped me outside the hospital."

She looked fondly at her friend. "God gave me a second chance when He threw me in your path."

When the story ended, the room became as silent as a graveyard. A pall of sadness permeated the air. Finally, when he was able to speak, Malek promised he would do the utmost in his power, with the help of his wife, to obtain amnesty for Mei Lin and to help her obtain an identity card, which was a new registration scheme introduced in September 1948 to keep track of genuine civilians.

With the support of her devoted friends, Mei Lin gradually picked up the pieces of her life.

The efforts to eradicate communist activities and ideology took much longer. The activities of the communist terrorists did much to destroy the infrastructure and to put fear in the minds of the people. They frequently ambushed and attacked buses, lorries and trains.

Numerous counteroffensives were taken by the government. The Malayan armed forces, together with the police, were supported by Commonwealth armies commanded by the British. The action taken by Sir Gerald Templar to win "the hearts and minds" of the people had contributed immensely in blocking the spread of communism in Malaya, preventing it from escalating to a dangerous militant level and gradually eroding even their ideologies. Moreover, communism failed to gain a strong foothold among the Malay community, as its ideologies contradicted the teachings of Islam.

The end of the state of emergency was declared on 31 July 1960. However, The Malayan Communist Party was still active. Communist insurrection persisted intermittently until their enigmatic leader, Chin Peng, signed a truce with the government of Malaysia to "terminate hostilities" on 2 December 1986.

# CHAPTER 4

K ATARINA RECALLS …

I was very excited at the prospect of having a picnic. Early that morning, I joined Mummy in the kitchen to help her prepare *laksa Kedah*, Daddy's favourite dish. Grandma seemed to be under the weather, and fortunately I managed to persuade her to rest.

"Don't worry, Grandma," I said to her. "I can help Mummy peel onions and prepare the fish. I'm good at it; you know that."

Thus amply persuaded, Grandma napped in her garden.

I loved talking to Mummy. She's a good listener. When I got tired of talking, I started humming the hit song "Azizah", which was being played on the air several times a day. The song paid tribute to a pretty girl that the singer, P. Ramlee, had fallen in love with. As I helped Mummy pack, I danced and sang to entertain my sweet mother.

The lyrics went like this:

*Rupa kamu yang cantik*

(Your face so beautiful)

*Mata kamu yang bulat*

(Your eyes so round)

*membikin pemuda jadilah gembira*

(Drive men crazy)

*Senyumanmu yang manis*

(Your sweet smile)

*Gigi kamu yang putih*

(Your teeth like pearls)

*Oh nonaku …*

(Oh my lady …)

Before I could end the song with the word *Azizah*, Daddy, who had tiptoed into the kitchen while I was busy serenading my mother, sang in a very high note, "Suraya …"

Trust Daddy to make everything about Mummy. But I didn't begrudge Mummy, who Daddy adored totally. Mummy deserved all the accolades. She was a wonderful mother, loving and caring and an accomplished cook, aside from being a dedicated nurse. What's more, she was beautiful. I noticed how often men turned to look at Mummy in admiration, but she had eyes for no one, except Daddy.

The drive to the picnic spot took twenty minutes. We continued singing in the car. Both my parents loved Nat King Cole, and throughout the journey, I—and even Grandma—would join them singing; but when Daddy gave his rendition of "I've Grown Accustomed to Her Face", we became silent because we felt as though Daddy was serenading Mummy in his husky and fabulous voice. The way he turned to look at her, bringing tears to her eyes, and then he took her hand and held it until the song ended …

We picked the most scenic spot along the river, where the ridge rose slightly and afforded a generous view of the cool water rippling in the gentle breeze. To the left, several miles away, an island of mangrove hugged the banks of the river. Far across the river, amid the green trees gently billowing in the breeze, several houses of the well-to-do dotted the landscape.

A few yards away from our picnic spot, slightly hidden by a clump of *kedondong* trees, was a bathing spot for the inhabitants of the nearby area, for they still were not supplied with piped water. Here a platform was constructed for people to wash their clothes or to bathe.

We spied a number of children swimming; their shrieks and laughter made Grandma smile. Occasionally we heard the blare of the horn of the barges transporting rice from Thailand. On several occasions, boats carrying passengers across the river would toot their horns as they chugged along and the children would gleefully wave and scream their acknowledgement. One or two *tongkangs* would pass quietly by, like shadows amid the hustle and bustle along the river. It was a remarkable sight!

While Mummy and Grandma unpacked, I made a beeline for the river, closely followed by Daddy, who had given me a couple of swimming lessons in the shallow parts of that river. I had taken to swimming like a duckling to water, and I was fearless, as Daddy would block me with his body when the ripples developed into large waves with the passing of a boat or a ship. I would confidently float without fear of drowning because he was there to protect me. He never allowed me to be in the water alone.

"The river has taken its victim once in my lifetime," Daddy warned me. "You're never to venture out alone. Promise me, Gina," Daddy insisted.

"I promise, Daddy," I responded obediently.

A pledge once made was never to be broken. Daddy had always insisted upon that. He turned to look at me with his crooked smile, his eyes twinkling. "A man, or woman, or a little girl is as good as his words or her words!" His tone was serious though. His words were indelibly imprinted in my mind and they guided my life long after he was gone.

When I grew tired, Daddy and I joined Mummy and Grandma, who had laid out the plates and glasses. They were in deep conversation but welcomed us with cheerful smiles as we neared. I slumped on the mat and proceeded to grab nuts to munch, as I was starving. Daddy immediately placed a record over the portable gramophone, and the sweet, dreamy, wonderful melodies of Tchaikovsky's music floated in the breeze. I loved *The Nutcracker Suite*, and I would plead with Daddy to repeat that piece again and again, until everyone vehemently protested out of boredom.

I didn't know it then, but it was to be the last of the happy times we spent together as a family for a long while. Daddy ceased to sing or to whistle, and for a very long time, our house became shrouded in sadness and grief.

I kept turning to look at Grandma, who seemed to be tired. Grandma and I were very close. We shared one bedroom, and she told me stories from the *Qur'an* ever since I could speak and comprehend what was being said. At times when I was fearful, she would hold me until I fell asleep. Recently I completed the *Qur'an* under Grandma's tutelage, and Mummy held a small *kenduri* to celebrate my *khatam*.

Grandma was only five feet in height, diminutive compared to Mummy and me. I was already two inches taller than she was by then, but she had a genteel air about her that commanded respect, and when she opened her mouth to speak in that soft but firm voice, people listened. I guess she acquired that authority through the hard knocks of life. Daddy used to tell me how poor they had been and how he had to help his mother earn their livelihood selling *kuehs*.

That day, she wore her hair tied in the shape of a ribbon. Not many people could carry that style. It was difficult to manage that *sanggul lintang* unless one practised it often. I know because Grandma taught me how to do it and I became quite an expert. Grandma was fond of wearing *baju Kedah*, a loose blouse with wide sleeves paired with *kain pelikat*, a sarong which originated from India, mostly worn by Indian men, though it looked natural on Grandma and other old ladies of that period.

I was extremely exhausted when we went home. Mummy advised me to go to bed early after a good shower. At bedtime, Grandma gave me a big hug and told me that I was the best thing that ever happened to her and that she loved me very much. She looked deep into my eyes and told me that I was to listen to my parents and never disobey them. "I will always look out for you, Katarina—remember that."

What Grandma said didn't register with me. I was ten, after all, but I hugged her back and went to sleep immediately.

The next morning, Mummy entered our room to wake me up and get ready for school. She was surprised that Grandma was still sleeping. Usually she'd be out of bed, and after her *subuh* prayers, she'd be in the kitchen getting breakfast ready. Mummy went over to Grandma's bed, touched her, and put her fingers to Grandma's pulse. That's when she started crying. "Get Daddy, Katarina. Please get Daddy." Mummy tried to help Grandma, but I think it was too late. Allah must have taken her when everybody was fast asleep.

As soon as Daddy entered, he knew immediately that Grandma was gone. He fell to the floor on his knees and hugged Grandma's lifeless body. I had never witnessed a death before. Grandma looked as if she were smiling, and she looked so much younger and calmer than usual. Her lips were pink, like that of a young woman.

Mummy hugged me tightly to her, her eyes full of tears. "Grandma's heart gave way, darling," she told me. "She died peacefully. We must thank *Allah* that she was not in pain."

It took a long time before I was able to come to grips with the loss of my grandmother. Most nights Mummy would patiently hold me in her arms and sing endlessly until I fell asleep. Often we would say a short prayer together.

The pain of loss, through death or through separation, would haunt me repeatedly. Those unhappy experiences gave me the courage and strength to face whatever life doled out for me, for deep in my heart, I believed that every cloud had a silver lining.

***

Malek sipped his tea slowly, his eyes thoughtfully watching his daughter as she was absorbed in teaching her cat, Ching, to jump. Her mother had found her the cat, a domestic Malay cat with no determinate pedigree, saving it from the wet market after it followed Suraya around as she was shopping for the week. The cat and Katarina immediately took to each other. When asked what name she would bestow on her new pet, she immediately retorted, "*Kuching.*" That drew much laughter from her parents, as calling a cat that was much like naming a dog "Dog." So it came to be that they finally shortened it to Ching, to which Katarina immediately agreed, for she had read about the Ching dynasty in China. To her, the cat became the emblem of an emperor.

"You made a wise decision, Sue, in finding the cat for Gina to love and care for. She has been so distraught after the loss of her grandma."

"I don't know, *bang.* I think Ching chose to follow me. I didn't even notice him until he sidled up to me and meowed endlessly," she replied as her eyes followed their daughter's antics with the cat.

"She's grown a lot in the last year, hasn't she?" He wasn't expecting an answer. It was obvious to anyone that his daughter had grown about two inches taller since his mother passed on. Now he was looking at his wife, wondering whether it was the correct time to discuss the idea that had been fixated in his mind for some time. He had given it a great deal of thought and desperately wanted her to support his decision.

"There's something I've thought about a great deal lately," he began. He took another sip of tea to wet his throat, which had gone suddenly dry.

He hated to admit to himself that he dreaded his wife's answer. *What if she doesn't agree with me?* He loved her too much to go against her wishes, but he had come to the crossroads of his life, at which time he needed to make the necessary changes if he wanted to move forward.

She focussed her full attention on him, the games played between the cat and the daughter temporarily forgotten.

"What is it, b*ang*?" she replied, her tone betraying her concern. "I notice that you've been preoccupied lately. Is something wrong?"

"Please listen to me carefully, Sue. I'm not going through a midlife crisis, I swear." He took hold of her hands across the table. "I'm getting bored with my life at the office. The work is pretty mundane, and the salary is mere pittance. I'm thinking of our future, especially Gina's."

She opened her mouth to intervene, but he shook his head. "No, *sayang*. Listen to me. You're the best wife and partner a man could ask for. I'm not dissatisfied because of you. I'm dissatisfied because I won't be able to give you and our daughter what you both deserve."

He turned to look at their daughter, who was holding her pet in her arms and talking to him in a motherly manner, her fingers gently stroking the cat's fur as it purred in contentment.

"See how smart she is. She deserves the best education we can provide, but I'm not earning enough to be able to finance her education once she completes her Senior Cambridge," he mused disconsolately.

She got up, went to his side of the table, and pulled out a chair so that they were sitting close together, knee-to-knee. She took his hands and held them tightly on her lap. "You've been the most loving and caring husband a woman could ask for," she began. However, their conversation was interrupted by a screech from their daughter.

"Mummy, Daddy. Look! Ching jumped. Ching jumped," her voice was high-pitched and excited, her hands clapping in glee.

Her parents clapped their hands to cheer her on. "Well done, sweetheart." Malek applauded. Then he turned to his wife, the fond smile still lingering on his face.

"She's such a joy, Sue. I want to give her the best: the best education, the best opportunities. I want to take her on a trip around the world, show her places we've only read to her about, but I can't go gallivanting around the world on my meagre salary," he explained to his wife with enthusiasm.

"I've saved up some money from my salary, but you've never allowed me to use it," she protested.

"Shush," he hushed her. "That's yours to do what you want with it."

"Then what do you propose we do?" she countered.

He answered cautiously. "I met up with an old classmate, Calvin Soo, who migrated to Perak after the war ended. Calvin's in the logging industry, and he's doing rather well. Right now he's looking for a Malay partner because he thinks that it would expedite the business," he explained.

"That sounds good, bang, but I don't want you to make a rash decision without careful consideration. I know logging is a lucrative industry, but is this Calvin trustworthy? Won't he cheat you? After all, it's a new field for you."

"You know me by now, Sue. I'm not afraid to learn and to work hard. Anyway, if we don't try, we'll never know, right? But ..." He stopped and drew a deep breath.

"But what?"

"You'll have to give up your job ... and we'll have to move to Ipoh. That's where Calvin's company is based. The logging areas are in Perak. Calvin will obtain a license once I've agreed. We'll set up a company and work together."

"You don't have to worry about whether I'm agreeable or not. If your mind is already made up, I'll support you a hundred per cent. With regards to my job, well, they do have a hospital in Ipoh, don't they?"

# CHAPTER 5

They MOVED TO Ipoh at the beginning of the year so Katarina could attend school at The Convent. They bought a modest house close to the golf club, which Malek considered a gift since the old Chinese couple who owned the bungalow had planned to move in with their daughter's family close by and wanted a good neighbour to inhabit their house, which carried many beautiful and happy memories for them. So when Malek requested that they lowered the price to suit his pocket, they were quite happy to let it go. The fact that he had a small family was in his favour, as the couple did not fancy having a neighbour with noisy, boisterous children who would keep them awake at night.

The house had been lovingly maintained, with a magnificent garden, beautifully manicured, prolific with fruit trees and an innumerable collection of frangipanis in various shades, their unique scent filling the cool evening air. A small fountain had been erected at the corner close to the bedroom window. At night, the sound of water falling over the rocks, soothing and sensual, created a pleasant ambience that would lull them into a deep, peaceful sleep.

The house in Alor Star, where they had resided for more than thirteen years, was carefully restored and repainted. They still referred to it as George's house, for Malek had not given up hope that his friend would return one day. Despite numerous enquiries, he had failed to find closure regarding George, but his hopes of seeing George again never diminished.

"George would love you, Gina," he told his daughter, who was old enough to understand his attachment to his old friend. "He's one of the finest men I know. He's five years younger than me. I feel as if I've known him a lifetime, as though we were brothers in another life. You'll meet him one day, sweetheart. I have a strong feeling about that." He said this confidently.

So George's house was left in a better condition than when he left. Malek's mother had tirelessly planted hibiscus hedges around the compound. They had grown to more than five feet, and they were neatly trimmed. The garden was resplendent with flowering trees. *Cempaka, kenanga,* and *tanjung* flowers perfumed the early morning air as a gentle breeze drifted through the leaves.

Ipoh was a well-planned town, with good roads that connected all parts of the state. The nine-hole golf course, which was within walking distance from their home, had initially been built on the racecourse in the 1930s, and as a result of its burgeoning membership, it had acquired more land to enlarge it to an eighteen-hole course, with a clubhouse added. The Japanese occupation had destroyed much of the course and the building, but by the time Malek moved to Ipoh, it had been completely renovated and upgraded. Malek would spend many happy hours practising his skill, and it was not unusual for him to rush home minutes before *iftar* during the holy month of *Ramadhan*.

Sending Katarina to the Convent School was a collective decision. Apart from it being known as an excellent school for girls, with its strict discipline, they liked the idea of its interracial composition, as Chinese and Indian parents made it their first choice. Malay girls were few and far between because Malay parents were suspicious that the school could be the centre of Christian efforts at spreading Christianity, though their suspicions had not been proven, for though it had been set up in 1907, initially known as the Sisters of the Holy Infant Jesus, there had been no conversions among Muslims. In the beginning, it was a co-educational establishment. Boys were also admitted until 1912, when they got their own school. It was only in the 1950s, for social and political consideration, that the school was renamed The Main Convent, from the original "St Nicholas' Convent."

Suraya was happy working at a nearby maternity clinic. It had regular hours, and the pay was good. Malek was reluctant to allow her to work, but she convinced him that a little addition to their now-depleted coffer would be necessary. They had spent almost all their savings, plus the inheritance from Malek's mother, to pay for their new house. He had felt completely emasculated as the provider and as a man at having to utilize his wife's savings.

"It doesn't make you less of a man, *bang*," Suraya told him impatiently when he expressed his dissatisfaction at having to "borrow" from her. "Anyway, if it makes you happy, consider it as a loan at forty per cent interest." She laughed. "Come on. Be practical. You need the house as collateral for your business loan. If we didn't spend the money to pay for the house, you wouldn't be able to get the loan, right?"

She had no idea that he had taken it so seriously until years later, when he repaid her.

Katarina, the apple of his eye, did him proud, for after the mid-year exam, she was awarded a double promotion, as her results were excellent. She was to excel in all her school's extracurricular activities as well, right to the end, when she completed her Senior Cambridge. Besides being a prefect, she led her team and won most of the interschool debates, apart from leading the badminton team to glory.

***

His business partnership with Calvin was registered, the license to carry out logging was obtained, and a large logging concession was designated and approved, totalling hundreds of acres. Calvin had an excellent reputation as a decent and honest businessman, who had never succumbed to illegal dealings or unhealthy practices, like cheating and shortchanging the government, as some were wont to do. Despite the many new precautionary steps taken by the government, many cases of under-declaring the quantity of logs harvested still persisted, and logs in areas that were not allocated were "stolen".

As soon as Malek informed her that he would take a study trip into the forest to check on his *kawasan*, Suraya became sick with worry. She had read of armed clashes between the security forces and the communist guerrillas in the jungle of Grik, where her husband was planning to go with his friend and business partner.

At breakfast, she watched him enjoy his cereal, half-boiled eggs, and honey on toast and wondered why he didn't seem apprehensive at all. She had been so distressed that she could hardly sleep the night before, when he had explained his plans to her in detail. Contrarily, Katrina seemed to be as excited as her father was, asking him persistently when she would be able to join him.

"It would be a wonderful adventure, Daddy," she announced as she fluttered around the room like a drunken butterfly.

"One day, poppet," he replied, mussing her hair affectionately.

But his wife was not pacified. "Is it really safe, bang?" she persisted. "*It is* in the wilds. There are tigers and snakes, not to mention communists. What if you get lost?"

Her frowning had begun to line her smooth forehead ever since he informed her of his plans.

"Well, for one, I won't get lost, *insya Allah.* There's a *kepala*, a guide who knows the jungle like the back of his hand. There's also an *Orang Asli* who will act as a guide and advisor as to the dos and the don'ts, according to *their* laws of the jungle. On top of that, there's a platoon of the Malay Regiment patrolling the area. Then of course there's Calvin, who's been in and out of the jungle God knows how often." He hugged her lovingly and stroked a stray hair into place. "I'll be gone for two nights only, Sue. Promise me you won't worry unnecessarily." Then he continued thoughtfully, "To be a successful businessman, I can no longer work from eight to four. I have to be hands-on so I can be familiar with the nitty-gritty of the job."

If she understood, she kept her own counsel. Nevertheless, when he kissed her goodbye, she clung to him like a wounded child.

The four-wheel drive travelled for several hours along the main roads before it veered off into the narrower countryside roads, passing small villages of *Orang Asli.* Children rushed excitedly to their vehicle as it stopped by the roadside to wait for the guide. It was quite rare for them to come across strangers from faraway places. There were no amenities for them, no schools or playgrounds, but they seemed to make do with the little they had and were happy.

Malek and his team continued their journey for several miles more, until they reached a logging tract that could hardly be seen from the main road. Those tracts were narrow lanes that had been cleared for vehicles like the one carrying them and for the lorries that ferried logs to their destinations. According to Calvin, as recently as two years before, buffaloes had been used to transport the logs before being replaced with *the sun tai wongs.*

"Those buffaloes were one of a kind," said Calvin, and Malek listened with rapt interest. "They were males between four and eight years old. Every two weeks, each was fed ten eggs and one bottle of Guinness stout. The buffalo's head would be propped up like so." Calvin demonstrated, holding his chin up so that his face was staring up at the sky. "This was to prevent him from throwing up. After that, he would be given a bath in the river, something I'm sure he loved. You noticed how the buffaloes would wallow in the mud in the *paddy* fields back home in Kedah?" he asked with a grin.

Malek nodded and smiled, thinking back of his childhood days playing in the paddy fields with his cousins. In his mind, a picture appeared of a herd of buffaloes in a mud pool, thrashing about in the clumsy way of buffaloes, soaking themselves lazily for hours on end until their minders came for them.

"But there's one thing, though," Calvin added with a chuckle. "A male is still a male. If he caught sight of a female, *habislah*, he'd abandon the log and run helter-skelter after the female, making that gawd-awful mating sound only buffaloes are capable of."

The mental scene of a six-hundred-pound buffalo crashing through the trees in the forest painted such a comical picture that the friends burst out laughing uproariously.

The vehicle picked its way cautiously along the track. The drive was extremely uncomfortable, for their bodies bumped up and down and swayed this way and that. They crossed a rickety bridge put together clumsily with sawn logs, with the river flowing silently below.

The jungle was never silent. The twitter and chatter of birds created a harmony of sounds in the background. An owl hooted. A monkey screeched. In the distance, a herd of elephants trampled loudly through the trees.

The vehicle meandered crazily along the path, dodging potholes and protracted roots that had grown across the path. The journey could have been worse if not for their driver, who was experienced and skilled in jungle driving.

The trip opened Malek's eyes to the hitherto unseen beauty of the jungle. Large trees with their abundant foliage at times obscured the view along the path. On his left, a gap appeared where the monsoon rains had flooded the area and swept away rotted old trees and fallen trunks. This allowed sunshine to filter through, casting warm rays of light, thus giving new trees and shrubs sufficient time to rear their heads and, with sufficient time, to grow into bigger trees, thereby darkening the clearing again with their rich foliage.

All too soon, they came across a patch barren of trees and shrubs, a desert in the midst of lush green and a wealth of foliage. The guide motioned for them to speak softly as they neared and warned them not to pass remarks that would anger the *penunggu* or all kinds of spells would be cast on them. The lightest would be to suffer from diarrhoea. If the more serious taboos were ignored, like spitting, the victim might not be able to speak for days, until a *bomoh* helped remove the curse.

Calvin broke the silence after they passed the sacred spot. "We picked the right time to visit. This is the best time to appreciate the forest," he asserted. "Later on in the year, when the monsoon starts, it will rain nonstop. Storms will tear across the trees and uproot them. The water level of the river will rise and carry away the log bridge. It is normal for us to construct new bridges after every monsoon. That's the season when we don't carry out our logging activities."

He turned towards the forest on his side and drew his friend's attention to the spectacle before him, pointing to the gaps among the trees where several monkeys were having a grand time swinging from one tree to another. "Look at those monkeys, will you? Those are common monkeys found in our country. Do you know, Malek, that there are hundreds of types of monkeys? Some of them can be found in our jungle," he remarked.

"We're fortunate that our jungles are rich with flora and fauna; some are as yet undiscovered," Calvin continued thoughtfully. "You're lucky today, Malek. Normally monkeys aren't easy to see as they devour their food in the canopy of trees; they can only be detected by the movement of the branches." He smiled at his friend and added, "Or by the braying of the male monkeys."

The driver turned to him and pointed to the footsteps made on the wet patches of the path. "Look, *tuan*. Those are the footsteps made by tigers, probably from last night. They've not been disturbed."

"Do they attack humans? What about timber workers?" Malek asked with some apprehension.

"So far, our workers have been safe. I've heard of one or two incidents. But generally these wild animals leave humans alone, unless provoked," Calvin explained calmly.

As they came closer to the areas of their concession, bigger trees came into view. They alighted from the vehicle as the forest ranger started to point out various trees and identified them according to the variations in their leaves, barks, trunks and sap; the *keruing*, the *meranti*, and the *cengal* were a few of the hardwoods they would harvest. It was a wealth of information for the new logger to take in, and he made sure he paid complete attention to the new lesson for future reference.

***

Night came early in the jungle, heralded first by the untiring cicadas. It was so dark that one could hardly see the back of one's hand. The party stopped at the makeshift base camp erected by the labourers days before. It had been carefully chosen so as not to invite sudden attacks by wild elephants. This had been known to happen before. The campsite was not too far from the river. The luminescent light from the logs over the bridge shimmered eerily, as the glow-worms floated in the air, like a thousand fairies.

Four bamboo poles held the camp together and a large canvas was stretched across, tied carefully at the four corners. Two specially raised beds with mosquito nets were strategically placed in the centre for the two bosses, while the rest of the group made do with tarpaulins laid out on the floor.

As they were enjoying dinner by the roaring fire, several soldiers of the Malay Regiment, fully armed, stopped by to check their identities, and once satisfied that they were bona fide loggers, they smartly marched away after warning them to be on the lookout for strangers who might turn out to be communist guerrillas and to be wary of their booby traps.

The forest rangers who had joined them for the night had a treasure trove of jungle stories and strange happenings. Malek wasn't sure whether to believe them or to treat them only as tales by the campfire. One story that fired his imagination was that of a young forest labourer who had been enticed by the *Orang Bunian* community that lived in the jungle fringes. He had disappeared one night from the camp, and as it was too dark, they stopped searching after walking a few yards off the perimeter of the camp.

The next morning, they found him sitting on a tree stump in complete stupor. The *Orang Asli* guide submerged him in the river several times and proceeded with some rituals that brought him back to normal. As he was emerging from his stupefied state, the young man muttered that he had married a *Bunian* princess in a large ceremony attended by all the *Bunian* community.

Sleeping in a new environment, a jungle at that, was an unnerving experience for Malek, though the forest guide had ensured that one person was on guard duty at all times. The silence was deafening. Once he thought he heard the patter of a cat moving about, accompanied by a low growl, deep and menacing. A glow-worm found its way into the tent and hovered about desperately before it found a means of escape. An owl hooted intermittently— or was there more than one?

At the dawn of a new day, what seemed like a thousand insects exchanged greetings, at times interrupted by the hoot of a gibbon calling for its mate. Rats scurried among the dried leaves around the tent. All kinds of weird sounds that had kept him awake throughout the night returned tenfold to plague the morning.

Adversely, the bath in the river made up for all the discomfort suffered throughout the night. The cool, clear water cascading gracefully down the rocks to his left was music to his ears. As he swam leisurely, his ears were trained to the twitter and chirps of the birds that were flitting from tree to tree. He could identify one or two, but the others seemed alien to him. He was delighted to spy a hornbill, its gorgeous colours brightening the morning.

His wandering eyes caught sight of a host of wild orchids in their full glory, in hues of purple and orange. They brought memories of his wife, who loved flowers above all his other gifts. A little to his right, a gnarled old tree stood proudly, displaying trunks that were coated with rich, velvety moss of various shades of green. A smorgasbord of ferns of all shapes and sizes, moving sensuously to the dictates of the wind, left him entranced. He thought they would make a lovely bouquet for his beloved Sue. He spent several precious minutes gathering them.

Later, as they were watching workers sawing at the mammoth trunk of the *keruing*, Calvin said by way of explanation, "Our timber industry is very old and lucrative. Wisely, the government, ever since the British, in the early twentieth century, had ensured that the forests were not over-logged. It is important to retain the forest cover at eighty per cent, not only as our heritage to our children but also to maintain nature's equilibrium. That's why the government metes out severe punitive action against illegal logging. Heavy fines are imposed." He paused for breath. "One could also be imprisoned," he added.

The loud screech of the chainsaw drowned out his words and reverberated through the forest. Malek wondered aloud how those monstrous trees had been cut before the introduction of the chainsaw.

"In the beginning, it was with the humble axe," Calvin replied, "then with the handsaw. It was hard work. The older generation was a very tough breed, Malek. They put us to shame."

Logging had been in Calvin's family for two generations, albeit on a smaller scale. As a student, he had followed his father and grandfather on their jungle trips during the school holidays and had enjoyed those trips. He learned that it involved hard work, but it was rewarding. Having his father and grandfather as his role models, Calvin had made up his mind, even as a teenager, that he would follow their lead.

Later on in the afternoon, Malek and Calvin watched as one single log of gigantic proportions was slowly winged onto the lorry, popularly referred to as *sun tai wong*. They left the forest as evening descended. It was an enriching experience which Malek would repeat often in future, in a much better frame of mind, as he became more knowledgeable about the industry that would make him a rich man indeed.

# CHAPTER 6

"DADDY'S GOING TO be ravenous after his game of golf, sweetie," Suraya said, her face wreathed in a smile as she watched her daughter's serious countenance while preparing the sauce for her dish. "He's going to love your *gado gado*. It certainly looks mouth-watering."

Katarina's face lit up at her mother's words of praise. At fourteen, she was mature for her age. Thankfully, she was never a chameleon with changing moods, like some of her friends' daughters. To Suraya's delight, that evening Katarina decided to be her sous chef. There were times when she would shoo her mother out of the kitchen so she could "experiment". At those times, they would sample her ingenious concoctions, which were not always pleasantly palatable, though both Suraya and her husband were too considerate to admit it to her.

The doorbell chimed.

"Daddy must have forgotten his keys," Suraya commented as she walked swiftly out of the kitchen towards the main door. She saw him standing at the open door.

"Did you need to announce your arrival, *bang*?" she asked in mock annoyance, wiping her hands dry.

"No," he replied. "I just wanted to announce the arrival of an old friend."

Suraya craned her neck to identify the shadow behind her husband. When Malek propelled his friend forward, Suraya could not believe her eyes. "George?" she whispered. Yet it could not be George. The last time they saw George had been at least sixteen years earlier.

"Suraya," he replied, as he crushed her in a bear hug. "It's been a very long time."

Any further conversation was interrupted as Katarina sailed in with her plate of *gado gado* to show off to her daddy.

"Look, Daddy ..." At the sight of the stranger, she stopped abruptly. There, beside her Daddy, stood a tall man, thin and wiry, with a wide forehead and a receding hairline that nonetheless made him look distinguished. He was looking most amused.

"Come, darling," her father said, breaking the awkward silence. "I want you to meet Uncle George." Gently he pulled his daughter forward and introduced her to him. "George, this is your namesake, Nur Katarina Georgina."

She turned to her mother to pass the plate she was holding and, like the well-brought-up young lady that she was, extended her hands in the Malay fashion to *salaam* with George. Having lived and breathed in their community for several years, he had not forgotten how to respond.

"Hmm ... That's an interesting choice of names. I'm honoured that I was remembered by your daddy when he named you. What may I call you, young lady?" George asked in a sonorous voice with an accent that was alien to her.

"Well, since you're Daddy's best friend, you can call me Gina, like Daddy does," she answered with a flourish. "I'm happy to meet you at last, Uncle George. Daddy always said that you'd be back one day." She prattled cheerfully, instinctively warming up to him.

Suraya and Malek looked at one another. It was a major concession on their daughter's part to allow someone else to address her in the same way her father did.

"A pleasure to meet you, Gina. I had always known Malek and Suraya's daughter would be a beauty," George replied. "Your daddy was always a smart man who could look into the future."

That statement, which complimented her and her father's wisdom, won George another point with Katarina. By the time the four of them were sitting at the dinner table, conversation ran as smoothly as if they had never been apart all those years and Katarina was talking as effusively about her school and her extra-curricular activities, as if she had known George all her life.

Once dinner ended, Katarina excused herself, pleading homework, extremely pleased that her father and her new uncle had demolished her plate of *gado gado* with gusto.

Malek was impatient to find out what really happened in the years George disappeared, but he was content to let his friend direct the course of their conversation. It seemed that he had stopped by Malaya after having made a trip to Thailand, where he had worked during the world war. As he had wanted so much to catch up with Malek and his family and he could not wait to find out about them, he took the train to Alor Star, only to discover that his friend had moved his family to Ipoh. Meeting up with Malek at the golf club was a calculated risk, as he was confident the latter would be perfecting his golf skills, just as he, George, would be doing on a Sunday.

The reunion was epic. The two friends shamelessly shed tears of relief and happiness as they hugged and backslapped one another. Now, sitting down comfortably in his friend's sitting room after a hearty meal, George was mellow and calm as he began his story.

"I needed to make that trip to Thailand in order to fumigate the horrors, the hatred and the bitterness that darkened my soul the past sixteen years," he began. "It proved to be therapeutic, as my friend who was also a prisoner of war, had assured me. For years, I could not put paid to the horrible experiences, the pain, the torture and depravity that we suffered. It affected my marriages. I married twice—neither marriage worked out, Malek. I'd wake up in the middle of the night screaming. Tell me, what woman would put up with that kind of life?"

Malek shook his head in sympathy, his mouth pressed in a tight, grim line. He sympathized with his friend who had experienced so many traumas in his life, whereas he himself had enjoyed much love and harmony. What's more, he had been extremely blessed with a lovely wife and a lovelier daughter.

Suraya had prepared a pot of coffee in anticipation of what would be a long night for the three of them after Katarina said good night and left for her room. She had not pestered George for information that he may not feel ready to talk about, allowing him to ramble on in any way he liked. *You banish the pain and grief when it's shared with people you love and who love you*, she thought.

"I left Alor Star the day the Japanese conquered Jitra. I didn't want to take the risk of being captured after I left my letter to you," George began. His face broke into a grin. "By the way, Malek and Suraya, thanks for looking after the house. I meant it when I said that it was yours. You both did a magnificent job of maintaining the house in such tip-top condition. I stopped by, and your neighbour told me where to find you." He grinned at Suraya affectionately. "She told me that you've been a wonderful friend and that during the war years, you shared a lot of food with her family. She sends you her love."

The news of her former neighbour and the fact that they still remembered her with affection brought a warm glow to Suraya. She smiled in appreciation.

George took a long puff at his pipe before he moved on with his story. "Anyway, I drove nonstop for several exhausting hours and made a beeline for Singapore. Like most Englishmen at that time, I was convinced that the Japanese would attack from the sea and that there was no chance they would be able to demolish our defences in Singapore. We were convinced that it was impregnable. Unwittingly, we facilitated the speedy conquest of that island." He gave a long, mournful sigh. "I took a job at the garrison there as a clerk and was there until the day the Japanese soldiers rounded us up. Some were bayoneted. I was punched and slapped as I resisted them. We were shepherded to the Changi prison, where we huddled together—fifty thousand men in a place meant for four thousand."

He looked at Suraya with concern, as she seemed horrified at the picture he was painting. "Sue," he said gently, "this may be too traumatic for you."

"No, George, I'm okay. What I'm feeling now is nothing compared to what you went through, I'm sure," she responded gently.

"The worst is yet to come," he said sadly. "I can't remember exactly how long we were incarcerated there, as days and night merged into long hours of pain, agony, and hunger. I was told later on that it lasted for eight months. Starvation, dysentery … you name it … affected us at one time or another." He paused. His eyes scrunched up with the pain of remembering.

Malek poured a glass of water and handed it to George, who seemed too upset to continue as he recalled his experiences.

"Then one day," George continued as he put down the empty glass, "we were shepherded out of the prison and crammed into a train which travelled for several days. The carriages were tiny, and we suffered from the heat as we were trussed up like pigs in a pen; moreover, we could not quench our thirst, for there was no water. There were also no toilets, so we had to answer the call of nature as best as we could. By the time the train stopped, we had been infected by vermin that caused unbearable itchiness. Some vomited nonstop. It was horrendous. Some of us prayed for the end." He took a deep, shaky breath. "If only we knew then what the Japanese had planned for us!"

"I'm so sorry, George. How you must have suffered!" Malek's voice was soft and full of sympathy, which George acknowledged with a semblance of a smile.

"The worst was yet to come, Lek," he said. "I think it was on the sixth day, when the train stopped and let us all out. We thought our suffering was over, but no, the soldiers made us march through the jungle paths for hundreds of miles until we were half dead with exhaustion. Those who refused to go farther were bayoneted and left as fodder for the wild animals. We only realized at the end of that long track that we were supposed to build a railway line for them to join Bangkok to Burma, for the Japanese army to transport their cargo." George inhaled long and hard, and then exhaled, as gently and softly as the breeze that whiffed the perfume of the flowers through the open window.

"Sixteen months of torture and hard labour followed. We utilized whatever energy we had left to break the ground manually, using pickaxes and shovels. Stones were crushed with hammers. Trees were cut down and sliced into planks for the sleepers, and some were lugged to the river to build a bridge across the *Mae Klong River*, famously known as the bridge on the River Kwai. It's said that for every plank of wood laid, one POW died." He winced as he recalled the rampant cruelty of the Japanese soldiers.

"And you had to do all those things?" Suraya wondered aloud, a tortured expression on her face.

"Oh, yes, Sue. No one was exempt, even if you were sick, or you'd get the feel of the rifle butt on your head. I was lashed with wire whips on my back once because I stopped working due to exhaustion. I have the marks to prove it." George stood up and lifted the back of his shirt.

His skin had healed, but the mark of the lashes across his back was a grim reminder of the pain he must have endured. Tears welled up in Suraya's eyes and trickled down her fair cheeks. He watched transfixed as Malek tugged his wife to his side, his cheek pressed against hers, his right hand sliding up and down her arms in his effort to comfort her.

George closed his eyes as he felt a significant wave swamping him, and as it receded, it washed away the debris of pain and hatred that he had carried in his heart for years. When he finally opened them, he felt absolute relief and light-heartedness, which had been absent in his life since the war. He stared at the couple before him, and as Suraya dabbed her tears dry, from the well deep down in his heart, in that poignant moment, love overflowed for her, his best friend's wife.

The knowledge hit him hard. He felt shaken to the core. Slowly he lowered himself onto the sofa. He became silent for a long time. He realized that his hands were shaking, and he could not look in their direction. In his heart, a myriad of emotions threatened to spill out. There was joy in the knowledge that he could feel love again and that the pain and anger had receded. Her tears had been cathartic for him. There was apprehension that he would not be able to remain as affable as he should be without betraying his true feelings. There was a feeling of hopelessness that he could never display anything more than pure friendship.

Malek noticed that George's shoulders had begun to droop. He interpreted George's continued silence as his friend being exhausted. He suggested they rest for the night. As Suraya dutifully cleared the table, Malek solicitously showed his friend to the guest room for a much-needed rest, and as his friend got ready for sleep, he checked on his wife in the kitchen.

It was a long night for George. The taste of fear and pain that had reminded him of those long years of incarceration had diminished, to be replaced by an intense longing for something fragile and unreachable. Those long hours of sleeplessness and introspection failed to bring any respite to his chaotic mind.

Their game of golf the next day was lacklustre. It was an easy victory for Malek, which did nothing for his self-esteem, as George's mind did not seem to be on the game. Malek attributed that to George's depressed frame of mind after recalling those terrible experiences in his life the night before. In those pre-war days, George had displayed his mettle on the golf course and it took a lot of concentration and skill for Malek to defeat him. If only he could read George's mind and know the kind of war that was raging inside!

At dinner that night, Katarina was excitedly discussing the film that she had seen with her friend in the afternoon. "It's based on a true-life event,

Uncle George," she said, not noticing her mother's warning glare. "It's called *The Bridge on the River Kwai*. Did you know that?"

George smiled at her exuberance. *It's wonderful to be young and innocent,* he thought. He had only known her for a couple of days, yet he knew that he loved her as if she were his own. He put down his fork and spoon and grinned.

"Of course I know about the bridge. I helped build it." He infused his statement with a modicum of pride for her benefit. "I was one of the sixty thousand prisoners of war who were forced to construct the bridge. We spent eight months completing that project."

"Were you tortured too, the way it was shown in the film?" she enquired with childlike innocence.

"Well, you know what they do with films. They exaggerate a little bit to make it more interesting," he lied, forcing a smile that did not quite reach his eyes.

She looked too sweet and innocent for him to recount the barbaric treatment he and the other prisoners were exposed to. Water boarding was a favourite form of torture. Then there was the way the *Kempeitai* cackled with laughter when prisoners with skin injuries were tortured with sharp bamboo strips that left them screaming in absolute agony. There were also rampant diseases that killed more than twelve thousand POWs. He was lucky to have survived. To regale to her all those gory details, when their captors glorified in their brutality, would ultimately wipe away the light dancing in her dark eyes. She would probably not be able to sleep, and he wouldn't have that.

She seemed to be satisfied with his answer, for she didn't refer to it again.

The discussion soon reverted to the day Malaya would achieve her independence from the British and its celebration on 31 August that year, which was months away, to be held on a large scale in Kuala Lumpur, the capital city.

"Uncle George, you're joining us, aren't you? Daddy is planning a family trip to KL. We're going to celebrate with other Malayans. It's going to be great!" she announced.

This placed him in a quandary. It would be wonderful to spend time with them, but could his heart take it? He thought it was the right time to inform them of the decision he had made the night before, after he had agonized for hours. It was best for him to leave and learn to come to grips with his new discovery before he destroyed his precious relationship with Malek's family and corroded their beautiful relationship based on trust and mutual respect. However, he was sure he would miss the little temptress he had grown to love. He forced a smile when he turned to her.

"That sounds wonderful, Gina. But I'm thinking that I should move on now. When I left England, I didn't plan to be away too long. I'd like to get my affairs in order, maybe travel to Alor Star and find out if I can continue where I left off before the war. Or maybe start something new. Whatever it is, I should start the ball rolling," he explained.

Katarina jumped in before anyone could respond. "Whatever you decide, Uncle George. I hope you decide to stay in Malaya."

"Gina's right, you know, George. You don't have a family in England, but you have one here," Malek stated, his upturned right hand pointing to himself, his wife, and his daughter. "And there are many opportunities for you here … Why, you could get into rubber plantation or tin mining. The possibilities are endless."

"You guys are very persuasive …"

"You already have a house, George," Suraya interrupted. "Half the battle's won."

He swallowed hard. Her voice was music to his ears. *I must get away fast,* he thought, *before I make a fool of myself and destroy this precious bond I have with this family.*

He forced a laugh, his eyes avoiding hers. "Well then, it's settled. I'll take a train ride tomorrow back to my house—or the house that you left for me—and then … we'll see," he added thoughtfully.

The train ride was long and surprisingly pleasant, with no rekindled memories of his tragic past. He had dreaded the trip for fear it might invoke memories of his enforced journey from Singapore years before, packed like sardines in a tin can. The monotonous thumping of the wheels as they rolled over the rails, the engines sputtering to a regular beat in the background, while intermittently the horn blared to announce the train's arrival in the vicinity, became music to his ears. He found the discomfort of swaying to the left and right, as the train zigzagged around a curving track, to be pleasant. The railway track passed by a couple of "New Villages", so named because the government had resettled the Chinese community who used to live at the edges of the forests, the better to monitor them to reduce the chances of their being harassed by the communists for food or information. The endless rows and rows of rubber trees evoked a feeling of nostalgia as he recalled the times when he used to run a plantation for a large British company. He even enjoyed the cacophony of sounds of the various languages and accents spoken when the train stopped to drop off passengers or pick up new ones. At the smaller towns, passengers would board with their chickens and a multitude of farm products. That too was vaguely comforting.

As he closed his eyes to savour the pleasant interlude, his mind reverted to the predicament he was in. Granted, he was hopelessly in love with Suraya. It should not detract him from carrying on with his life as long as he kept his distance from her. To be able to love again, albeit an unrequited one at that, and to know that the object of his affection was a person so worthy of that love, after the failures and experiences he had been through, was a miracle. The taste of fear and pain that inhabited the crevices of his mind and rendered him helpless and inadequate had somehow faded away, leaving him energized and eager to move on.

When he stepped off the train hours later, he was in a better frame of mind. He had resigned himself to his fate, and the future was beckoning him. He would engineer that future for himself, he vowed.

# CHAPTER 7

SURAYA WAS GOING through the guest list scheduled for the *Merdeka* celebration on Saturday, 31 August 1957, which was slated to start late Friday evening. Malek had chartered a bus to ferry his grandfather's followers from Alor Star to Kuala Lumpur, where he had booked a hotel for them. His family would be staying at the bungalow he had bought for Suraya at the upscale area close to the city. She remembered the incident clearly.

It was a Friday. He had gone to the office as usual after sending Katarina to school. She caught them whispering like two schoolchildren who were hiding something up their sleeves. Curious, she asked suspiciously, "What are you two whispering about?"

"Nothing, Mummy," Katarina replied innocently.

"Oh, Sue," Malek said, as if in an afterthought, "could you pick up Gina by four? I don't think I can make it in time."

Father and daughter got into the car and drove away, smiling like two conspirators. As she drove to work, she wondered what her two loved ones were up to. Nevertheless, she arranged for her colleague to take over her shift so she could leave earlier, as her husband requested.

Around four o'clock, when she arrived home with her daughter, Malek was standing by his car, two suitcases already packed. Surprised, she enquired of her daughter, "Is Daddy going somewhere?"

"I don't know, Mummy," she replied. She almost blurted out her father's plan.

Suraya parked the car carefully and emerged from the car perplexed. "Are you going somewhere, *bang*?"

"No," he replied, his expression almost comical as he attempted to keep his laughter in check. "*We* are going somewhere."

"Oh, Mummy," Katarina giggled. "Don't you remember it's your birthday today? Daddy has got a surprise trip for you."

Malek wagged a finger at his daughter. "That was supposed to be a secret too."

"*Kesihan,* Mummy," his daughter replied. "She looked so confused, Daddy." She immediately threw her arms around her mother and gave her a bear hug that almost squeezed the breath out of her. "Happy birthday, Mummy."

Suraya stepped away as her husband moved to take her in his arms. "Not you," she said, "not until you tell me what you plan to do."

"Well, we're going to KL to celebrate your birthday. We'll spend the weekend shopping and going to the movies. I thought you might like that." As her frown disappeared, he pressed his advantage. "Now, can your doting husband give you a k—?"

He didn't have to ask, for even before the word left his lips, she had already flung her arms around his neck and smothered him with several loud kisses.

The journey took almost two hours. They kept themselves occupied with their plans to bring their relatives to KL for the celebration. Malek was to arrange his grandfather's transport and accommodation. Even before they reached the city, Malek veered off to the left into a quiet road where several large houses were situated, each surrounded by a spacious compound.

"Are we visiting someone?" Suraya looked around with curiosity.

Her husband didn't answer but carefully swerved his Volvo into the nearest garden. "It's a beautiful house, isn't it?" he said. Without waiting for her reply, he jumped out of the car and opened her door with a flourish. "Welcome home, darling!"

Katarina hopped out and circled her mother in a dance that she alone could choreograph.

"Do you like it, Mummy? I helped Daddy pick this house."

She was at a loss for words. The bungalow was erected at the far end of the driveway, with a fountain facing the front porch. Tall cedar trees lined the driveway. The front entrance was impressive. When she recovered her voice, she said softly, almost inaudibly, "You bought this house? Why?"

"Why? Because I love you. Because I promised to pay you back as soon as I could. Because you're the most wonderful wife and mother a man could ask for. Now, is there any other reason that could convince Mummy, Gina?"

He was talking to her back, for his daughter had wandered off to the front door.

"Mummy, come and look!" she beckoned imperiously.

Suraya turned to her husband with shining eyes. "I love you too, bang. You needn't have to prove your love in this way, but I'm very grateful," she said, as she stood on her tiptoes and kissed him so tenderly that it brought tears to his eyes.

Gently he took her hand and led her to where their daughter was creating a ruckus. "Mummy, look!" There on the left wall beside the main door was her name, *Suraya*, written in the most beautiful *khat,* in gold lettering, over a dark bronze base.

"I helped Daddy choose this too, Mummy. Do you like it?"

As an answer, she drew her daughter into her arms and hugged and kissed her. "Yes, my Katarina, I love it. I love it very much. Thank you. You have great taste."

The rest of the five-bedroom house was spacious, but Malek had not retouched or repainted it. "I want you to decide on the interior and the decor, Sue." He pulled out some documents from the valise he was carrying. "Here is the title to the house."

She took the documents from him with reverence, her eyes carrying a message only he could decipher.

"You can thank me later," he whispered softly in her ear, his teeth giving it a meaningful nip.

They spent many happy holidays in that house. Suraya, with her "magic wand", according to her daughter, had transformed it into a modern hub for the family and for close friends to meet and enjoy each other's company.

It was here that she planned to invite her friend, Mei Lin, to stay for the two days they planned for the Independence Day celebrations. Malek couldn't understand why she had to invite her old friend.

"For George," she replied simply.

"Oh, no, Sue. It won't work," he said confidently. He found the idea humorous.

"Why?" she protested. "What's so funny?" She stared at him, wide-eyed with incredulity.

"She's not his type," he replied confidently, shaking his head.

"*Bang*, she's pretty. She has a lot in common with George," she reasoned. "They went through such horrendous tragedies in their lives. They would have developed that sangfroid, for want of a better word, to overcome anything. You know, like two birds of a feather and such?"

He burst out laughing. "Your analogy sucks," he replied when he was able to control his laughter.

"Think about it," she continued, ignoring his merriment. "They're two lonely people who went through failed marriages—well, maybe not in Mei Lin's case ... But you know what I mean. I want George to have a happy marriage, like the one we have. That's not too much to hope for, is it?"

"I'd like that for him too, but I don't think she's the one for him. He'd probably like her as a friend."

"Want to bet?" his wife challenged him.

She seemed so convinced of her chances of success that he didn't have the heart to tell her that he knew George well and that Mei Lin was not the cure for his ills, but not to burst her bubble, he gallantly extended his hand to her.

"Deal," he said.

Malek underrated his wife's determination as she engineered various opportunities for their two friends to be together, starting with *Merdeka* Day. Mei Lin had accepted her invitation to stay in her house for the celebration, but George, to her disappointment, declined, pleading that he had to take care of the company's guests that would be in Kuala Lumpur to observe the occasion. He had been offered a position in the old company that he had worked for before the war, this time holding a more senior post.

Katarina was unhappy that her Uncle George was not going to celebrate it with her, or so she thought, but she was kept busy playing host to her great-grandfather and his wife as well as her grandmother on her mother's side.

At eighty-six, her great-grandfather was still sprightly and lucid. If not for the slightly advanced Parkinson's disease that caused such degeneration in his muscles, making him tremble uncontrollably and his head to shake, he was still a force to be reckoned with. His sense of humour did not abate, though it was painful to watch him struggle with his speech. She loved him and appointed herself his nursemaid when he was at their home. She insisted in pushing his wheelchair when they attended the Merdeka celebrations, despite her father's protests.

On Friday, 30 August 1957, Kuala Lumpur took on an air of festivity. Busloads of Malayans from all walks of life and from all over the country converged in KL to celebrate. The Royal Selangor Club Padang, which was to be the venue for the historic handover of power by the British to the Malayans, had been packed with excited people of all races and creed, eager to witness this once in a lifetime event. Early in the evening, a crowd of tens of thousands of people poured into the streets, finally converging on the field, in anticipation of participating in the much-awaited ceremony that was not due to start until a little before midnight.

By eleven thirty, Katarina and her parents wheeled in her great-grandfather, politely making their way through the multitude of people to the place where her great-grandfather's followers had grouped. Most of the dignitaries had arrived, even the King and the Tunku, the prime minister designate.

"Where *is* Uncle George?" Katarina mumbled for the tenth time.

"Gina, he has guests to look after. Don't fret. He'll be here when he can make it," her father consoled her.

"Here I am!" the latecomer's voice boomed. "Sorry. I couldn't see where you were with all these people. There must be tens of thousands of people here," he said as he gave her a hug. "Phew. I've never seen so many people."

Before anybody could respond, the lights went out. The field was in total darkness. The crowd cheered. So did she. She put two fingers in her mouth and whistled like a tomboy. As the lights went on again two minutes later, every one of her family members stared at her in surprise. George found it highly amusing.

At the stroke of midnight, the Union Jack was lowered. The symbol of colonialism was down, and the flag of a free nation, *Jalur Gemilang*, was raised.

The response was tumultuous. The Tunku, in a voice laden with intense emotion and pride, raised his right hand high up in the air, his fist tightly closed, and shouted *"Merdeka!"* Shouts of *"Merdeka"* reverberated across the field. The seventh one rang the loudest. The crowd erupted with joy and unwavering patriotism. Katarina egged her Uncle George to follow suit. Her unflagging enthusiasm and her boundless energy dragged him to the peak of excitement of the crowd. His voice was as hoarse as hers was after the seventh *Merdeka*.

Even Great-Grandpa didn't want to be left out. As the Tunku gave his speech, his voice at times at the breaking point because he was overcome by emotion, Great-Grandpa also shed tears of joy in total harmony with that great man. Clearly, patriotism was not defined by age. When the function ended at 1.00 a.m., Katarina was skipping happily, buoyant with the feeling of being at one with the whole nation.

Later, when they were at home, Malek turned to his wife. "Well, how did it go?" he asked, his eyes trained on his wife's graceful movements as she lathered her face with night cream.

She pretended ignorance. "How did what go?"

"Your matchmaking." He grinned mischievously. "I was right, wasn't I? There wasn't a tiny bit of a spark. I told you. There's no chemistry between those two," he said with the tone of the victor, the one who was convinced he was right.

Her beauty routine complete, she slid sensuously into bed, and as she put her arm around his middle, she burrowed her face in his shoulder. "Give them a chance," she mumbled. "Can you allow me to sleep in peace now?" She yawned loudly, a long and exaggerated yawn.

He denied her request. "No peace for the wicked," he said as he started tickling her, "unless you admit you've lost the bet."

"Never," she replied, responding in kind. Soon their light-hearted banter turned into something more serious, and shrieks and laughter turned into moans and groans of pleasure.

**\*\*\***

Not giving up hope because she knew that Mei Lin was not indifferent to George, Suraya tried several times more in her effort to match the two. A small and exclusive birthday dinner for her husband was attended by George and Mei Lin only, apart from their daughter. A quiet family barbecue held under the romantic light of the stars included George and Mei Lin too, with a picnic by the waterfall and a swim by the beach. Though he was polite, gregarious, and full of charm, George didn't follow up until finally, having suspected Suraya's true motives, he hinted to his friend that he was not on the lookout for a mate.

Suraya could not understand why all the plans that she engineered to bring her two friends together had failed. They had seemed to be so well-matched. At least, she thought, they would understand and appreciate one another, having undergone similar life-threatening experiences, mental and physical torture that left indelible imprints in their memories and punctured their sleep with horrible nightmares.

"I don't understand," she said with a frown, having admitted defeat. "Together they would be a perfect team, like us, *bang*. We understand one another so perfectly because we come from the same background."

"That may be so, Sue, but we fell in love with one another the first time we saw each other, remember?"

"Well..." She was hesitant. "I have a secret that I never told anyone, not even you."

His heart missed a beat. He wondered whether she was going to confess that she had been in love with someone else before they met. He waited nervously, a sudden fit of jealousy hastening the beating of his heart.

"Well?" he asked impatiently when she didn't continue immediately.

"I hate to admit this, but ..."

"But what?" he interjected.

She smiled shyly. "I was in love with you ever since I saw you jogging in the college field. I was in Standard Two. You never even noticed me."

"You were only, what, seven, eight? Sue!" He roared with laughter.

"I know, *bang*," she responded with a smile. "But that didn't stop me from dreaming about you. I told my childhood friend Sheila that I was going to marry you when I grew up. I was lucky. Our *jodoh* brought us together. Now I'm the happiest woman on earth."

"And you've made me the happiest man on earth," he added with alacrity.

Not to submit too quietly, she challenged him, "Now who's got the last laugh?"

"We both do," he replied succinctly, drawing her into his arms for a demonstration of his happy state of mind.

After an enthusiastic response, she persisted, "*Bang,* why can't George and Mei Lin find love with each other like we have?" She stubbornly reverted to her pet peeve, which was gradually getting on his nerves.

He sighed with barely subdued impatience. "You yourself said a while ago that *jodoh* plays a very important part in finding a life partner, Sue. They are not destined to fall in love and be together." He shook his head at her stubborn insistence. "Give it up, Sue," he advised her, feeling sorry that all her efforts came to naught. "Maybe it's not meant to be. Maybe one day George will find happiness with the woman he loves. Only time will tell."

# CHAPTER 8

M Y TEENAGE YEARS were the happiest and most remarkable years. Daddy overwhelmed Mummy and me with his unstinting love and generosity. His star was on the ascendant. His business was doing extremely well. His circle of friends was expanding and he had spread his wings into the local politics. With his success came respectability, but one attribute that placed my father above other men was that he never let his wealth and the accolades he received make him forget his roots or his family. Through it all, he remained the charming and charismatic man he had been, yet his needs were simple. Though countless women threw themselves at his feet, he remained true and faithful to Mummy all his life.

To my mind, my parents' marriage was ideal. I recall with nostalgia the great love and respect they had for each other. Their marriage certainly had its difficulties, but I never heard Daddy raise his voice, much less his hands, to Mummy.

I remember distinctly two classmates I had when I was in Form 2: May and June, twins who were born a few minutes apart. May was born two minutes before midnight on 31 May, and June was born two minutes after midnight on 1 June. They were the most beautiful girls in the school, with dewy brown eyes, shiny brown hair, luminescent skin and sparkling white teeth. Moreover, their voices could draw a nightingale out of hiding. At our concert at the end of the year, they brought the house down with their rendition of "When the Nightingale Sang in Berkeley Square."

They loved to play pranks on us by misleading us about their identity, and it became almost a daily game for us to identify them. I was privy to their secret, which I've kept until this very day. May had a birthmark behind her left ear, and she was the more protective of the two, being the older sibling. Her voice was huskier, and she was more sensitive than her younger sister was.

I was drawn to them, and for two years, we were firm friends, so I was the only one who knew the suffering and hardships they went through because they had a drunkard for a father. On more than one occasion, the twins would come to school with puffy red eyes, having cried their hearts out whenever their father became inebriated and took out his anger on their mother. Whenever this happened, they would cower in their room in fear and helpless anger as their father slapped their mother and screamed at her for whatever it was that had aroused his ire.

I had no idea how to handle the problem then, so I did the best I could by being kinder to the twins and by pretending I was ignorant of their predicament, studiously avoiding their eyes and speaking in soft tones.

As May and I became closer, I gradually became her sounding board. Although I felt completely helpless, I would listen quietly as she poured her heart out. In hindsight, I wish I had done more, but as a young teen and living in a society that did not interfere in the domestic affairs of others, there was no recourse.

On my home front, nothing could be better. Every year, true to his promise, Daddy arranged numerous trips that made me look forward to the end of the year holidays. We started with South-East Asian countries like Thailand and Burma, to be followed by Indonesia. Then came France, Italy and Spain. One year it was the United States, followed the next year by Canada.

Nothing could ever mar the unique and exciting experiences impregnated in my mind of the two similarly exotic, yet completely different places we visited: Cartagena in Colombia and Istanbul in Turkey.

Daddy had been looking forward to visiting his business counterparts in Colombia for some time. That country on the northern tip of South America was not considered a safe place to visit. People talked about drug cartels and frequent kidnappings, but we decided to take the risk anyway.

Safety being the major issue, Daddy took the necessary precaution by arranging for two bodyguards to take care of Mummy and me while he reluctantly left for his meetings, leaving us to go sightseeing on our own, his firm warning to stick to the scheduled trip, ringing in our ears.

I remember Cartagena well because that was the first time I saw a sloth; it was at the hotel compound. I stood transfixed when I saw this mammal that had clung to the tree when I left after breakfast and that was still there when I returned at night. No wonder a lazy person is likened to a sloth. I learned that sloths sleep fifteen to twenty hours in the same tree and they mate and give birth in that tree. Wow, I was entranced!

Like all tourists, Mummy and I went on cruises to the islands in the Caribbean and visited the centuries-old historic town, which had been declared UNESCO World Heritage, but what was special to me was the chance to visit the extinct *volcan de Tutomo*, about one hour's drive from the city.

It was a never-to-be forgotten experience. Mummy and I spent hours soaking in the bubbling hot mud in the crater of the volcano, fifty feet above the ground. In order to reach the crater, we had to climb tiny stairs, which became quite scary once you looked down from the top. From the crater, the view of the surrounding was breathtaking. We were in awe of the spectacular view of Santa Catalina in the far distance. The surrounding mountains and lakes were a painter's masterpiece on a palette of greens and blues.

There were not too many tourists that morning, for we had started early. We had the pool to ourselves. Mummy giggled like a schoolgirl. It was an uncanny experience floating on the surface of thick gooey and slimy mud, our whole bodies except our faces completely swathed in mud. Legend had it that a priest had sprinkled holy water onto the lava of the spewing volcano and tamed it. It seemed like a natural spa, and we were told that the mud had natural healing powers, as the minerals within would rejuvenate the skin.

It was the best time I had with my mother because we had a mother-daughter conversation which would have been uncomfortable under different circumstances. I had never felt as close to my mother then or since.

Istanbul was next. In my mind, I had always conjured romantic pictures of Ottoman emperors in their rich flowing robes with huge turbans on their heads, which distinguished them from other potentates, followed at a discreet distance by their concubines of a multitude of races and denominations. What utter debauchery!

Mummy and I must have visited the five-hundred-year-old Grand Bazaar four times during that visit, drooling over myriads of "stuff", as Daddy called it, as we browsed in over more than three thousand shops within that ancient building! It was a maze of labyrinths which made us lose our way several times, so engrossed were we with the objet d'arts so characteristic of

Turkish culture and traditions, magnificent carvings, and bric-a-brac which we couldn't find anywhere else: a vase, a set of teacups, porcelain figurines. We went crazy!

Daddy would accompany us on those shopping trips, patiently standing by as we bargained and haggled. He didn't feel that it was safe for two women to be "gadding about" the city with armfuls of shopping extravaganza.

The cruise along the scenic Bosphorus was a once-in-a-lifetime experience which I relive in my mind's eye time and time again. In the dark of the night, when sleep evades me and my heart is heavy with feelings consciously suppressed, I distract my thoughts to scenes of the vastness of the deep blue ocean with clear waters that lap gently to the whispers of the wind. Visions of the grandiose ancient palaces and mosques, with high minarets and domes that we passed by, as the cruise ship meandered along the twenty-mile strait from the Sea of Marmara to the Black Sea, soothe my aching heart, until finally I'm able to close my eyes and my mind to dreams that could never be.

It was wonderful to see my parents' reaction to the beauty that surrounded them. They held hands and smiled into each other's eyes, like two young lovers. At seventeen, I was mature and wise enough to appreciate the love and devotion my parents had for one another. It was something that I too dreamed of having one day, when the right man came along.

No visit to Istanbul would have been complete without paying tribute to the Dolmabahce, which to me was the most symbolic of all the architectural marvels of the thriving, albeit decadent, Muslim Empire. The Topkapi became the court of the Ottoman kings for four centuries, from the fifteenth century to the nineteenth, Constantinople having been conquered from the Holy Roman Empire in 1453 and renamed Istanbul. One can only gape in wonder and bemusement as one walks along the corridors of Topkapi and imagines the intrigues and plots that were hatched behind its walls, where concubines and eunuchs played their role with hidden hands.

We had the rare opportunity to view the Topkapi's collection of Chinese Caledon porcelain, which was renowned for its beauty as well as its magical power of changing colour if filled with poisoned food. We did not miss the Hagia Sophia Museum, which, to my mind, could have been the eighth wonder of the world.

It was a dream come true for me.

As a little girl, I used to rattle off the monuments and structures that made up the seven wonders of the ancient world, and to be able to touch one that was a wonder in itself was a dream come true. The Hagia Sophia, the guide explained, had been built in 537 BC by the Byzantine kings and had been worshipped as a church for the previous one thousand years. In 1453, when the Turks captured Constantinople, they converted it into a mosque.

On looking up at the massive dome, which was fifty-five metres from ground level, it transported me into another world. Gold mosaics that obliterated the original Christian symbols glittered in the sunlight that filtered through the forty windows on either side. The crescent, the symbol of Islam, had replaced the Cross on the summit of the dome. The altar and the pulpit had been cleverly disguised.

The fact that the church had not been totally demolished spoke well for the wisdom of the Ottoman rulers and the ingenuity of the architects of the period.

In 1935, when Kemal Attaturk became the first president of the Republic of Turkey, the building was converted into a museum.

I could never in a million years forget my trip to Istanbul. It was so picturesque and memorable that it eclipsed all other places that I ever visited with my devoted parents.

Years and years later, I would travel again to the dream city of my youth and marvel at its architectural masterpieces with my beloved, who would share my fascination and awe. He would patiently explain to our children and me the significance of each feature through his eyes, the eyes of a connoisseur. But that would be a long way into the future.

Our last trip together as a family was to London. I suspect that Daddy was living his dreams through me. Fortunately, I didn't let him down. England was his first choice for me to continue with my studies. My success was his success. When I opted to continue completing my sixth form in my hometown, he supported me, and when I obtained good results in the finals, he rejoiced. When I was awarded a scholarship, he could talk of nothing else.

I suspect that he regretted not having the opportunity to further his studies in some of the renowned universities overseas like some of his friends, who returned with the much-desired scroll and who rose to prominence in the country's administration and politics.

Studying at an English university, I suppose, was, to many Malayans of that era, the culmination of a lifelong dream of achieving academic success and climbing the top social structure, as a degree would guarantee respectable jobs in the administration of the country. I grew up clapping my hands and tapping my feet to the rhythm of English nursery rhymes like "Baa, Baa, Black Sheep", "Ding Dong Bell", and many others that I still remember today. In secondary school, we were exposed to English novelists and poets, like Emily Bronte, Keats, and Wordsworth, whose works we learned to appreciate. Little wonder that to some Malayans, English was proudly upheld as their first language.

There is a favourite saying among Malays to explain the feeling of awe that accompanies a person's first exposure to a place foreign to him: *macam rusa masuk kampung*, like a deer lost in a village. That was exactly how I felt when I first stepped foot in London and absorbed the environment, the atmosphere, the scent and the sounds. Everything was totally alien, yet something I could identify with. Batu Road was the shopping haven in Kuala Lumpur, but it was nothing compared to Oxford Street. There were people of all races speaking in various tongues, but almost everyone understood English. Imagine my excitement at my first glimpse of the Tower of London or the London Bridge, when at eight I joyfully tapped to the rhythm of the song. The underground system and network was scary, albeit exciting to travel. The train journeys were a welcome experience as miles and miles of the green expanse of the English countryside swept by.

We dined at restaurants that offered various cuisines, after which we would walk tirelessly along the streets. Sometimes our feet would lead us to Broadway as we watched and listened with excitement to the tunes of *Oh! Calcutta!*, *Fiddler on the Roof*, *Hello, Dolly*, and *My Fair Lady*. That was my first exposure to live entertainment of such magnitude, and I became totally addicted.

One Sunday we walked to Hyde Park and stood by at the speakers' corner. It was a unique experience for us. Nowhere in the world was there a place where one could stand and spout anything that one desired, short of insulting the British royalty. In our country, no such thing would have been tolerated! The pomp and ceremony associated with the Changing of the Guards at Buckingham Palace was an eye-opener. Not only was the ritual uncommon, but it was certainly attention grabbing, as the guards in their red-and- white uniforms and tall fluffy black hats, marched so smartly that I was tempted to march as well.

Like the average tourists, we too unfailingly took the Thames River cruise and the city tour. Daddy wanted us to visit the many locations of the universities that he hoped would accept me. So we went to Cambridge, Newcastle, Bath, York, and Birmingham. After some time, I told him I would be content to study at any institution that I was sent to. Mummy and I wondered why Daddy appeared to be too anxious to see me settled. We attributed that to his concern for my well-being and happiness, my being his only child and all that.

If only we knew then what lay ahead for us.

# CHAPTER 9

THE WEEKS AFTER the London trip were filled with happiness. Upon their return, Katarina received the confirmation for her entry to the University of Newcastle, just as her father had wished for. They hugged each other in joy. They had a thanksgiving dinner that weekend, and the local *imam* led the prayers for her continued success. Malek was walking on air, as his dreams for his beloved little girl were about to materialize. Together the family sat down to plan for their trip to Mecca to perform the *umrah*, which would cover twelve days. That would give them ample time to spare for her trip to England.

That fateful Sunday dawned like any other Sunday, except that it changed the very fabric of their lives. George had driven down from Sungai Petani, where he was stationed, for their monthly game of golf, a routine which had cemented the friendship of the two friends ever since. They returned just before m*aghrib,* joyfully singing and laughing like two drunken sailors celebrating their furlough. Katarina and her mother rushed to the door, wondering why the two men were causing such a commotion.

"Congratulate me, darlings," Malek said as he hugged them in jubilation. "I made it finally!"

"Made what, Daddy?" Katarina asked curiously.

"He scored a hole in one," George answered before his friend could, sharing Malek's achievement with enthusiasm and pride.

"Isn't that wonderful?" Malek continued after a brief glance at George.

The two women hugged the victor as George looked on with nostalgia and regret. He felt he would never share that moment of triumph with the woman he adored. Much as he loved and respected his friend, at times like these, he felt a stirring of envy for Malek, which he tried vainly to suppress.

Dinner was a joyful affair. Suraya had baked a special two-tiered chocolate cake, decorated with a golf ball supported by two golf sticks leaning on the side. The two men found it hilarious. They enjoyed the dessert, and their conversation was interspersed with jokes and a great deal of laughter as they poked fun at one another.

After dinner, Malek, buoyed by his lucky streak, challenged his daughter to a game of scrabble. They had played the game many times before, but after she turned sixteen, he had never been able to defeat his Gina unless he openly cheated. It would draw much laughter as she wrestled with her father for the tiles which he openly pilfered.

"If we are playing, Uncle George will be the judge," Katarina had demanded in a tone that brooked no objections. "And you, Uncle George, must make sure Daddy plays by the book." She stated this imperiously, in the manner of one who knew she was truly loved.

"Yes, ma'am," George answered with a fond smile. "Your wish is my command." He made a semblance of a bow, with mock deference.

The two men smiled at each other, amused at this young lady who had recently turned eighteen and who seemed to know where she stood with them; each secretly marvelled at how she was able to capitalize on the great affection they had for her.

Thus the game began. It started well for Katarina. As usual, with her knack for picking good tiles and turning simple words, as well as placing them to her advantage, she was able to lead. However, at one juncture, fifteen minutes into the game, her father, to his delight, playing by the book as she commanded, was able to get a triple word score, which left her eighty points behind. Malek found it amusing, and he started clapping and laughing uncontrollably, mussing her hair affectionately. As they joined in the merriment, to her consternation, her father started coughing. She watched with horror as, with his hands clutching at his chest, her father sputtered and choked before collapsing.

"Uncle George," she screamed, "what's happening to my Daddy? Mummy! Something's happened to Daddy!" Her agonizing screams echoed through the house. She heard frantic cries, unaware that those heart-wrenching screams were escaping from deep in her throat.

Suraya rushed into the lobby as George was in the midst of applying CPR. Without a word, she pushed George aside and tried desperately to resuscitate her husband. Katarina stood by sobbing heartbrokenly. It seemed to go on forever, and when all seemed fruitless, George touched her and gently pulled her away.

"He's gone, darling," he said gently, the endearment escaping his lips unconsciously and as automatically as if he had applied it to her all his life.

"No!' Suraya screamed in anguish. "No!" She struggled in his arms.

When George finally released her, she pulled her husband's lifeless body into her arms and howled, *"Bang! Bang!* Why? *Why?"* She sobbed long and painfully.

Katarina watched, horrified, her mouth agape, as her uncle and then her mother failed to revive her father. She fell to her knees beside her mother and howled, tears streaming down her cheeks unchecked. She hugged her father as tightly as she could, calling out to him in loud terrifying wails, as if by doing so, she could bring him back to life.

George, who was in a state of shock as well, went down on his knees and put his arms protectively around them both as he too gave way to tears for the man who had been more than a friend and brother. If he could, he would take Malek's place so that the two women he loved most in this world would not be deprived of the man *they* loved.

For days, as if they were in a bad dream, mother and daughter moved through the motions of living. The sound of his voice and raucous laughter echoed through the house and in their dreams. For a long time, their life was shrouded in grief. Katarina would wake up in the middle of the night calling out for her Daddy. At these times, they would hug and hold each other as if their lives depended on their being together. They talked about him every day, and each time their conversation would dissolve into anguished tears. They could not accept the fact that he had been taken so abruptly, he who had so embraced life. He had been a man of such vitality, taking great care of his health. He was as fit as the proverbial fiddle. To discover that his heart had given way so suddenly was beyond comprehension and acceptance. He would never see all his plans and dreams for them come to fruition. To them, the future seemed empty.

The saddest part of it all was that he had been only two months shy of fifty-two. He had so much to live for. They regretted that they had not insisted that he rest a little, for after those hectic trips, he still rushed about his business trying to deal with the problems that surfaced while he was away, as an immeasurable number of logs had been stolen from his logging concession.

"If only I had insisted that he took more time to rest," Suraya told her daughter sadly.

"Daddy would have laughingly told you off, Mummy. He always thought he was invincible," she remarked, a tinge of bitterness and regret in her voice. Sometimes she felt angry with her father for leaving them and not finding out sooner that he had a weak heart. However, her love for him outstripped her anger at his early demise.

Her mother understood her well. The tragedy had cast a pall over their lives, and though at times despair and misery made their lives seem unbearable, they still had each other. She assured her daughter that her late father would want them to carry on with their lives and for Katarina to fulfil his dreams he had for her.

Two months after her father's demise, her first year at the university would start. The thought of leaving her mother to face the prospect of living alone without her soul mate was daunting, and it nearly derailed Katarina from pursuing her tertiary education overseas as planned. She began to discuss the possibility of continuing her studies at the local university, but her mother would have none of it. With her gentle persuasion, so characteristic of her, she finally managed to convince Katarina to follow the path set out by her late father.

***

True to form, Katarina plodded through the first few months at the university with determination. It was a tough period in her young life. She was still grappling with the grief of losing her beloved father to that sudden fatal heart attack. Living alone in a strange and new environment amidst strangers who may have similar ideals, but who were from different cultures and backgrounds, took a certain amount of adaptation, and without her mother, from whom she had never parted and who had unfailingly been her most ardent supporter and counsel, it was doubly difficult. But her father's words rang constantly in her ears: "You're a tough young lady. You're my daughter, and to us nothing is impossible, by the grace of Allah."

Hard work, patience and fortitude, saw her through her academic life at the university. Gradually she was absorbed in the throng of student population and established herself as one of the smartest students in her faculty. As predicted by her father, she began to enjoy her life. Together with her father, she had decided upon a course in business administration. She assumed that she must have inherited some of his business acumen and her mother's tenacity, for she succeeded in overcoming her weaknesses and emerged stronger than before, in both her studies and her personal life.

She had made quite a number of friends in her sojourn at the university and had graduated with honours. There were a handful of admirers too— young men of different nationalities—for she had that air of vivacity and a caring nature that drew people to her like a magnet. Despite being an only child and monopolizing her parents' total attention to herself all her life, she had learned at a young age that others too had problems and needed a willing ear. She was not self-absorbed. She had never been attracted to any man, maybe because her standards were high, she thought, as her father was her yardstick. Would she be able to find that someone who would be to her what her father had been to her mother and what her beloved mother had been to him?

Katarina and her mother had remained extremely close. If she did not return home for holidays, her mother would spend them with her in London as she did that memorable year after her graduation, when they spent an incredibly enjoyable Christmas holidays together. For a month, she enjoyed a hectic—albeit joyous—time with her mother, who had picked a hotel at Piccadilly Square to stay, to enable them to have easy access to London's extremely efficient underground system.

At forty-three, her mother still looked fabulous, and as they trundled along the streets, window shopping or merely for the pleasure of walking, they drew admiring glances from men from all walks of life. They looked more like two sisters, being almost identical in complexion, height and gait.

They visited many places and reminisced about her father. They cried and laughed as memories of him and his devilish humour were relived. They chatted like two loving friends who had nothing to hide from each other.

It was during one of these chats that her mother confided in her that her uncle George had asked her to marry him. Surprisingly, the news did not shock her. Young and immature though she had been years ago, she had always suspected that Uncle George's affection for her mother was more than brotherly.

Suraya recounted to her daughter that George had paid her a visit recently, something he had not done for months after her husband's demise, for fear that society would hold her in contempt. A widow did not entertain a man who was not her *muhrim*. That was frowned upon. And for her sake, George had respected the tradition. He had kept in touch with her via telephone, though, and he was well informed about how Katarina was faring. He paid his Gina a visit on every business trip, and though the visits were brief, he made her feel loved and treasured. He never forgot her birthdays, and he would buy her little presents that he knew she would treasure.

'What did you say to him, Mother? Did you accept?" Katarina asked.

"I told him it was too soon after your father's death and that I never thought of settling down again," she replied thoughtfully.

"How do you feel about Uncle George, Mother?" Her eyes scrutinized her mother intently.

Suraya was taken aback by her daughter's question. She thought for a while as she inspected her nails in concentration, her mind absorbed with images of George.

"I have never thought of him in any other way except as a friend. And I told him that," she added.

"Mummy …" Katarina had reverted to her childhood term for her mother. "I love Uncle George. I think he's a wonderful man who's been in love with you forever. Remember the times when you tried to pair him off with Auntie Mei Lin? When that failed, you tried a few other women as well. I remember that he used to get extremely annoyed with you."

Suraya looked at her daughter in surprise. It never occurred to her that George would confide in her, as she was only in her early teens.

Katarina continued, unperturbed. "You wonder how I know this, don't you? Do you remember that Uncle George used to take me bowling? Well, one day he looked at me and said in frustration, 'Gina, some women are so dense sometimes. When a man has fallen deeply in love with one woman, there's no one else for him …' It didn't register then. I guess he was so frustrated with your interference that he had to let off steam somehow, thinking that I wouldn't be able to read between the lines. He was right. I didn't see it then …" Her voice softened considerably.

"He always treated me with deference. Not once did he display any untoward behaviour," Suraya said as she thought back to the times when George visited them.

"I know, Mummy. That's because he loved and respected Daddy and he valued Daddy's friendship," she reminisced. "He said to me one day, 'I never had a brother, Gina. Your daddy is my friend *and* brother. I would die before I'd hurt him.'"

Suraya softly explained to her daughter that though she still missed her life with her father, she had started picking up the pieces in the years that he had left them. She enjoyed her work, and recently she had been promoted as a staff nurse at the hospital.

"I'm glad for you, Mummy," Katarina replied as she congratulated her mother with a hug. "I loved Daddy. No one can ever replace Daddy, for you or for me. I know that for sure. But you're still young and beautiful, Mummy, and Uncle George is a wonderful man. Next to Daddy, I don't think there's any other man who can hold a candle to him where you're concerned." She paused as she watched her mother's face for her response. "Will you please consider Uncle George's proposal? I'd love to see you happy and taken care of," she begged her mother earnestly. "Uncle George deserves to be happy too, Mummy."

Suraya studied her daughter thoughtfully, her teeth biting her lower lip in concentration. Then she smiled. "You really are an ardent advocate of George Smith. What if I tell you that I'll give his proposal some serious consideration? Would that make you happy?"

"It would, Mother," she replied, her tone changing to that of the adult Katarina, her eyes brightening hopefully. She stood up and gave her mother a smothering hug. "I'm sure Daddy would approve too. I don't know of anyone who's as selfless as Daddy was."

They spent the rest of the holidays as actively as any other young women did. The theatres were their favourite haunts, and they watched one play after another without fail. *Funny Girl, Fiddler on the Roof*, and *Hello, Dolly!* were their favourites.

The *"Swinging Sixties"* was a decade of revolutionary culture that started in Britain and gradually spread to other parts of the world. It was a period when youths determined which way the wind blew and during which time, the restraints imposed by society that had limited their freedom were broken. That era of unlimited freedom and self-expression bred a culture of permissiveness, drugs, hippies, and mod fashions, as epitomized by *"Swinging London"*—the centre of fashion, art, and *hippiedom*, where Jean Shrimpton and Twiggy became famous faces adorning the pages of fashion magazines, wearing their miniskirts and bell-bottoms.

Suraya breathed a sigh of relief that her daughter had not been inclined to follow the trend blindly. Her only weakness was the bell-bottom pants, which, to her credit, did give her figure an added fillip, as she was tall and slim.

It was the age of the Beatles, and their music blared from the shops and stores. Even little children sang *"She loves you, yeah, yeah, yeah ..."*

It was a world of changes on the political front too. In September 1963, the Federation of Malaysia was formed; in the same year, John F. Kennedy was assassinated and Martin Luther enunciated his famous speech *"I Have a Dream,"* which became a battle cry for African Americans; Neil Armstrong landed on the moon in 1969. There were social changes too. The birth control pill, introduced in 1960, was a welcome invention for those who advocated free sex. The first James Bond film, entitled *Dr. No*, was released in 1962, and the list went on ...

***

"I'm late, I'm late," she mumbled breathlessly as she struggled with her backpack, a sling bag dangling across her left shoulder, her right hand tugging laboriously at a heavy suitcase, her bell-bottoms swinging merrily in the breeze. She was running frantically, balancing precariously on her high-heeled knee-high boots, hoping to be on time before the lecturer arrived. It would be an embarrassment to enter the hall late, when the professor had already started; all eyes would turn towards the door when she entered. That would not be a befitting end to her wonderful holiday spent with her beloved mother, to whom she had bade a tearful farewell earlier as she put her in a taxi that would take her to the airport and thence home to Malaysia.

The train was punctual as usual. It was just difficult finding a cab that would take her back to campus so early in the morning, thus the delay. She had run helter-skelter as soon as the cab dropped her off at the front entrance.

As she was rounding a corner, suddenly, without warning, she stumbled and hit what felt like a block of granite. She would have fallen on her face had not two strong arms reached out and wrapped her around the shoulders in a tight grip.

"Hey, hey, hey," a deep, melodious voice sang out, laced with laughter. "Look out!"

She was transfixed as she looked up and encountered the bluest pair of eyes she had ever seen, bluer even than the Mediterranean, just inches from her own. No words escaped her lips, for she couldn't find any. She was struck dumb. For what seemed like an eternity, she didn't say a word.

"No woman has ever thrown herself at me with such force before," the voice continued huskily, the laughter still apparent, the blue eyes searching her face with complete absorption, the strong hands still holding her up by her shoulders, steadying her on her feet.

When she was able to match the voice with the face, she blinked stupidly. His was the handsomest face she had ever seen. Her breath caught in her throat. Her mouth opened, but not a whisper passed through her vocal chords. She cleared her throat repeatedly and replied in a squeaky voice that she had never heard before, "I'm sorry …" She continued to stare.

The magic of the moment transmitted strongly between them, for he too was at a loss for words as he looked into the black pools of magic that shone with a blinding light.

From what seemed far away, they heard a concerned voice asking, "Hey, you guys. Everything okay?"

That rudely brought them down to earth.

Gently the handsome stranger released her. "You're not hurt?" His resonant voice was heavy with concern. She shook her head.

The young student wordlessly helped pick up her bags, handed them to her, and quietly left, whistling cheerfully, after she murmured her thanks.

She straightened up quickly and adjusted her clothes, which had twisted askew. With dark red colour mounting her cheeks, she mumbled an apology in total embarrassment, pleading that she was late for class. Hastily she picked up her bags and attempted to walk sedately and nonchalantly, as if crashing bodily into a stranger was an everyday occurrence.

As she clumsily dragged her bags up the steps, she heard him say, "I'm Josh Reynolds. Let me help you."

She pivoted towards the voice. He was standing at attention, tall and ridiculously elegant in dark jeans and a brown jumper, hands placed snugly in his pockets, both eyes trained on her, a vision of ruffled elegance, an endearing grin branding his aristocratic features.

"Katarina," she replied briefly, pronouncing it with an exaggerated European accent. "I'm fine, Josh. Thank you for offering."

She turned around the corner and promptly disappeared.

For several long minutes, he continued to stand stock still, his eyes unblinkingly focussed on the spot she had stood before dashing away. Shaking his head as if he couldn't believe in such an encounter, he slowly turned and walked away in the opposite direction.

Countless sleepless nights followed as two mesmerizing onyx eyes followed him while he was awake and continued torturing him in his dreams. The incident played and replayed in his mind's eye—those large shining eyes staring deeply into his own, which had become so blinded that he feared he would never be able to see anything or anyone else again.

For days, he walked around the university grounds, searching in despair, hoping to catch sight of her again and to feel the weight of her warmth against his body. He wondered where she had disappeared to. While conducting tutorials, he became distracted with the slightest movement out of his peripheral vision. Jogging in the weekends used to be a pleasurable activity. That had turned into an obsessive need to search for her. In saner moments, he would ask himself if, by some coincidence, he was turning into a lunatic and teetering on the brink of madness.

Then one day it unexpectedly happened—in the bookshop, of all places. He was engrossed in an article in a popular magazine on the explosive popularity of the new pop group known as the Beatles and the background of its members, when he stepped back and accidentally collided with a soft body that was passing behind him. With the quick reflexes of the athlete that he was, he pivoted promptly, stretched out his arm, and steadied the young woman he'd almost knocked down.

"Oh my God." He was completely apologetic. "I'm sorry." He bent down to pick up the books that she had dropped.

He heard her giggle in that voice that he had heard in his dreams countless times. She said huskily, "We have to stop colliding with one another, Josh."

Ah, that achingly familiar voice, that heart-stopping smile! He felt a rush of exuberant pleasure. How often had he dreamed of meeting her and how hard he had practised the smart remarks he was going to make. However, at that juncture, all he could do was to gape mutely at her as she smiled brilliantly up at him.

When he still had not said a word but continued to stare stupidly at her, Katarina assumed that he did not remember her. She stretched out her hand and smiled faintly. "I'm Katarina. The last time we *collided* with each other, it was I who crashed into you."

Short of getting a slap in the face, Josh refrained from expressing the feelings that threatened to explode from his chest. The blue flame in his eyes burnt brightly. Her radiant smile was going to be the death of him yet, he thought. He remembered those tantalizing lips with aching clarity. His pulse raced with his mounting adrenalin, but only one word escaped his lips: "Katarina …" It was so soft that it was almost inaudible. He took her hands and held them as if he would never let go.

For a long while, they stood facing each other, completely oblivious of their surroundings as students bustled around them. Finally, as if she were suddenly awakened, Katarina became aware of a few giggles and blushed as she realized that they must have presented a ludicrous picture: like in a melodrama, two people holding hands right in the middle of the aisle, staring into each other's eyes, neither saying a word. With an embarassed laugh, she gently tugged at Josh's hands, and when he *did* come to his senses, Josh reluctantly released hers.

Afraid that he might not see her again, Josh quickly suggested that she accept his apology by letting him buy her a drink. For one tense minute, he panicked, as she appeared to be debating whether to accept his offer.

His face broke into a joyous grin when she said hesitantly, "Just for a short while, Josh. I have to see someone in half an hour. He's come all the way from Kuala Lumpur."

His heart plummeted to the bottom of his stomach. *She's spoken for,* he thought wildly, but he kept his smile plastered to his face as he engaged her in a fact-finding conversation. He loved listening to her voice—it made him feel warm and fuzzy—and when he became cognizant of the train of his thoughts, he forced himself to pay greater attention to what she was saying. His drink was left untouched as his eyes observed every feature of her face: those lively intelligent eyes, that pert nose, those luscious lips and the glorious coal-black hair that cascaded down her slim shoulders.

"Daddy passed away several years ago. There's only Mummy and me," she was saying, "but I'm boring you," she hastened to add as she rose from her chair.

He stood up as quickly, his hands reached out to stop her. "I'm making an idiot of myself again," he chided himself. He was frantic as she picked up her handbag and files. "Please stay a few more minutes. You're not boring me at all. I can repeat every word you've said in the last ten minutes verbatim, if you want me to. Please?"

He smiled, his face brightening with the sheer pleasure of holding her attention. "You began by saying, 'I have only twenty minutes to spare, Josh, then I have to rush. It's funny the way we seem to be crashing into one another,'" he parroted, mimicking her tone and hand movements to a tee.

"Stop, stop." She burst into peals of laughter, the likes of which he had never heard before. Slowly he released her hands. The smile on his face was reminiscent of the little boy he must have been, portraying pure and unadulterated innocence.

As her laughter subsided, she wiped her eyes and stated with a smile, "Okay, you made your point, but I have to go. Thanks for the drinks."

"Let me walk you to wherever you're going," he offered.

She looked at him thoughtfully. It felt as if she were looking into his soul. His stance was that of a man fully in control, strong and confident, but his eyes were pleading her not to reject his offer. She drew a deep breath and suddenly felt that instant connection that she had never felt with anyone before.

In that instant, she knew without any doubt that she had found her soulmate. Her legs trembled uncontrollably. Slowly she sat down again. He followed suit, his eyes on her. Her heart was beating furiously. She swallowed, her mouth dry. She wet her lips.

His eyes followed her every move.

"Kat ..." he breathed. "May I please call you Kat?"

She nodded wordlessly, her eyes searching his face.

"I know we've only met and we hardly know anything about each other. Can we please continue to see one another so that we can get to know one another better?" He was on tenterhooks.

"I'd like that," Katarina replied, her voice hardly above a whisper.

Josh's worried face broke into a grin. Jauntily he walked over to her chair, and as she stood up, he pulled it out behind her, took her arm, and led her out of the cafe. This was a different Josh from the one who had escorted her twenty minutes before. His face was wreathed in a smile that brightened his whole countenance.

"I'll accompany you to meet this gentleman, and then I'll have to rush off to conduct my tutorial," he offered, brooking no resistance, and she willingly acquiesced.

It felt good to walk with him, his hand gently guiding her at her elbow. It felt as if they had been walking together forever. She stole a look at him as he talked about the school of architecture that he was a part of with so much passion that she was surprised when they finally reached the arches at the main entrance in what seemed to be only a few minutes. When she caught sight of George walking briskly towards them, she quickened her steps, her hands waving frantically at him, her face alight with joy.

"That's my Uncle George," she told Josh without preamble and ran towards him like a little girl. Gone was the gorgeous beauty who'd walked sedately and gracefully on the arm of her gentleman. She was quickly enveloped in George's arms as his laughter rang out loud and clear.

"My darling Gina," the voice boomed. "How are you?" He released her and studied her from top to toe. "You're as beautiful as ever. Come give your Uncle George another hug. How I've missed you."

Over her head, he caught sight of Josh, who had silently sidled up to them, studying Katarina's uncle George with interest. Josh was quite surprised that Katarina's uncle had no resemblance to her at all. He was totally English, not only in his appearance and demeanour but also in his accent, whereas Katarina had the exotic looks of a Middle Eastern beauty, with a mixture of Asian features that he couldn't put his finger on. She was just unique, he thought.

His musings were interrupted when George, who had spied him with Katarina earlier, released her from his embrace, and turned towards him, his arm loosely around her waist.

"Ah, who have we got here?" He studied Josh with interest.

"I'm sorry. This is Josh Reynolds, Uncle George. Josh, this is my uncle, George Smith. He was my father's dearest and closest friend."

That explained the loving embrace which had caused a deep frown on Josh's forehead.

The two men shook hands while sizing each other up.

"Josh and I have the habit of running into one another," Katarina explained with a laugh. George looked from one to the other, expecting an explanation for that quirky remark.

Josh smiled ruefully. Katarina dismissed it with a wave of her hand. "It's a long story, Uncle George."

Josh excused himself, explaining that he was going to be late for his class, after promising to call on her later in the day. As the young man hastily walked away, George studied his Gina with an affectionate smile and drew his own conclusions with regard to the young man he had just met.

# CHAPTER 10

GINA TOOK HIM around campus as George cheerfully updated her on his business affairs and the political developments at home. The confrontation between Indonesia and Malaysia was of particular interest to Katarina. President Soekarno of Indonesia, George explained, had started a move towards *Ganyang Malaysia*, a campaign which had recently been formed to crush Malaysia, as the new federation included North Borneo, territories which *he* had planned to include as a part of the Republic of Indonesia. During that campaign, Indonesia carried out raids in Singapore and inspired the racial riot on that island, which was easily put down. Earlier that year, there was an attempted coup by the PKI, the Indonesian Communist Party, which was crushed, and Soekarno, who had the base support of PKI, was forced to transfer power to General Soeharto, who proved to be a friend to Malaysia.

However talkative and informative George was, Katarina had a feeling that there was a greater purpose for his visit with her. He took her to lunch at the Vermont, where she enjoyed a typical English meal of roast beef and Yorkshire pudding. Once they had their fill, they went for a walk to view the splendid Tyne Bridge. By the side of the river, George invited her to sit and enjoy the view. She turned towards him and smiled. In that smile, George spied the little girl he used to entertain, the one he taught to swim and to bowl, the one he grew to love as if she were his own. There was mischief in that smile. It was as if she knew what he was up to. It seemed that she alone had been able to glimpse the real man under the unintelligible mask he wore.

"Come on, Uncle George. Out with it," she said, a hint of laughter in her voice. "It's about Mummy, isn't it?"

"Gina, is there nothing that you don't know?" he questioned her in that affectionate tone that he reserved for her alone.

"About you and your affection for Mummy?" She stared at his weather-beaten face, a face that had carried the brunt of suffering that few would have survived, a face that was not in the least handsome but had character and strength stamped upon it. "I've known all along that you loved Mummy, Uncle George. That's why you never married, isn't it?"

George shook his head at her and stared at her ruefully. "How would you feel about me and your mummy should we decide to tie the knot?" He had always known that Gina loved him, but nobody loved their father the way Gina did. Would she resent it if he took her father's place? That possibility had been bothering him all the while that he contemplated asking Suraya to marry him.

She laughed gleefully, a happy, cheeky laughter that never ceased to lift his spirit. "I talked to Mummy about this when she was here in January. Have you approached her again, Uncle George?"

He shook his head. She continuously amazed him with her astute observations.

"All these months when Mummy wrote to me, she didn't mention you at all. You're a slow worker, Uncle George," she nagged at him with the confidence born of their strong ties.

He tugged at a shiny curl, the way he used to when she was a young teen. "This time I wanted to consult you first and get your support, Gina. If you had already talked to her, you'd know that I proposed to her once and she had rejected me." His tone was sad.

"It's been three years and eight months since Daddy died. I loved Daddy dearly, but he won't be coming back. Mummy needs someone to take care of her, Uncle George, and who better than you? I know that if we could ask Daddy now, he would tell us the same thing. Daddy was a selfless man who did everything for us and would have sacrificed everything for us. You're of the same mould, Uncle George."

She stopped abruptly. Her voice ended in a sob. Silently she wiped the tears from her eyes. She took his hands in hers and looked at him as he too wiped a tear.

"Yes, Uncle George, I'd love you to become a member of my family, and though you'll be my stepfather in name, you'll always be my Uncle George."

That statement drove George to tears. He pulled her into his arms and sobbed. Katarina had never seen a grown man cry. Overwhelmed with a myriad of emotions, George cried as if his heart would break, his pitiful sobs loud and hoarse, but she knew it was not due to sadness or pain. She had glimpsed the real man ever since she grew up, for he had always been himself when he was with her. She understood that his tears were an expression of happiness and relief to be able to achieve what he had dreamed of and yearned for during a period of many, many years. She held him in her arms as she would a little boy who was overwhelmed on receiving his most precious gift.

When the storm of weeping passed, George gingerly wiped his face and apologized, a little shamefaced.

"I'm sorry, Gina, that you should see me at my weakest moment. I didn't even cry when the Japanese tortured me. It's just that I've loved your mother for so long, and she, bless her soul, never had any inkling of my feelings towards her." He looked at her and grinned. "Remember those days when she tried to pair me off with this person and that? I wanted to scream at her to leave me alone. It was tough to pretend that it was a big joke," he added through his teeth.

"You're a strong man, Uncle George. Please go home and ask Mummy again. This time do it the proper Malay way—you know with a little bit of *hantaran*. Better still, wait for my holidays and then we'll arrange a small, meaningful wedding for you and Mummy." Then, as if an afterthought, she asked, "Have you gotten a Muslim name ready?"

He laughed, a loud joyous laughter. "I have … already."

She covered her mouth in total surprise, her eyes wide. "You haven't!" she said, a tinge of her old impish nature emerging as she hugged him with total abandon.

He nodded, returning her hug, his smile wide. It made her wonder how good-looking he must have been as a young man before the Great War messed up his life, his face, and his fortune.

"I converted to Islam some time ago, just before your father passed, but there didn't seem to be any opportunity to tell you about it. I haven't been a completely practising Muslim, but I'm learning," he confided.

"Mummy will make sure you become a true one, Uncle George," she said gleefully.

George returned home a happier man than when he left. Armed with Katarina's blessings, he approached Suraya and asked her again if she would marry him. This time her answer was "Yes".

It had been a long thinking process for Suraya. She had prayed long and hard for divine guidance so that she would make a wise decision for herself, her daughter, and especially for George. Katarina had opened her eyes to the possibility of finding happiness again. True, she was not attracted to George in the way that she had fallen for Malek, the love of her life, who had been a charming man, exuberant and full of warmth. George was tall and lanky and, in her eyes, far from handsome, but that was far outweighed by his kindness, his generosity, his strength of character, and most of all, his boundless love and devotion to his Gina.

George and Suraya had a long talk. George confessed that he had been in love with her ever since they reconnected again after he returned from the war. He even enacted the incident when he realized that he had fallen deeply in love with her.

"You have to be patient with me, George." Suraya said truthfully. "I've never looked at you in any other way except as Malek's friend."

"I'm a very patient man, Sue. The fact that you've agreed to marry me is one battle won. I promise I'll take care of you the way Malek would have done, had he lived. I live for the day when we're married and become a family."

That day came sooner than expected. In July, Katarina returned for her holidays as promised, and she roped in her mother's family, the assortment of aunts and cousins, and arranged a memorable wedding for her mother and George, who, by tacit understanding, agreed not to go through the fanfare of ceremonies befitting young couples in the Malay community.

It was a memorable day, especially for George, who had dreamed of the privilege of looking at his love without trying to hide his true feelings. For that, he was grateful to his Gina, and when the *imam* cited the *doa* for him and his new family that night, he unfailingly said a silent prayer for his dear departed friend.

The day before the wedding, he had quietly visited Malek's grave, which Suraya had meticulously maintained. Gina too had visited her father's grave as soon as she returned from England. He felt totally blessed to have her support, for he knew Suraya would not have agreed to his proposal, had she objected.

He sat heavily beside the tombstone of his departed friend. "Lek," he said, loud enough for his late friend to hear if he were sitting beside him, "you must have known that I've loved Suraya for a long time, ever since my return after the war. I know you did, but you were too honourable a gentleman to make a fuss about it, for you must have known that our friendship mattered a lot to me and I wouldn't have jeopardized it for anything in this world." He felt tears pricking his eyes and dabbed at them impatiently. "Now that you're no longer with us, I'm asking your permission to marry her and take care of her and Gina. I promise I'll do my very best to make her happy. I'm willing to accept the fact that she may not love me as much as she loved you."

A cool breeze swept across the grave and silently disappeared. George smiled. It was a good omen, he thought, that his friend had given his blessings. A monarch butterfly hovered over the grave and slowly fluttered away.

"Thank you, Lek. You've made me the happiest man today."

After dinner that night, once the modest marriage ceremony ended and the guests had left, George told the two women of the incident with apprehension, wondering whether they would attribute it to a figment of his imagination, but to his surprise, they accepted his tale without question. In fact, Katarina contributed her own experience with her father in a dream that she had on the night she returned.

"In the dream, I was sitting on the steps by the pond with Daddy," she recalled. "Daddy looked happy and fit. He was wearing his favourite golf T-shirt and he said to me, 'George will take care of you and Mummy, darling. Treat him with respect. He'll be a good father to you.'" She stopped abruptly as tears cascaded down her cheeks.

Suraya burst into tears. George went over and enveloped them in his arms, feeling extremely vulnerable but at the same time grateful that finally he was given the right to comfort and to take care of the women he loved, who were now his to love and to protect.

"You've stayed only for four weeks, darling," George said at breakfast that morning, after Katarina informed her mother and stepfather that she was planning to leave for England soon.

She smiled as she glanced at her stepfather. *How much he has changed,* she thought. His face was a picture of happiness, and the way he looked at her mother was priceless. The stern lines of his features had softened, and his cheerful voice rang loud and clear around the house.

"Why the rush, Katarina?" Suraya asked. "You still have a few more weeks of holidays," she stated as she poured George his second cup of tea. He looked up at her adoringly and caressed her arm as she passed by him to get to her seat.

Katarina stole a look at her mother. A smile adorned her beautiful features as her eyes fell on her new husband. The honeymoon had done wonders for her. She carried a glow that spoke volumes of their new relationship. It wouldn't take a magician to conclude that the marriage had been a blessing for both.

"It's got to do with those aerogrammes that she has been getting regularly, doesn't it, Gina?"

"Uncle George," she protested, a blush suffusing her cheeks. "Is there nothing that goes on in this house that doesn't escape your notice?"

"Certainly not," he rejoined with a grin, "especially if it has anything to do with you." He turned to his wife and, by way of explanation, said, "Gina's been receiving letters from her young man nearly every day."

Katarina stared at her stepfather in mock displeasure. She had not taken the opportunity to have a mother-daughter chat since the marriage, not wanting to deprive her and George of their newlywed status and precious time together. They had gone on a one-week honeymoon to the Cameron Highlands at her insistence, even though they had been reluctant to leave her alone in the house.

"I'm a grown woman, Mother. Surely I can be left alone at home. You and Uncle George need this time together," she said persuasively.

Now, looking at her mother and that questioning look on her face, she felt slightly guilty that she had not used the opportunity to exchange confidences as they used to do. George looked expectantly at her, inclining his head slightly towards Suraya as a silent pressure for Katarina to take her mother into her confidence, as she used to, so that she wouldn't feel slighted.

"I've found someone, Mother," she said softly. There was a lilt in her voice which Suraya did not miss. She felt her heart rise in happiness. She stretched her hands across the table, palms up. Katarina took them in hers, smiling from ear to ear.

"I'm so glad, darling. Tell me about him," she insisted.

"His name is Josh," she replied, her eyes like twin stars blinking in a dark night. "He holds a master's degree in architecture and urban planning."

Suraya turned to George accusingly. "You knew about this all along, didn't you?"

"It's not my place to betray our daughter's confidence. Come on, Sue. Tell her you're happy for her," he wheedled.

"Of course I'm happy for her. Now tell me more about this young man," she cajoled.

"Uncle George … No, I think I'd better call you Dad. Is that okay with you, Mummy?" she asked anxiously, unconsciously reverting to her affectionate childhood term when asking for a favour from her mother. She could feel George tensing up as he remained deathly still, holding his breath, waiting for his wife's reply.

Her hesitance seemed to last for a long time for the man waiting. He wondered silently how he would feel if she discouraged her daughter from referring to him as Dad. He had assured Gina that it would have been all right if she continued to address him as "Uncle", but as the precious word slipped from her tongue, he experienced a surge of happiness. His throat was parched, and he swallowed hard.

After what seemed like an hour, Suraya turned to look at him, a smile creasing her cheeks in the way that made his heart somersault dangerously in his chest. "If George doesn't mind being saddled with a grown-up daughter so soon."

"Mind?" He almost choked on the word. "Why would I mind?" He stretched out his hands and held each one of his darlings' hands. "I'm so blessed to be loved by both of you. It makes me feel that all the tortures I went through were in preparation for this very moment."

George's words struck deep in their hearts. From that minute, it seemed that their relationship was inextricably linked together much more than blood and heredity could ever do.

"Well then, *Dad*," she said, gingerly testing the word on her tongue, "you've met him. What do you think of him?"

"I only saw him for a minute, *daughter*," he replied with considerable affection, his tone teasing. "It's not possible to judge a person within such a short time. *You* tell us about him."

Katarina and Josh had only been seeing one another for a few months since, but they seemed to have a close rapport. They were mutually attracted to one another, but they both agreed to take their time to get to know one another before they committed themselves to one another. She felt rather embarrassed to speak of her feelings to her mother and her new dad, but the little that she did speak of, and the light shining in her eyes every time she mentioned Josh's name, betrayed her strong feelings for that young man.

"I'm happy that you're not rushing into this relationship, darling," George said with relief. "Whatever you decide, we'll support you a hundred percent because we know you have a good head on your shoulders."

***

It was a very happy woman who landed at Newcastle airport early that afternoon. Her mother and George had sent her off at the Kuala Lumpur airport. They made a lovely couple, she thought. Anyone could tell her stepfather was a happy man who loved his family dearly. *He deserves everything he has*, she thought fondly as he hugged her and promised to visit her on his next trip to London, this time with her mother. He was rewarded with an affectionate kiss.

"I'll hold you to your promise, Dad." As always, his heart gave a jolt every time she addressed him as such.

The flight from Kuala Lumpur to Heathrow was smooth but long. In-flight service was excellent and the food served was without par. She fell asleep almost immediately and even when the plane stopped in Dubai, she didn't budge from her seat. She would need to board the connecting flight to Newcastle in London. She was looking forward to seeing Josh, whom she'd missed a great deal and whom she would not have left had it not been for her mother's wedding. Josh had written nearly every day, letters that she would treasure forever, for in those letters he had poured out his heart to her.

In the dark days of the future, she would cling to those words as a drowning man would cling to his life buoy in a turbulent sea.

# CHAPTER 11

S HE CAUGHT SIGHT of him first as she pulled her luggage sedately—a lone solitary figure, his back ramrod straight, his hands tightly clenched together behind his back. He was shifting his feet impatiently, his eyes darting quickly towards the door as passengers trooped out. She was hidden behind a giant of a man, so she was able to spy on him before he saw her.

As always, her heart thumped erratically at the sight of him, tall, lean, solid as a rock. His handsome face with its carved cheekbones, his slightly flared nose, and his full sensual lips overshadowed his cold and emotionless blue eyes, which lit up as soon as he saw her, the blue flame now burning hot and bright.

A small thrilling shiver ran through her as it always did at the first sight of him. She flashed him a smile, a shiny, shimmering smile that was radiant with love and joy.

*Yes, yes, I do love him,* she thought ecstatically. The enforced one-month separation and the happiness that she witnessed following her mother's marriage to George had become a symbol of the enduring love that her stepfather had for her mother.

True love, she surmised, elicited the best in a person: loyalty, strength, compassion, and most of all, self-sacrifice. She wondered if her newfound love would stand the tests that George went through for a seemingly endless time.

"Josh!" she cried out, a joyous lilt to her voice, her left hand waving frantically. Within a second, she was engulfed in his arms as, with one long stride, he unceremoniously pulled her aside, out of the path of the hurrying passengers.

"Let me look at you," he said, his eyes scanning her face inch by inch as he reverently placed her chin in the palm of one hand so that her face was completely exposed to his scrutiny. "God," he whispered, "how I've missed you." His voice resonated with intense longing.

Still shy of public displays of affection, she placed her hand gently over his wrist. Immediately he released her chin, but his other hand still held hers tightly.

"I've missed you too, Josh," she said, when she was able to find her voice. He promptly guided her out of the airport to his car, his strides so fast that she almost had to run to keep up with him.

Once he had placed her luggage in the boot and shut the door, he turned to her. Leaning back against the car, he gently pulled her into his arms and held her for a long time, her face buried tightly against his chest.

"It feels wonderful to hold you in my arms again, Kat," he whispered hoarsely. "I've always been a lonely man, but I've never experienced the emptiness that threatened to devour me when we were apart."

"Oh, Josh," she sighed as her eyes focussed on his face, which was taut with emotion, her thumb gently caressing his lips, which followed and nibbled at it like a cat trailing after a wily mouse. She understood the depth of his loneliness, though it was beyond her own experience, having been loved and spoilt every day of her life.

"I missed you too, darling," she reiterated. "That's why I returned as soon as I could." She returned his kisses with abandon.

They adjourned to their favourite cafe, where they ordered coffee and sandwiches. He wanted to keep her by his side as long as he could. He listened with rapt attention as she talked, his eyes never leaving her face, his hand holding on to hers, his thumb gently caressing the little heart-shaped mark above her right thumb. Occasionally he would lift her hand for a kiss.

"That's my brand on you," he had said emphatically the first time he caught sight of the spot, and she confessed that she couldn't remember when the mark appeared.

As she sipped her coffee, her voice lilting with excitement, she talked about her mother's marriage to George. He gazed at her, a besotted look on his face, marvelling at the beauty of this love of his life, with her ivory skin, her flawless complexion, her lush lips that drove him crazy, and that sweet voice which was demanding insistently whether he was listening to her.

"Of course, my love," he replied, his lips curved in a whimsical smile. "You were saying..."

"Okay, okay," she interjected, giggling like a ten-year-old, her fingers on his lips, which he promptly kissed one by one.

Their love swiftly blossomed. No longer was she reticent in declaring her love for him openly as before. In the months they had been seeing each other, she had refrained from professing her love for him, and she had elicited a promise from him not to talk about their feelings for each other until they were certain. In that one month at home, she had noticed how love had blossomed for her mother with George's verbal protestations, and when words were inappropriate or when others were present, a look or a gesture from him was sufficient to make her glow like a candle in a dark night. An overwhelming sense of possessiveness assailed her whenever she cast her eyes on Josh, a feeling he completely reciprocated to the extent that at times it worried her.

They basked in the glow of their newfound love. Every free minute spent together brightened up the hour, purposely delaying the time when each had to bid the other good night in order to prolong the time they were together, as he respected the limitations that she had set for them.

Josh had begun to introduce to her the spectacular beauty and history that was Newcastle. At ten years old, she had learned of Newcastle in her geography class. She became familiar with the expression "carrying coal to Newcastle", never imagining that one day she and the man she loved would visit the mines that had produced that commodity.

In the previous years, she had been completely unaware of the special features of the city, as she had been totally immersed in her studies and scholarly pursuits. Josh introduced her to the picturesque bridges that spanned the stunning River Tyne, explaining to her the marvels of architecture and engineering that went into their reconstruction. The statuesque Tyne Bridge, the landmark of the city, so reminiscent of the Sydney Harbour Bridge, had originally been constructed during the Roman times, he explained. It was an architectural marvel which had the longest single span bridge at one time. In addition, trams used to cross to Gateshead, on the other side of the river.

He took her out one day to watch the *kittiwakes*, the white-and-grey gulls that built their nests on the tower of the bridge. In a moment of thoughtless prank, he had even dared her to jog across the bridge one Sunday, and when she gaily accepted the challenge, he changed his mind for fear she might not be able to complete it. To his chagrin, he was not able to withdraw his challenge, for she wouldn't hear of it. He had to eat his words when she completed the 389-meter jog huffing and puffing, to his immense pride.

That night after dinner, they walked hand in hand along the quayside. He had never loved or admired her more than he did then. Sitting on a bench at their favourite spot, he held her hands tightly in his and professed his undying love for her as the water echoed his words, lapping gently in the breeze, the lights across the river blinking and twinkling in the cool night air.

That year, the Christmas holidays became the most joyful time for them, as George and her mother joined them in Newcastle. By then, Josh had landed a job in one of the up-and-coming architectural firms in the city.

He had always declared himself an orphan. Strangely he never alluded to his childhood or his family. He would deflect her questions if she should touch on his background, and out of her love and respect for him, she did not persist or risk seeing the deep frowns on his forehead deepen more and his sadness destroy his mood.

The happy foursome spent that fortnight together. Josh appointed himself their tour guide. George had a perpetual smile on his face. Unsurprisingly, Katarina thought, Dad looked distinguished and happy as his eyes continuously turned to her mother or followed her around when she walked away. Once he caught her looking at him with wonder in her eyes.

"I love your mother, Gina. I'm totally blessed that she has learned to love me," George explained, a blissful smile brightening his grey eyes.

At fifty-one, George had achieved a measure of peace after years of turbulence. The stern lines that marked his countenance after the war had given way to soft creases that came with the tide of fortune that had finally risen in his favour.

The two men got along well together. George sensed that the younger man had a tough childhood while growing up and had little or no role model to follow. For that, he sympathized. He himself had been an only child, and though his father had passed on at a young age in a factory accident, his mother had brought him up with tender, loving care. He looked at the young man sitting across him at the dining table as the women excused themselves. Like him, Josh's eyes were following the women's retreating backs.

"You love my Gina, don't you, Josh?" George questioned, fully expecting the answer the young man would give.

"Very much, George," Josh replied briefly and with absolute honesty.

"You must promise me that you will take care of her," the older man replied. "She's very precious to me."

"She's very precious to me too, George. I'd do anything to keep her from harm," he vowed. "I would sacrifice my own happiness if only to protect her." He spoke with disarming sincerity.

George looked at him strangely and silently mulled over Josh's statement, but he refrained from elaborating. Later, he would truly begin to comprehend the young man's words, uttered in a moment of honest self-reflection.

Suraya put an arm around her daughter's shoulder as the latter applied fresh lipstick and combed her fingers through her abundant hair. They were standing side by side in front of the mirror in the ladies' room, and she was impressed by her daughter's striking beauty. Katarina seemed oblivious of the picture she created as she gracefully patted her hair in place.

"What do you think of Josh, Mother?" Katarina turned towards her mother and waited anxiously for her reply.

Suraya hesitated for a second before she responded. "I think he's a very nice young man—handsome and smart—and he seems to be head over heels in love with you …"

"But? You seem to have some reservations, Mother."

"Darling," her mother said wistfully, "your daddy was a simple man and had no hang-ups. His young life was uncomplicated." She thought carefully before continuing the conversation. "How much do you know about Josh's background?" She hugged her daughter with deep affection. "Please forgive me for saying this, but Josh appears to have a dark side to his nature, which he seems to try vainly to overcome."

Katarina looked at her mother thoughtfully. She was not offended by the latter's observation. She knew her mother was an astute woman, but she prayed that this time she was wrong in her assessment. She told her so.

"I do hope so," she responded. "My advice, for what it's worth, is that you take your time and learn about each other. Don't rush into a commitment that either of you is not ready for. I'm not saying that Josh is a bad man," she hastened to add. "Don't get me wrong, darling. Dad and I like him very much, but I have a feeling that he has certain issues that need to be resolved."

She gave her daughter a final hug and took her hand. "Come on," she said gently as she spied a frown beginning to appear on her daughter's smooth forehead. "Things have a way of working out for our benefit, *sayang*." She readjusted her daughter's hair tenderly. "Let's go now. The men must be wondering whatever has happened to us. George will be sending a team soon to look for us."

True enough. George and Josh were loitering by the entrance of the restrooms when they emerged.

***

During the first week, they traversed the university grounds and pried at every nook and corner. Josh, who acted as their driver cum guide, took them to the original locations established by the Romans, which later grew to become shipbuilding centres. In those days, Newcastle was a major trading hub for wool. Josh's commentaries were interspersed with words in the *Geordie* dialect, which he seemed to have picked up in his sojourn in Newcastle. The small group happily hailed *haway* to one another when they learned that the word meant "come on". The women shivered in empathy as they walked along the limewashed walls of the seven hundred metres of the Victoria Tunnel, which had been dug four kilometres below the city streets, each imagining the sweat and grime enveloping the weary labourers when coal was being mined and transported along those tunnels.

They enjoyed the 360-degree view of the city from the top of Castle Garth Keep, with the splendid view of the bridges spanning across the historic river and its sweeping panorama of buildings and mountains in the distance, so awe-inspiring that it took their breath away. Josh explained that its vantage point was of prime importance in the Middle Ages, as the views it commanded would give ample warning of any imminent attack.

The two men patiently escorted them around as the women peeked into one shop after another and then tried on new dresses and pants, parading for them with unique poses that drew much laughter. They spent hours at the Laing Art Gallery, browsing through its fascinating and extensive collection of paintings and sculptures. Mother and daughter yawned with boredom as the men became absorbed in the displays of windmills, steam engines, and turbines.

The two weeks were an invaluable opportunity for Josh to get to know Katarina's family and, for once, to experience a familial bonding, something which had been sadly absent in his life. It was a time which he treasured most. With their cheerful dispositions and affection not only for one another but for him as well, they drew him into their orbit. They accepted him without reservation. It was enough that Katarina loved him, but her parents also gave him a sense of belonging that obliterated his feelings of loneliness, abandonment, and instability. He wondered whether this was the reason he loved Kat so much—the fact that she was comfortable in her own skin, ready to laugh at herself, and extremely giving and forgiving. He saw her in a new light. She was still the most beautiful woman in his eyes, something that had initially drawn him to her, but now he loved the inner Kat that radiated from her being.

After dinner that night, before he left for home alone, as Kat was staying in her parents' hotel suite, he held her with total reverence. "I love you, Kat," he said, "like I've never loved anyone or anything in my miserable life." She opened her mouth to respond, but he shushed her gently. "I've never known that family life can be so rewarding, considering that mine never lived up to any standard, though my mother, bless her soul, tried her best."

His eyes misted. She wiped them tenderly with her fingers, her own eyes dewy with unshed tears, as she pictured Josh's lonely life—so bereft of close interaction with his parents.

"I'll never, ever hurt you, Kat, the way my father did my mother. I'd remove myself from your presence should I inherit his cruel streak." he vowed as the spectre of his bullying father taunted him.

"Shh, Josh," she murmured. "What brought this about? Mummy and Dad are very fond of you, darling. We all have our weaknesses, I assure you." She hugged him as her fingers caressed his cheeks. "I love you very much, Josh. There's never been anyone else for me. There never will be," she asserted. "We'll try to work things out together. I promise."

"Hold me close, Kat. Never stop loving me," he said, a tinge of desperation in his voice as he pulled her close and held her tightly in his arms.

Their holiday extravaganza culminated on Christmas Day.

Josh had organized a three-hour boating trip for the family along the Tyne. Thanks to Josh's clever negotiations, they were able to hire a boat, as many operators were not too keen to go out on Christmas Day. Suraya was initially afraid to board because the boat was a small vessel bobbing in the waters, but George assured her it was safe. He made sure the life jackets were available and that she was comfortably tucked in one. Josh gave an excellent narrative of the historical landmarks, which he spiced up with humorous anecdotes. So funny was he that Suraya actually forgot her fear and began to enjoy the experience. They shared a light lunch as the boat gently swayed to the dance of the water.

Dinner was special. George had insisted that they all dress up for dinner in order to celebrate Christmas with Josh. The men were in tuxedos, while the women were elegant in long evening dresses they procured on one of their shopping trips. George had reserved a special table for his family, and as they walked into the dining room, all eyes turned to look at the two exotic beauties on the arms of two similarly dashing men who walked jauntily with pride, grinning like two Cheshire tomcats.

The dining room was decorated with a massive Christmas tree in the centre, a thousand lights blinking gaily, with Christmas decorations adding glamour and allure to the tree. Christmas music was playing, loud enough to create the mood but soft enough not to deafen the ears and kill off all conversations. The melodious voices of Bing Crosby and Frank Sinatra, with their rendition of "White Christmas" and "Silent Night", contributed to the nostalgia of Christmas for the two men.

Dinner was an extravagant affair. The main course consisted of traditional turkey with stuffing, mashed potatoes, turnips and carrots, topped with delicious cranberry sauce. It was preceded by Mulligatawny soup, which Josh loved. "Mom used to make this on special occasions," he said softly.

Kat turned to him and smiled gently as she took his left hand and squeezed it. *Poor Josh*, she thought sadly. *He must have missed many Christmases without his family.*

A Christmas pudding brought the delectable dinner to a close.

To all intents and purposes, they looked like a loving family of four that had decided to celebrate Christmas together in a genial and festive atmosphere. After a leisurely dinner, having been waited upon by efficient waiters in crisp uniforms, they adjourned to the hall to wait for the midnight hour, and when it arrived, they hugged and wished each other a merry Christmas. They danced until the wee hours of the morning, and when her parents excused themselves, Katarina and Josh were still embraced in the magic of the night.

Later they walked hand in hand along the esplanade, joining several other couples enjoying the crispy, albeit chilly, early morning air. It was a wonderland of lights and colour, as the trees had been adorned with a myriad of colourful lights that transformed the atmosphere into a magical and mysterious world.

Josh broke the silence. "Kuala Lumpur isn't as chilly, is it, Kat? I know so little about Malaysia," he confessed a little sheepishly.

"Oh, Josh," she replied, "it's the rainy season now. It rains every day, and if it doesn't rain, it gets terribly hot. But Europeans like our weather. I know Dad does. He's debating whether to open an office here in Reading, his hometown, but he doesn't want to put up with the fickle English weather."

"George is a good man, Kat. I wish I had a father like him," Josh said wistfully. "It was so good of him and your mother to plan such a delightful Christmas celebration in my honour, considering that you're all Muslims." He shook his head as he tried to recall the last time he celebrated Christmas. "I haven't celebrated Christmas for I don't know how long."

"We had a good time, didn't we, darling?" She tried to infuse some cheer into the conversation. It would not be a fitting end to the evening if he was allowed to feel depressed upon recalling his unhappy past.

"We did," he concurred. "You're a pretty good dancer. I didn't know you had so much energy. It took a lot to keep up with you."

"You're a good dancer yourself. Must be those dances that you used to practise with those beautiful girls." She was surprised to feel a tiny spurt of jealousy.

"There won't be anyone else, Kat. Those girls were mere distractions," he hastened to convince her. "I'm sure as I stand before you this morning, with all that expanse of the sea before us and the blue sky above us, as God is my witness, I have never loved anyone the way I love you, nor will I ever love anyone else." His voice shook a little for its intensity.

She got on tiptoes to reach his neck, which she encircled with strong, steady arms. "I love you too, Josh." Her voice took on a captivating femininity, which made her tremble. "I've my mother as my role model. She loved my dear departed daddy with so much devotion that she couldn't function for some time after he died. She took great care of him while he was alive. She gave him her all."

Josh led her to a bench and gently guided her so she could sit, and as he tried to make her comfortable, he asked her curiously, "How did it happen between her and George?" To look at them, one would be impressed by the way they spoke to one another with such extreme deference and respect. George was extremely attentive to the two women, more specifically to his wife. He was obviously very much in love with her.

"I persuaded her to give Dad a chance. I've always sensed that he had loved Mummy all those years when Daddy was alive." She laughed in recollection. "Dad used to get pissed off with her when she tried to matchmake him with other women."

"But she cares for him a great deal—I can see that," Josh observed.

"Dad is a wonderful man. She can't help but learn to love him, maybe not the way that she loved Daddy. She was only eighteen when she married Daddy. I wanted Mummy to be happy again with someone who loves her, and no one can love her the way Dad does."

"And nobody can love you the way I do," he affirmed forcefully, pulling her none too gently into his arms.

It was almost daybreak when they strolled slowly back to the hotel. She persuaded Josh to stay the night, for she was reluctant to part with him. They bunked down together on the floor of the sitting room of the suite after divesting of their evening attire. And that was how George and Suraya found them at midday, fast asleep with their arms about each other.

***

In the following months, life returned to normal—or did it? With his new discovery of the extent of his feelings for her, did she sense a change in his attitude? She felt increasingly that Josh had become more controlling and short-tempered. His love for her did not change; in fact, it seemed to have bordered on the obsessive. He plied her with gifts and took her to various places of interest to sightsee or simply to enjoy a dinner. They went for shows, picnics, and long walks. They even went to see the World Cup at Wembley Stadium when England was crowned winner for the first time.

They had a lot of fun together, yet at certain moments, she felt tension emanating from Josh, which would spoil the fun of being with him. The incident after the birthday party, when he unceremoniously threw the vase against the wall, never did happen again. However, she gradually became more disenchanted with their relationship and his increasing need to control. He loved too much and too excessively. His strange behaviour seemed to have escalated. He needed to know her whereabouts all the time. His insane jealousy was driving her up the wall.

"Josh, you need to see someone about your recurrent anger. Your behaviour is unnerving. I don't know how to deal with this anymore," she said one day after he lost his temper yet again.

"Please be patient with me, Kat. I'm fighting my demons the only way I know how. I need you to be with me." As always, he would be contrite and ask for her forgiveness.

Soon, even he opened his eyes to the possibility of endangering her with his selfish demands on her. He was hanging on precariously to his sanity. He thought long and hard. He couldn't bear the idea of living without her, yet he knew one day he would hurt her the way his father had hurt his mother. His love would become a two-edged sword which would ultimately hurt them both, and he couldn't do that to her.

That night, he took her to their favourite restaurant. He watched her eat as she chatted cheerfully, not realizing that he was unusually quiet as he pushed his food around on his plate. He watched her with total absorption, silently recording in his mind every one of her gentle moves for the time when he would need to recapture the memories, that smile, that voice, and that gentle touch that he would not feel anymore once he put his plans into action. He was convinced that he would hurt her more if they stayed together.

She broke into his thoughts. "Josh, you haven't heard a word I said."

"Sorry. I was engrossed by the way you gorged on your food," he replied in an attempt at levity, his smile stiff on his lips. He had always complimented her as having the most elegant eating habits.

"You have something on your mind?" she asked, concerned. "You've hardly eaten a thing."

He didn't reply to her question. Instead, he said, "Finish your dessert, darling. We'll take a walk by the river. Then we'll talk." He pondered endlessly how he was going to inform her of his decision without sounding heartless and thereby breaking her gentle heart.

*God, please give me the strength to let her go,* he prayed silently yet fervently, he who had stopped praying at six. *It's better that she's free of you now,* his alter ego reasoned. *"Would you be strong enough to see the love in her eyes turn to fear and hate?"*

So he led her by the hand, his heart heavy, dreading the hour when he would have to tell her of his decision, forced upon him by circumstances beyond his control. It would hurt him much more than it did her, but it would be he who would pierce her heart with the cruel arrow. If he didn't, he would cause her endless suffering. That well of anger, that uncontrollable rage, that endless stream of jealousy that had been inflicted upon him, causing him to spew vitriol from his mouth and causing her pain, had to be stopped. He didn't know how, but he would remove himself from her so that she could find someone who would love and respect her the way she should be loved and respected.

He remembered the number of times her eyes flickered with hurt and pain and how often her lips had trembled at his churlish behaviour. It was often too late to ask for forgiveness, and though she had forgiven him as often as he begged, he felt that through his callousness, he had almost destroyed that fine thread of love and respect she had left for him.

As he was guiding her along the riverbank, he was immune to the beauty that surrounded them. It had never failed to bring joy to his heart before. He told her how much happiness she had brought into his life and how much his perception of life had changed ever since he became acquainted with her family. Then he sat her down gently on their favourite bench. He was on his knees before her, his hands holding on tightly to hers.

He started to speak, but no sound escaped his lips. He cleared his throat and tried again. It was getting harder for him to tell her what he needed to do. She was looking at him as she always did, her eyes shimmering with love and a smile so amazingly disarming that he almost became dissuaded from his hard fought decision that had taken him countless soul-searching and sleepless nights.

"Kat ..." The syllable was a mere whisper. He cleared his throat again. "Kat," his voice stronger this time, "these few months have been the most wonderful time of my life." He paused and inhaled long and hard. "But it brought havoc into your peaceful existence."

She opened her mouth to speak, but he quickly forestalled her. "Hush, darling. You must listen to me, for both our sakes. Promise me you'll be strong for the two of us."

She frowned, perplexed. "What are you trying to say, Josh?" Her eyes darkened with confusion.

"Please never, ever doubt my love for you," he pleaded. "I've always loved you, Kat, and I always will; but instead of making you happy, I have degraded and desecrated whatever is good and pure in you with my bouts of anger, jealousy, and insecurity." He broke down and sobbed. "Forgive me, forgive me," he begged between sobs.

She held him quietly in her arms, her heart beating painfully, for she understood his pain.

"I hated it when you so much as smiled at another man. Even I know it's unnatural. Your beauty draws people to you like ants to honey. I know you're blameless. Yesterday, when you were talking to Bert, I was out of my mind because I knew he was attracted to you, and somehow I blamed you because I thought that you encouraged him. It took a stupendous amount of willpower for me not to hit him and to drag you away." He wiped his eyes impatiently, a tortured expression blanketing his face. "I know I have a sickness that I have to find a cure for. I can't condemn your life to these crazy episodes any longer."

She was startled by his sincere confession. Her face paled, and her lips trembled uncontrollably. A storm of weeping shook her. In her heart, she knew they had reached the crossroads from which there would be no turning back. The road ahead would be grim and lonely without him.

"Don't say anything, my love. Just listen." He forced himself to continue. "I'm going to take a long leave, and I'm going wherever my feet lead me." He sighed. "Maybe this cruel streak in me will evaporate, maybe it will not, but know this: I'm doing this because I don't want to hurt you anymore. I could never forgive myself if I so much as laid a finger on your tender skin or lashed your sensibilities with my acid tongue. It hasn't come to that yet, but I know it will ..."

The shock of hearing those words from him made her silent for some time. Finally, in a tiny voice, flat and without expression, she asked, "And I have no say in this matter?"

On detecting the hopelessness in her voice, he pulled her into his arms and lost whatever self-control he had left. "I've thought long and hard about this, Kat," he said hoarsely, his hands stroking her face with all the tenderness overflowing from his heart. "You're my most precious love. I absolve you of all the vows we made to one another. And if …" The words stuck in his craw. He swallowed yet again and tried once more. "And if … you find another man worthy of your love … I want you to marry him."

As he uttered those words, an avalanche of pain swamped him. He laid his head on her lap and cried. They were hoarse, painful sobs that seemed to have been wrenched from his heart.

Tenderly she held his head in her hands, her fingers gently threading through his hair. "Oh, Josh. Tell me you don't mean those words," she begged. "If you're bent on going, I won't stop you, but I'll wait for you." Her gut-wrenching sobs almost weakened his resolve.

"No, my love. No!" he persisted. "I don't want you to waste your youth and your beauty on what could be or what should be. You're an incredibly beautiful woman, a loving and caring person. I would destroy that essence in you, the way my father did to my mother." The long shadow of his tyrannical father cast its tentacles on him, still palpable after those long years. He inhaled deeply as he took both her hands in his and looked into her eyes, now puffy and blurred with tears. "Promise me, my love, that you won't wait for me," he pleaded, his voice breaking in his anguish.

She sobbed hysterically while he continued to hold her tightly, his tears and sobs mingling with hers.

They stayed where they were for hours, hardly saying a word to each other but continuing to clutch each other in desperation, for each had accepted that their separation had become inevitable. Even though their love for each other was strong, it would not withstand the problems they faced.

He drove her back to her apartment in silence. There was little left to say.

At her door, he held her and whispered a heartfelt goodbye, but she clung to him and would not let him go. "Please don't leave me. I won't know what to do without you," she cried, swallowing the aching lump in her throat and pleading in a ragged whisper, "Love me, love me, please, Josh." She whimpered as her body sagged against him.

Gently he lifted her in his arms and carried her to her bed. Her vice-like clutch belied the limp body that had sagged against him, and as he tried to comfort her, their need for each other defied the promises they made to each other in saner moments, a very long time ago it seemed. For that night, nothing seemed to matter but their need to be one. He gave her all of himself, as did she too. Finally, when she fell asleep out of sheer mental and emotional exhaustion, he kissed her tear-stained eyes and cheeks, knowing in the deepest part of him that he would never hold her again. Tenderly he covered her with a blanket and with tender fingers smoothed her lips reverently upon hearing a sigh.

"Be strong, my love," he whispered softly, quickly making his way to the door. At the door, he turned to look at her bedroom once more, swallowing the impulse to hold her once again. He walked back to her desk and on a piece of paper wrote his final massage.

*Kat,*

*By the time you wake up, I'll be gone. I feel like a heel leaving you, the only love of my life, but I need to, for both our sakes. Making a clear break is the best way I know how.*

*Remember, try to find happiness with someone who can take care of you as I should but could not.*

*Maybe one day we'll find each other again. I love you desperately; you know that.*

*Josh*

Three months later, what had kept her in suspense from the time Josh left became a fact. She was pregnant with Josh's baby! Her initial feeling of euphoria at the thought of having something precious that belonged to Josh lasted only for a while. It soon was replaced with remorse and despair as other issues cropped up.

Her mind became preoccupied with the ramifications of her plight. She was carrying a child out of wedlock, totally forbidden within her culture and religion. The baby's father was lost to her. How would her mother and stepfather respond to this new development, which was totally unexpected of her? Would they abandon her to her own devices or would they accept it as something inevitable, even though their society at home would mock her as the fallen woman? The only way to find out was to return home and face the music.

# CHAPTER 12

FOR TWO HOURS, the storm tore through the trees, uprooting those weakened by age, snapping off branches and trunks, creating havoc, mimicking the tempest in her heart. In her ears, she heard his deep voice wrecked by emotion, whispering, "I love you, Kat." The tears, held in abeyance by sheer willpower when the *mak andam* was dressing her up for the ceremony, gushed down her cheeks unchecked.

Then, just as quickly, the storm outside died, but the one in her heart continued unabated. "Josh," she sobbed, "how can I go on with this?" Marrying someone other than the man she loved was a terrifying prospect. She felt as if her heart were pulverizing into little fragments and her world had fallen off its axis.

Those deep blue eyes bore down on her. "I can't be there for you, darling. Marry the man who loves you," she seemed to hear him say. His voice, like velvet, reverberated in her mind. His words, callous as they seemed then, still sounded as cruel and they burned her like acid. After those nights lying awake, twisting and turning in chasms of loneliness and yawning emptiness, and those days that were filled with misery as she went through the motions of living, how could she forget?

Gradually the last drops of rain petered away, leaving a vacuum of absolute stillness. One by one, the birds emerged from their hiding, chirping merrily, sending happy messages to one another. From the *surau* nearby, the words of the *Qur'an* blasted away as *isyak* drew near. The trees stood immobile as if transfixed by the magic of the hour.

A knock on the door heralded the arrival of her mother. She seemed to have grown more beautiful as the years went by. Her second marriage had given her the stability and confidence only an adoring husband could provide. He spoilt her with everything a woman could ask for, and more: when all she ever wanted was to have her family by her side. With one look at her daughter, Suraya knew what she was going through.

"Katarina," she said, addressing her only child in the accent that was hers alone. Gently she held her daughter in her arms as she unfailingly did on occasions like these; she was her baby once more, who had taken on more burden than she could carry. For the umpteenth time, she wished she had murdered Josh, who was the cause of it all.

"I can't go through with this, Mother," she confided between sobs.

"Katarina," she repeated patiently. "Your dear departed father was a strong man, physically and spiritually. He always said you were a lot like him, and you are. You're a strong woman, *sayang*." She dried her daughter's tears. "Jamal will be good for you," she said convincingly. "Daddy, like Jamal, was twelve years older than me, and he was a wonderful husband and father. Jamal will be too." Katarina's sobs slowly subsided, and after blowing her nose repeatedly, she began to inhale slowly.

"One advantage in marrying a man a lot older than you is that he's more mature, as Jamal is. He'll be more accommodating and more considerate than a younger man would be. He'll treat you with kid gloves." She adjusted her daughter's headdress carefully. "He won't expect too much from you, trust me," she assured her daughter. "Daddy would have been very proud of you," she added, a catch in her voice.

"I love Dad dearly," Kat said, referring to her stepfather. "Still, it would be wonderful if Daddy were still here." She missed her late father often, especially now, when she needed his wise counsel.

The conversation with her mother comforted her immeasurably, and it strengthened her resolve to marry her betrothed, even if she was sure that she could not give her heart totally to him. How could anyone compete with Josh? Josh had such vibrant intelligence. Her Josh was tall and commanding. He made other men seem insipid. His smile for her was so alluring that he overshadowed everyone else.

*But he was too insecure to make a success of your relationship, and he threw your world out of kilter,* her common sense whispered.

Jamal was strong and steady, with a good head on his shoulders. He was always solicitous of her.

*So what if your heartbeat does not escalate upon seeing him?* her common sense questioned. *At least you know where you stand with him. He'll keep you and your daughter safe. And he loves you; there's no doubt about that.*

Thus convinced, she firmly closed that one chapter in her life, retouched her make-up, linked her arm with her mother's and made way to the nursery, where George was playing with his little granddaughter.

George's eyes lit up with pleasure as his stepdaughter entered. "My, my! You're a sight for sore eyes," he said fondly, kissing her on both cheeks. At the sight of her tear-stained eyes, he looked questioningly at his wife, who blinked her eyes repeatedly and shook her head in warning.

Katarina missed this byplay. Her little daughter had run up to her and hugged her around her legs. Little Bella was nearly two years old, a chubby-cheeked little doll who looked nothing like any of them. Her blue eyes twinkled with merriment, and her golden curls swished around as she turned this way and that, begging her mummy to carry her.

Bella had saved her life and her sanity. In the darkest hours of the night, when misery and utter dejection threatened to swamp her sanity, it was the thought of the baby she was carrying that made her strong. When Bella was born, those deep blue eyes, so reminiscent of the man who sired her, filled her with such immense love that it obliterated the pain of loss that she had endured.

As Katarina bent to pick her up, Suraya said, "No, let me carry her. We don't want to mess with your make-up."

Katarina covered her mouth with both hands in an effort to stem a cry of pain, her eyes following her little daughter, whereupon George immediately hugged her. "It will be all right, Gina," he said comfortingly. "Jamal loves her like his own daughter—you know that. Anyway, your grandpa loves you, doesn't he, my angel?" He tickled the little girl's cheeks. He was amply rewarded when the little sprite chortled in merriment.

***

It had taken a long time before Katarina could bring herself to agree to marry Jamal.

The day she returned home that summer after her breakup with Josh, George and Suraya hardly knew her. She looked extremely haggard and emaciated. She must have lost about twenty pounds. Suraya gave a keening cry at the first sight of her daughter. Why, she could hardly recognize her! It was a broken-hearted woman who returned, a far cry from the effervescent and vivacious young woman they bade goodbye to, that joyous Christmas many months before.

"What happened to you? Oh, my baby, why didn't you tell us you were not well?" she cried.

George hardly said a word, but his eyes looked worriedly at her. He kept himself busy with her luggage. He suspected it had to do with Josh. *I'm going to kill him,* he vowed silently.

She kept to herself for a long time, hiding in her room, unable or unwilling to speak about her predicament. Pain, anguish, and despair filled her days and nights. Her parents treated her like fragile china that might disintegrate at the slightest touch, until one morning Suraya heard a wail from her room. George was getting ready for work. With her heart thumping crazily, Suraya rushed into Katarina's room, followed closely by her husband. Katarina was standing by the bed, her eyes wide with apprehension.

"What is it? What is it?" she asked in panic. Still her daughter kept mum. "Tell me!" she persisted.

"Oh, Mummy. There's no other way to tell you this. I'm pregnant, Mummy. Forgive me!" She said this so softly that Suraya had to strain her ears to be able to hear her. "I've debated for a long time whether to tell you before I leave for England again to have my baby there."

The news shocked her mother, whose worst fears had been confirmed. She had noticed the changes that her daughter had been going through, so typical of pregnancy symptoms, but she had not broached the subject to her, hoping that Kat would confide in her voluntarily. She trembled with shock and anger.

"It's that good-for-nothing Josh, isn't it?" she cried vociferously. That vehement outburst came from her normally gentle and soft-spoken mother. Katarina was thrown aback, but she understood.

"Josh is not to be blamed, Mummy," she cried heartbrokenly. "It was me. I begged him to love me." Slowly, between tears and sobs, she described the last farewell with Josh and told them how she couldn't let him go. For as long as they were together, Josh had respected her wishes; even when at times she was willing, Josh was the one who pulled back.

The flood of tears and sobs racked her body like a dam that had burst its banks. Suraya held her troubled daughter in her arms as she sobbed out her story, leaving George shaking with impotent rage and disappointment with the young man he had hoped would be the one to take care of his Gina.

As her mother held her in her arms, she was twelve years old again, crying over the loss of her beloved cat, Ching, only this time the pain was so great that it was indescribable. He was the love of her life to whom she had willingly given herself—and she would never see him again. In the silence of the night, those blue eyes would penetrate her soul, his breath would fan her cheeks, and his voice would whisper like a gentle breeze, with such finality that it never failed to hurt, "My love, my love. We were not meant to be together."

"Daddy would have been disappointed in me, Mummy, but for my own reasons, I do not regret giving myself to Josh. I begged him to love me. I wanted something of him to cling to when we were no longer together," she explained plaintively.

"Josh is a good man, Dad." She felt she needed to explain to her stepfather. "But he is confused and in pain, through no fault of his own. I know he thinks that he is doing this for my sake, and I respect him for that. I can only pray that he will find that inner peace and redemption that he's looking for." She drew a long shuddering breath. "Allah, forgive me," she said sadly. "I will spend the rest of my life atoning for my sin."

That night she dreamed of her father. He looked as smart and debonair as ever. She was a little girl with pigtails. "My darling," he said, "don't let one bad decision spoil your life. You have so much to live for."

***

She picked up the pieces of her life with steely determination. They never spoke of Josh or even alluded to him in their conversation, even as his baby was growing inside her.

In the following weeks, the loving and caring George hardly mumbled a word of blame. Without much fanfare, he arranged for her to settle down and work in his office in Reading, where he had maintained the family cottage that he had inherited from his family, though in her interest and safety, he acquired a two-bedroom apartment close to the office. George had started a successful export business in the rubber trade after he retired from managing the company estates. When Katarina came home with a baby in her arms, she created very little waves and little Bella was accepted as the product of a broken marriage.

Her stepfather kept her busy, so she had little time to moan over her heartbreak. The baby was a delightful diamond that brought joy to their household. Katarina energetically threw herself into her new job, and there was no one as good as George to acquaint her with sufficient knowledge about rubber or who was as well trained in business dealings. She became well versed with the identity of latex and was adept at distinguishing it from the many grades of ribbed smoked sheet, and no one could convince her otherwise.

As time passed, the light that had died in her eyes slowly returned, especially when they focussed on little Bella. She met Jamal, a scientist, at one of the conferences held on the progress made on rubber research in Malaysia. They took an instant liking to one another and realized that they had many things in common. Their relationship remained platonic, not for want of trying on his part, and they often played badminton, went bowling, and attended several conferences overseas together. Jamal had a nine-year son from a previous marriage which had ended acrimoniously and he had sworn off marriages, until he met her. When he realized that his feelings for her had matured into full-blown love, he asked her to marry him, but she declined.

"I can't picture myself living with any other man except Josh, Mother," she explained. But Jamal persisted. There was not an excuse that she gave that he did not shoot down, even after she told him that she still loved Bella's father. For her daughter's sake and the fear that her name would be dragged through the mud when she grew older, she decided not to tell him of Bella's illegitimacy.

Finally, Jamal applied the policy of attrition. Slowly, as her defences began to crumble, he approached her mother and stepfather for support, until they became convinced that he was adamant in wanting to marry her.

George, who had suffered the pangs of unrequited love for a long time, saw a solution to his Gina's loneliness. He didn't want to see her living in the vacuum of loneliness and desolation, the way he did. Jamal was a good man who would be faithful and loyal. His lack of good looks was immaterial, he told his stepdaughter, for he was highly educated and conducted himself well at all levels. He spoke well, and most important of all, he treated her with respect. At a family powwow, George and Suraya discussed the possibility of Katarina accepting Jamal's proposal, as opposed to the disadvantages of remaining single for the rest of her life.

Suraya finally asked her daughter to consider her own situation when Katarina asked her to marry George. "I didn't love George then," she reminded her, "but you said he was a good man who would take care of me, and he has done so … beyond my wildest dreams … and I've learned to love him." She smiled affectionately at him.

Her husband took her hand, kissed it, and continued holding it in a tight grip.

She continued talking about Jamal. She sang his praises. "He's gentle, tolerant, understanding, and he's a great cook," she added wistfully. "Matchmaking has been a practice in our society for a long time, and in most cases, it has been successful. Married couples learn to love one another as time goes by. It's a question of having the right attitude towards the union." She said, with great conviction.

Finally, albeit reluctantly, Katarina agreed. Her one main consideration was that Jamal loved her daughter and if Bella grew attached to him, she would go through with the wedding.

"I don't want a huge wedding, Dad," she said adamantly. "Just a small one will do, attended only by close friends and family."

And that was how their marriage came to pass. She played her role as a devoted wife and mother to perfection. She took care of him as no other woman had done, preparing his meals, laying out his clothes in the mornings, and cooking for his guests. In turn, he treated her with love and respect. Even if the passion that she carried in her relationship with Josh was absent in her marriage, she kept it to herself. She doused all the feelings that had fired that first love and focussed solely on her husband, his health and his career, to the exclusion of all else, besides running the business that she owned jointly with her dad. Her other total and complete devotion was to her Bella.

Jamal was proud of her, and if there was a little piece of her heart that he could not possess, he made no issues out of it, nor did he make any references to it. She had been frank about that from the very beginning. She had supported his career, and he did not discourage her from carrying on with hers. She continued to manage the office in Reading, taking turns with her stepfather to visit. Having been born in a poor family of rubber tappers, Jamal understood poverty and the need to work to eradicate it; he also supported his wife's involvement with various charity organizations. His home was a haven that drew friends and associates like a magnet, and she made that possible. He couldn't ask for more.

***

Coming home from a gruelling week at the Reading office was a welcome respite. The sight of her husband holding Bella by the hand was a welcome sight. Bella was decked in all her finery. At five, she was a prissy little lady who loved to dress up in lace and ribbons, her golden hair diligently combed, especially when welcoming her mother home from her business trip.

The man and the child made an incongruous picture, being so different in looks that they constantly drew curious attention, which they became used to. The first time she became aware of those curious glances, Bella had asked Jamal, her new papa, why they were drawing such attention, to which he replied, "Because you're so beautiful, pet." She learned to take that in stride, accepting his explanation without question.

Since her marriage, Katarina had made countless trips overseas. Jamal was always there to welcome her home, with Bella in tow. She was gratified that the two got along well with each other and that Jamal loved her daughter as if she were his own. This time, however, she sensed a little difference in him. In the car, Bella, who was always full of chatter, talked incessantly about what she had been doing in the one week that her mother had been away, but Jamal was uncommonly silent. As she entertained her daughter, she made a note to draw him out.

Dinner was a happy family affair. It was customary for the family to enjoy dinner either at the family home or at her own house. Bella was enjoying her weekly playtime with her stepbrother, Saffian, Jamal's twelve-year-old son, a tradition which they faithfully adhered to so as to maintain close contact with him. Bella and Saffian became as close as if they were blood siblings.

Once the older couple had left for home and the children had gone to bed, Katarina broached the subject that had been nagging at her.

"You were so quiet throughout dinner, b*ang*. In fact, you've been very quiet ever since I returned. Is something the matter?"

Jamal didn't answer immediately. He had changed into his pyjamas and was sitting on the sofa in their bedroom, watching her as she busied herself unpacking. She went over to sit beside him when his answer was not forthcoming. She studied his features closely. He *did* look like someone with a problem, a big problem. She prodded him again. Finally, very softly, he replied, "I went for a blood test when you were away, and it wasn't very good."

"What do you mean, it wasn't very good?" she queried, feeling a little anxious.

"I have to do another test tomorrow to verify whether the previous test was correct," he told her quietly.

"Why did they think it was incorrect?" she insisted, her curiosity becoming more intense.

"There was a decrease in the red blood cells and platelets. If the test results are the same, they will have to do a CT scan to view the spine and the liver to see if they're swollen," he replied, a certain amount of fear lacing his voice.

"What does that signify?" she asked, fear knotting her stomach.

"I'm not sure," he replied, "but whatever it is, it's not a good sign. Hamzah looked rather worried." Dr Hamzah had been his classmate in school, a brilliant student, short, bespectacled and genial, characteristics he carried into adulthood.

"Oh, *bang*, I'm so sorry. I'll accompany you tomorrow. Tonight we'll pray that this was merely an error on the part of the health centre. It's been known to happen," she said hopefully, trying vainly to comfort him as well as herself.

They took the blood test again. The prognosis was terrifying. Just as Dr. Hamzah feared, there was an excess of white blood cells in his blood. A bone marrow test confirmed it. The shock of the test results rendered them speechless. There had never been any symptoms of such a catastrophe. After further careful and detailed examination, the good doctor concluded that it was a rare form of blood cancer, something that they'd never heard of before.

"I'm sorry, Jamal," Dr Hamzah said, trying to break the bad news as gently as he could. "There was a large amount of lymphocytes, or white blood cells, as we know them, produced by your bone marrow. We put these white cells under the microscope and they looked hairy, which is abnormal." Katarina held her husband's hands in an iron grip. He hardly felt it. So shocked and fearful was he with this horrific information he was receiving from his friend. "To put it simply, these abnormal cells kill all the healthy cells and weaken the immune system," the good doctor explained.

Jamal was silent. Only his face betrayed the tumultuous thoughts warring in his mind. He turned to look at his wife in a confused state of mind. She stood up and hugged him, keeping her eyes on the doctor as he purveyed the information with a multitude of graphs and diagrams.

"As a result of this interaction," the doctor said, "the red blood cells decrease."

"And how does that affect the body?" Katarina asked.

"The immune system weakens, and the patient becomes extremely susceptible to infections," Dr. Hamzah explained.

Jamal finally found his voice. "Is there a cure for this disease?" he croaked. He coughed to clear his throat.

The doctor was blunt in his reply. "I'm sorry, Jamal. So far, there has been no cure for hairy cell leukaemia. This is what the disease is called. There have been good responses to the treatments given. One or two have responded and have had long-term remissions."

"How long?" Jamal prodded brusquely.

"How long what, *bang*?" Katarina frowned, a tortured expression distorting her remarkable features.

"How long before the longest surviving patient succumbed to the disease? Come on, Hamzah. No pussyfooting around me," he persisted, as the doctor hesitated.

The latter looked at him sympathetically and replied briefly. "Five years, but with proper medication and diet, *insya Allah*, we can fight this disease."

Jamal smiled, a stiff compression of lips that hardly displayed his perfect teeth. "Now I know. At least I have some idea about my longevity." A certain amount of bitterness was reflected in his voice.

"We'll fight this, *bang*," Kat assured him. "Who knows—maybe soon they'll find a cure for this."

Consequent tests demonstrated that the disease had progressed rapidly. There was very little knowledge that they could gather as to the manner in which it could be halted. When talking to her friends or relatives, someone would refer to a friend or relative who had similar symptoms and had passed on without being cured. It was a trying time for Katarina, but she presented a strong front to her husband, who needed support and strength to face what they knew in their hearts would be inevitable.

# CHAPTER 13

G EORGE FLIPPED THROUGH the magazine disconcertedly. The plane was delayed yet again.

There were only a handful of passengers in the first-class lounge. It was quiet and peaceful, no children running around. He welcomed the respite. Normally his wife would accompany him on his monthly trips to Reading, but for the last several months, she decided to stay back to help look after Bella, as Gina was taking care of her husband. He missed Suraya's gentle ministrations, her loving care, her devastating smile that still had the power to turn his legs to jelly, and her warm body to hold at night. He smiled ruefully at his trend of thoughts. It was not as if they were young pigeons, newlywed. They had been married for several years now, and his love for her was boundless. She had learned to love him as he had hoped and prayed.

Gina was the one worrying him. She had been so immersed in the well-being of her husband that he wondered how long her own health would withstand the constant demands of his deteriorating health. In the initial stages, Jamal looked normal and he continued working without any signs of slowing down. Soon, however, the constant reliance on antibiotics, and then later, the regular chemotherapy sessions began to leave side effects. He began to complain of tiredness and weight loss. Gina was encouraged to take a leave of absence from their office so she need not have to rush, and for that reason, George had to take over the visits to the Reading office.

A tall, commanding figure strode in. There was something familiar about the man and the way he walked. His face was fashionably adorned with a well-trimmed beard. His expensive suit and tie bespoke of success. He was carrying a briefcase in one hand and a roll of important-looking documents in the other. He was vaguely recognizable. George stared unblinkingly. It began to dawn on him that it could be …

The younger man accosted him first, his voice in shocked wonder. "George?"

George stood up, and before he could utter a syllable, he was engulfed in a giant bear hug that threatened to smother him. He could see why his Gina could not forget him. This man oozed charm and charisma. After the repeated handshakes and shoulder thumping, they sat down.

As they sipped their drinks and indulged in small talk, Josh couldn't contain himself any longer. He needed to hear her name being mentioned and to speak of her himself.

"How's Kat?" he blurted out without preamble. *God*, he thought, *I still miss her so much.*

George felt his ire rise. He could not forget the days when his stepdaughter muddled through the storm of heartbreak and mangled emotions. His lips tightened immediately, but his upbringing and years of observing proper etiquette in his business dealings controlled his basic impulse; he answered Josh's question with a semblance of good manners.

"She's happily married to a local scientist," George answered carefully, watching the young man's reaction closely. "They have one child," he added chattily. With a cruel streak he was unaccustomed to, he thought, *So what if I stretched the truth a bit. He deserves whatever he gets.* He had an insane desire to smirk when he saw the flash of pain in those eyes so like Bella's.

"A beautiful little girl with curly hair and as smart as can be," he continued, embellishing his granddaughter's lovable quirks that would make anyone fall in love with that little imp, enjoying the discomfort and regret he could sense emanating from Josh. He desisted from describing the colour of her eyes or her hair for fear of confirming her paternity. *Let him broil in his jealousy and misery*, he thought maliciously.

"I'm happy that she's happy, George. That's all I ever wanted for her," Josh responded sincerely, his voice a little shaky. "I was a flawed human being. I take responsibility for my actions which impacted our relationship. Kat didn't deserve that."

Abruptly he excused himself. He wanted to run to the men's room to scream out his pain at the thought of his love with another man. As he entered the toilet, he leaned against the wall and closed his eyes, his hands bunched into tight fists. He started breathing deeply and slowly as he had often done, ever since he returned from his wanderings, and gradually his mind took over and he was in control again.

He was gone for quite a long while, and when he returned, it was the strong, confident Josh that emerged. They continued talking about things in general, never again alluding to Katarina. Josh's face, however, was pinched and drawn.

Josh's demeanour changed his perception. Instead of anger, George felt sympathy for him. He admired him for his selflessness, and they parted on good terms. When he recounted his accidental meeting with Josh to Suraya, it was with regret rather than anger. His kind and caring wife was never any meaner than when she referred to Josh, yet every time her eyes fall on Bella, she could not help but be grateful that such an angel had been foisted in their midst. So she rejoiced and forgave the father. According to George, Josh had started working for an architectural firm since he returned from his travels. He was in charge of a development project in Dubai, a contract which would be completed in the next five years.

"It was fortunate that it was you who came face-to-face with him, George. I dread to think how it would have affected Katarina had it been her," Suraya said thoughtfully, knowing deep in her heart that her daughter still carried a torch for Josh.

"I'm sure it would have been unbearable for her. I know she still loves him." He thought for a second and added, "And I have a strong suspicion that he too still loves her. When I told him that Gina is happily married and has a beautiful baby girl, he almost jumped out of his chair and the disappeared into the men's for a long while. When he returned, his eyes had this pinched look and I felt terribly sorry for him ..."

He felt sad, for he understood Josh's predicament. Didn't he too go through that painful period of love unfulfilled? Consequently, he was tactful in not blurting out to Josh that Bella was his daughter. To do so would have created more problems for everyone.

Looking at his wife, he knew that she was burning to ask him about Josh's marital status. He looked at her with a mischievous smile. "And the answer to your question is *no!*"

"What question?" she protested. "I didn't ask any question."

"You were burning to know whether he's married, Sue, or at least involved with someone." When she opened her mouth to deny it, he put his hands over her mouth and they both collapsed into laughter, which quickly turned into something more serious.

***

The hospital room was eerily silent. It had become their retreat as often as Jamal needed medical attention. He was finally resting peacefully after having fallen into a stupor. He had been warded for the past two days immediately after his return from a trip to China, as he was persistently coughing and running a high temperature. The room became her abode too, for as long as he needed medical care.

It had been a long and painful journey for both of them. In the initial stages of the diagnosis, he had been extremely confident that he could defeat the disease. He had worked like a Trojan, as he always did, despite her objections. He still attended meetings overseas. He still played golf, even though he tired easily. After two years, it began to take a toll on him. He became constantly tired, and his weight loss escalated, yet he stubbornly persevered. There were many hospital visits and enforced stays, to which she accompanied him without fail. He would still take his files, turn his room into his office and conduct his business. She gradually learned to understand that for a workaholic like him, it was a statement of defiance; as long as he was able to utilize his mental faculties, he could tolerate his weakened physical state.

But always he needed her by his side—a need he never vocalized, yet something she had learned to anticipate in the five years of their married life. Jamal was a proud man who didn't like to be seen as weak. He would fight tooth and nail to get what he wanted. He had wanted Katarina as his wife, and he had been successful. He had treasured her and loved her but never told her that he needed her. In the long months when the disease wrought its havoc in their lives, only his eyes betrayed that need; she had understood and supported him, to the exclusion of her own physical and mental comfort.

He was emaciated and dependent on medications and antibiotics. The numerous blood transfusions to increase his blood count and the countless chemotherapy sessions to kill the abnormal cells, in the end became futile attempts at combatting the disease. In one of her private chats with the haematologist, the latter sighed, saying that he was at his wit's end, as none of his treatments seemed to be effective. The bouts of fever and chills, nausea and lack of appetite plagued Jamal. His stubborn refusal to take a break from his office did little to help. The infections were getting more frequent. That was when Katarina knew Jamal's days were numbered. He too must have known that, but being a fighter, he refused to surrender.

She resorted to prayers. She took greater pains to monitor Jamal's diet. Special foods would be prepared at home, consisting of healthy vegetables and steamed spring chicken essence, which to a certain extent kept him stronger, for he could still walk and talk with a certain amount of energy. She brought the children to the hospital almost daily, and his eyes would light up as Bella inadvertently climbed onto his bed and put her arms around him, talking in the way only Bella could. During those times, his laughter could be heard along the corridors of the ward and the nurses would smile to one another, happy that their long-term patient could forget his pain, for a while at least. Saffian too would visit his father as often, though he was less likely to elicit that much cheer, being quieter by nature.

As the disease progressed, persistent coughs tormented him through the night, every night. There was no medication and no way that she could help alleviate his suffering. She tried to make him as comfortable as she could, but always to no avail. She read him verses from the Qur'an when he dozed off, but he was obviously not too deep in his sleep, for when he woke up, he would thank her for her prayers and support.

The doctor had despaired after having tried and failed all possible treatments. At one point, a special dose of medication was air flown from Europe and administered, but that too failed to have the desired effect. By this time, Katarina had begun to experience the caretaker syndrome. She suffered massive hair loss, her blood pressure was abnormally high and her blood sugar had risen to dangerous levels. Without much resistance, she too started on her own medical treatment.

That final Sunday was a day she would never forget. Jamal was wheeled out for a CT scan. He objected strongly. He had been subjected to the process once before. Had she known what would transpire after the test, she would have supported him, but she wanted everything possible to be done for him. She held his hand and talked softly to him in a calm manner, as if she were talking to a little boy. She was thrown into confusion when he started howling, as if in pain—long-drawn-out hoarse cries that reverberated along the hospital corridors. When the howling subsided, he immediately lapsed into a coma.

For the next three days, she never left his side in the intensive care unit, especially after the doctor informed her that there was no hope left. His internal organs had collapsed. She was crushed. Tears of regret and pain overtook her. Jamal was only forty-five years old, in the prime of life, too young to leave this world. He had so much to give. If she had not loved him as much as he deserved and had not given her heart totally to him, it was not because of his failings, though she had tried her best to give him her all.

That night, as the monitor beeped to the tempo of his heart, she took his hand and whispered, "I tried my best to be a good wife to you, *bang*," she said as tears coursed down her gaunt cheeks. "Forgive me if you found me wanting."

Carefully, she slid her right arm around the multitude of tubes that supported his breathing and laid her head on his chest, which had been rendered so emaciated that she could feel his ribcage beneath her cheek, her left hand gently combing his sparse head of hair. She felt a movement beneath her, an involuntary twitching of his right hand, or so it seemed then, and she took it as a sign that he had heard her and had forgiven her. She cried as she had not cried in a long time. This time it was for her husband of five years, who had given her stability and unquestioning devotion, demanding nothing that she could not give.

She left his side only to observe her obligatory prayers. Although it was against regulation to stay in the ICU, she managed to persuade the staff to let her stay. She made sure she did not get in their way. She read verses from the holy book and talked as if Jamal could hear her. Sometimes she told him humorous anecdotes from her life or excerpts from the papers; at other times, she would talk about his son or her daughter. She assumed that he could hear her.

One night as she was reading *surah Yasin* to him, she had an uncanny feeling that she should talk him into letting go. She looked carefully at his face. He was breathing calmly, inhaling and exhaling in a regular rhythm. She took his hands and held them, kissing them lovingly. "It's all right to let go, *bang*." She was amazed that she could speak so calmly to him. "I promise to take care of everything. I'll look after Saffian too. You know I love him as if he were my own," she assured him as calmly as she could. She received no response from him. She stayed awake throughout the night to ensure that he was not alone in the final hours of his life.

Early the next morning, he breathed his last. He inhaled gently, a deep breath which he expelled in an extensive sigh that she followed with her eyes as her ears listened to its sound. Was it her imagination or did she actually see his breath leaving him? All those he loved and who loved him were by his side. She had made sure of that. His was a life that was snuffed out in its prime, but he had died with dignity and grace. For that, she was grateful. *Inna Lillah wa Inna Ilaihi Rajiuun*: To Allah we belong and to Him we return.

The journey of pain, loss, and heartbreak started again for her. She had been resigned to a peaceful domestic existence that was devoid of drama and tantrums. She was even beginning to enjoy her life within the circle of her loving family, which made no demands, only to give and be given love. How ironic were the words of the famed American journalist Norman Cousins, and how relevant they were to her when she looked back at her journey thus far: "Death," he had said, "is not the greatest loss in life. The greatest loss is what dies inside us while we live."

*I died inside once,* she thought, *but I lived again when I had Bella. What else is there in store for me, ya Allah?*

She often wondered if her lot in life was destined to be marked by tragedies and losses.

***

Bella, who was almost seven, took the death of her papa badly. It was her first taste of loss. Katarina felt deeply for her, as she had never known her own father. She had never pestered her about it, but having started school and having been teased by her friends about her exotic and unusual hair colour, eyes, and skin tone, she had started to question her mother.

"Why do I look different, Mummy? Papa said I was God's gift, with my golden hair and blue eyes, and that I should never question that. Papa said he loved me more because I looked different and beautiful."

Her daughter's questions made her realize that she should at least explain to Bella about her father. So she made Bella sit opposite her in the quiet corner of their lounge. Slowly she began to talk about Josh to his daughter.

"Your father's name is Josh Reynolds," she began. "You have inherited his good looks, darling. He's a tall and handsome man, an architect by training. We met at the university where I studied for my degree, and we fell in love. He has light brown hair, not golden like yours, and gorgeous blue eyes, exactly like yours." *How could I tell her that she was a product of my own weakness,* she thought. Finally, she decided not to dwell on her daughter's conception. "He was smart and funny, and we were totally in love when you were conceived." She stopped when she felt a constriction in her throat, as she unfailingly always did, whenever the subject of Josh cropped up.

"Is he dead too, Mummy? Is that why you're not together?"

*Spoken from the mouth of the innocent,* she thought. *Allah, please let me say the right things and explain to her without confusing her,* she prayed silently.

"No, my darling, he's very much alive," she replied. *At least in my heart,* she thought. "Your father and I didn't agree on many things, so we finally decided to part and lead our own separate lives," she lied blithely, simplifying that complicated part of her relationship with Josh.

"When can I meet my real daddy, Mummy? Do you think he will love me like Papa did?" she asked, her little forehead developing a massive frown.

"One day you will, *insya Allah,* darling. Your daddy will adore you, not only because you are sweet and kind but smart and adorable too," she replied, as she hugged and kissed her.

Bella seemed satisfied with her mother's explanation, and she ceased to ask about her father, but she continuously talked to her grandparents about the day she would meet her father. It was making Katarina uncomfortable.

George, who had not breathed a word about his chance encounter with the younger man before, for fear it might complicate Gina's already complicated life taking care of a dying husband, finally decided to inform her of their meeting. He was exceptionally surprised when his Gina displayed scant interest and continued to chat as if it were a matter of no consequence.

***

Sitting on a large rock by the sea, watching the waves lapping against the banks that were partly shadowed by the dwindling light of the setting sun, she replayed the conversation she had with her stepfather, her hands idly sifting the blinding white sands as the cool evening breeze whispered among the sweeping majesty of the casuarina trees. She smiled to herself on recalling her attitude and valiant show of disinterest. She could win an acting award if her mother and George believed her. For years, she had hidden her true feelings from those she loved. She remembered reading an extract from Elizabeth Chandler, one of her favourite authors: *"When you love someone, it's never over. You move on because you have to, but you take them with you in your heart."*

It was like that with her. Her love for Josh never diminished in all those years. His voice alone could thrill her as no one else's could. She remembered with aching clarity how that voice would soften with tenderness, with its rich timbre, so distinctive of him, that her pulse would start racing and a thrilling little shiver of excitement would ripple through her when those deep, captivating blue eyes stared intensely into hers. Those memories were stubbornly embedded in her psyche. They only emerged at times when she woke up in the middle of the night, when dreams of him troubled her sleep. Oh, yes, she dreamed of him often and wondered, just as often, if he had found his salvation, if in his wanderings, he had been able to slay his dragons and his search for peace and enlightenment had been successful.

Oh, no! She was never indifferent to Josh. But she had fought hard to submerge her true feelings on account of her marriage to Jamal and her loyalty towards him. She had tried her best to make her marriage to Jamal meaningful. She remembered what he had said to her once, when they were friends in the boardroom and rivals on the tennis court. *"A marriage should make a man feel that he has come home when his feet have crossed the threshold of his house."* Throughout the eight years of marriage to his first wife, he had never felt at home with her. She understood what he meant, and when she finally agreed to marry him, she had unfailingly tried to make their house a home. Poor Jamal! She hoped in the five years with her, he had finally found the ideal home that he was searching for.

Did she love him? Undoubtedly, though not in the way she loved Josh, she corrected herself. A good man brings out the best in a woman. And Jamal was a good man, caring, loving, gentle, and undemanding. What was there not to love about such a man? What if her heart did not crash into her chest at the sight of him as it did when that other was strutting towards her or calling out to her in that deep voice that was music to her ears? At least her marriage to Jamal afforded her the stability and peace of mind …

*Oh, Josh, where are you?* her heart, engulfed in sadness, cried out.

A strong gust of wind threw a monumental wave against the shore. The loud booming crash shook her from her reverie. A spray of salt water rained down on her. She gently dabbed at the tears that had trickled down her cheeks unchecked. The huge orb that was the sun, so like a monstrous egg yolk, was slowly sinking in the far horizon. It was time to face reality. The words of *Rumi*, the thirteenth-century Persian poet, played in her mind.

*Oh soul,*

*You worry too much.*

*You have seen your*

*own strength.*

*You have seen your*

*own beauty.*

*You have seen your*

*golden wings.*

*Why do you worry? ...*

Her life had been a patchwork of tattered memories. There was no other recourse but to move on. At least she had a wonderful family, an adorable daughter, a loving stepson, and a rewarding career that she enjoyed. She must remember to count her blessings.

# CHAPTER 14

KATARINA ELECTED NOT to alight when the aircraft landed at Dubai, a short stopover on the route to London. This was the first trip to Reading for her since George suggested that she stayed back to look after Jamal. After Jamal's demise, she had arranged for his properties to be divided up according to *Syariah* law; everybody seemed to be satisfied, though she herself received little from Jamal's legacy. The children had been left behind in the care of their grandparents, as school was still running. She was still considering whether to transfer them to schools in England now that her trips would be more frequent.

She buried her nose in the novel that she had brought along from home. It was peaceful because she was alone in the cabin, until half an hour later, when passengers started boarding. Their muted conversations did nothing to distract her. The flight attendants welcomed them in the hospitable way so characteristic of the national airline, which made passengers feel very welcomed. As a frequent flyer, she was made to feel extra special every time she boarded the plane; because of this, she hardly ever travelled by any other airline.

Slowly the business-class cabin began to fill up. She was hoping the seat beside her was not booked so she could have more room to herself for the next eight hours. Passengers were making themselves comfortable, and there was no sign that the seat was going to be occupied. But soon her high hopes were dashed. Her ears perked up when a male passenger was enthusiastically welcomed by a flight attendant.

"Welcome aboard, Mr. Reynolds. It's good to see you again."

"Thank you," the passenger replied perfunctorily.

The gruff answer in that clipped accent almost jolted her from her seat: that sonorous voice, rich, deep, and husky, with a hint of authority.

How familiar she was with that voice from such a long time ago; yet never forgotten. It dragged up memories that she had unsuccessfully tried to forget.

"Sorry I'm a little bit late. The meeting took longer than I anticipated," the voice continued.

The flight attendant's reply was lost to her as her senses went haywire. Blood gushed to her face. Her heart pumped painfully and loudly, deafening her ears like an overly loud drum. Without conscious thought, she parted her lips and a pink tongue slipped out to wet her lips, which had gone suddenly dry. A lump lodged in her throat. She tried vainly to swallow in a mouth that had become parched.

It was still there. She could never deny it. The voice could still elicit from her that surge of excitement and thrill. Oh, the sight of that beloved face, now made more distinguished by a covering of a well-groomed beard; those deep-set blue eyes, the high straight nose; those chiselled lips that could break into the most heart-stopping smile, that lit up that severe countenance. How could she ignore them? How could she look away from that classic masculinity, that handsome man with light brown hair, impeccably dressed in an Armani suit and carrying a branded briefcase that looked heavy in his hands—the manly trappings of success.

He had not spied her yet, busy as he was pushing his hand luggage into the overhead compartment which he was unknowingly sharing with her. It was too late for her to run and hide, without drawing attention to herself. His presence created havoc on her emotions. There was no smile on that severe face; the lips were compressed in a thin line, as if he saw nothing to be cheerful about. Years ago, she had the power to make him smile. Would he smile now if she ran her fingers over his lips as she used to do? Her thoughts shocked her to the core. *He's a stranger to you now,* she chastised herself. *He probably has a woman waiting for him in London, maybe several of them, if he's not married yet.*

Seeing him again so unexpectedly gave rise to a multitude of sensations: pain, excitement, sadness … and hope. Dare she hope that he still loved her? Would he still find her as attractive as he did years ago? *He has probably dated countless beautiful women beside whom you'd appear drab and dowdy,* she reasoned. That brought her down to earth, and with a self-control born of years of practice, she looked down at the hands on her lap, pretending to be engrossed in the book she was holding.

Once he had stored his hand luggage, he accepted the ever-solicitous offer by the flight attendant to take his jacket for temporary storage. Then, with a sigh, he sat down beside her. When he attempted to fasten his seat belt, his elbow accidentally nudged into her. He turned to apologize. His eyes inadvertently caught sight of the heart-shaped birthmark on the back of her right hand.

*It can't be,* he thought; his eyes instantly flew to her face, which was studiously averted. He stared hard, stunned, unable to believe his incredible luck.

"Kat?" he whispered in a voice that was strangled with shock. A rush of excitement pounded into his bloodstream. His heart threatened to burst from his chest for its erratic pumping.

Having had the advantage of several minutes over him, Katarina was able to compose herself and pretended complete surprise. With hands clasped tightly on her lap, voice a little shaken but firm enough, she replied in a soft voice, "Hello, Josh. Fancy meeting you here."

Her greetings sounded false even to her ears; the words were inane, polite, and unemotional. She gritted her teeth together and kept a faint smile plastered to her face. Her pulses at the temples pounded so loudly that she feared that he could hear them. In her heart, a plethora of needs gravitated: to throw herself into his arms, to have him hold her again, to hear sweet and loving words from his lips. How often she had fantasized about those, but thankfully she was able to maintain a strong grip upon her inner self.

He still continued to stare at her, his lips tightly compressed, as though he had no words left to say. Silently he studied that beloved face that was remarkably unlined. The youthful beauty that used to enthral him had not diminished. In his eyes, she had always been perfect. Her skin was more tanned than he remembered, her nose just as pert, her full lips slightly glossed. Apart from that, that gorgeous face was devoid of make-up. He had always thought that she never needed it. He noted that her remarkable eyes, that had always held him spellbound, had a touch of mascara, which added a certain allure to her and threatened to demolish his manhood.

She smiled and extended her right hand. That smile nearly undid him. His heart jolted into a somersault. It took all of his willpower not to sweep her into his arms. With a control borne of years of self-restraint, he gently held it with both hands and continued holding it, his eyes boring into hers. Oh, the sheer joy and wonder of beholding her! It felt surreal!

"How have you been, Kat?" His voice was soft, caressing.

Out of his chaotic thoughts, those were the only words he was able to articulate after those precious minutes had elapsed. There was more he wanted to say and do, but how could he? His last words to her, an eternity ago, though still fresh in his memory, were to ask her to leave him and marry someone else, someone worthy of her, and according to her stepfather, she had. Their last wonderful night together would be forever entrenched in his memory. In those miserable, chaotic days, that memory of her was all that kept him going—the hope that someday, by a stroke of luck, he would be able to feast his eyes on her again, and if destiny willed it, he would be given the chance to hold her in his arms again.

Despite the chaos in their hearts, they managed to keep their conversation on an even keel, polite and deferential, two like-minded strangers heading towards the same destination. He explained to her that he had an office in Dubai, where his company was involved in constructing a new development project for a renowned sheikh. So he travelled often to that city. He was oblivious to his surroundings. His eyes were totally focussed on her ... and hers on him.

Even as busy as they were serving drinks and preparing for take-off, the flight attendants could not help but be drawn to this good-looking couple who seemed to have just met but who looked as if they belonged together, for the way their eyes were looking at one another spoke of a deep-rooted intimacy between them.

They were so absorbed in their conversation that they seemed hardly aware that the plane was taking off when it did.

She explained that she was taking her turn in place of her stepfather, visiting the office in Reading, a practice that she had been doing for years now. He told her he remembered meeting her father several years before and that they had a good chat. He was burning to ask her about the state of her marriage, but he resisted the temptation—only for the first twenty minutes or so, as it turned out.

His curiosity was too great to ignore. So he started by asking about her daughter. It piqued his interest when she took several long minutes before she replied.

He wondered why her answer was somewhat evasive, as if she found it difficult to talk about her daughter. After telling him tersely that she was fine, Katarina changed the subject quickly, not exactly like a proud mother who adored her child. That was not like his Kat at all. His Kat adored children and animals.

But what did he know about this exotic creature who seemed to be reining him into her silken web more and more tightly? There seemed to be some mystery about her that he could not fathom, and it left him feeling disconnected and dejected.

Their conversation was interrupted when the flight attendant brought the menu and soon after took their order. She turned to him and quickly, before she lost her nerve, asked, "What about you? Are you married? Do you have any children?"

She perversely enjoyed asking him those questions. Did he keep his word that he wouldn't settle down with anyone else but her? He had asked *her* to marry someone else, hadn't he?

"The answer is *no* to all questions," he replied emphatically. "I'm not married, nor do I have any children," he added, looking at her strangely.

The adrenalin that had engulfed her a moment ago in perverse pleasure abated, leaving her hopeful and energized. His gaze held hers as his eyes scrutinized every inch of her beloved face, which was now radiating with hope and unfettered joy.

*God, how I love her still, so much more than ever, if that's possible.* Without a blink, he said in a voice that was low and intimate, "I dated many women, but I never met anyone who could replace you," he added sotto voce.

Her lips quivered. For an intense second, the past and the present merged. "Josh," she whispered tremulously.

He took her hand and stared at those magnificent eyes that were brimming with unshed tears. He was at a loss for words. Gently he tried to dry her eyes with his fingers. "Darling ..." He whispered the endearment as automatically, as if an eon of time had not separated them.

Yet it didn't seem awkward to him. He had squired and bedded a string of women whom he addressed by their given names, even in the most intense physical moment, moments that had been exactly that—physical—and he had never forgotten himself or given them more, for there was nothing to give. He had lost his heart years ago.

The spell was broken when the flight attendant accosted them. "Your dinner, *puan*."

Josh reluctantly released her hand as he felt her tugging at him with hands that trembled. She felt enormously embarrassed at being caught in such a compromising situation. Her cheeks flushed. Eyes lowered, she busied herself with the tableware and helped to arrange the dishes and cutlery, while Josh tried to compose himself. He smiled his thanks when his meal was served, but food was far from his mind.

During the times they were together, she had introduced him to a multitude of Malaysian cuisine which he had grown to appreciate: the many types of *laksa*, the various ways of serving noodles or rice together with their *lauk pauk*, some of which he enjoyed, though there were others that were too hot, with *chillies* that he couldn't get accustomed to. In the years that they had been apart, he had sampled those foods at the many restaurants that he came across, but he enjoyed none of them the way he enjoyed the dishes that she had prepared for him. Maybe it was her love that added pizzazz to all the food that she cooked for him. Maybe his eyes were so blinded by love that whatever she did was perfection to him. How good those days had been and how totally in love they were.

His reverie was interrupted by the flight attendant, who enquired about his choice of wine. He made his preference known, while she opted for mineral water instead.

"I only drink wine," he told her by way of explanation. He had vowed to lay off liquor, she remembered. She smiled in acknowledgement.

They raised their glasses to one another silently, his smile softening the harsh planes of his features as his eyes paid tribute to her beauty; and for a moment, they were transported into the perfect world that was bereft of pain and heartbreak, unlike the one that had dogged them for years.

Simultaneously, as if by accord, they each picked up a chicken *satay* stick and dipped it in sauce. Before the delicacy reached their mouths, they turned to one another and burst out laughing.

"You remember!" she said amidst her laughter, displaying a perfect set of pearly teeth that glistened in the dim light.

"Yes, I remember!" he guffawed. "I started that meal with what I thought was the thickest soup I ever tasted but was too polite to say so, until you pointed out to me that it was the sauce that you dipped the meat in—elegantly, I might add." He wore an amused smile. "You also explained to me that in Malay cuisine, there are no courses and that all the dishes are served and eaten together. I never made that same embarrassing mistake again."

As the night wore on, the passengers settled down to a good night's rest; the stillness in the cabin was punctuated by an occasional snore. The soft drone of the Boeing 707 was at once soothing and comforting as it floated effortlessly through the clouds in a calm sky, creating a perfect ambience for love and for exchanging confidences. For the longest time, she had debated whether to tell him of her husband's demise, and on reaching the conclusion that nothing would be gained by hiding the truth from him, she finally decided to come clean.

After a lull in their conversation, she turned to him and said quietly, "There's something I have not told you." He gave her his full attention, wondering what she had been holding back from him. Then, without preamble, she blurted, "I'm a widow now."

His heart lurched in his chest. He wanted to jump for joy. His face broke into a grin, but her air of dejection tempered his exuberance. *How do I know that she is not still mourning his loss,* he thought unhappily. *Maybe she loved him too.* That thought felt like a knife twisting into his heart.

"I'm sorry for your loss, Kat." He managed to inject a modicum of sympathy into his tone. Despite his happiness that she was free at last, he had no inkling of her feelings towards her late husband. "Tell me how he died," he said gently, taking her hands and holding them with tenderness.

Slowly, with great sadness, she began from the beginning, how they had discovered that he had leukaemia at an already advanced stage and how valiantly he fought the disease for nearly three years before he succumbed to it. It had been a traumatic experience for her too, and she relayed to Josh how painful and difficult it had been for her to watch Jamal slowly descend into that moribund state, while she tried to remain strong for his sake.

Having Josh beside her, giving her his unstinting support and sympathy, was everything she could ever hope for. Her control was finally broken, and she sobbed softly in his arms. He had thought that he should have been the one participating in that journey with her and that all the adventure of marriage and building a family should have been theirs and theirs alone. He waited for that well of anger and uncontrollable rage to bubble and burst. Yet strangely, he felt only sadness and empathy for his love's late husband. He searched in his heart for the telltale signs of jealousy and anger, but there were none. He was only thankful that Jamal had loved her and taken care of her the way he, Josh, would have done. Therefore, as Kat cried, he showed her all the love and sympathy that he was capable of, until her tears dried.

The long flight and the emotional turbulence must have exhausted her, as her eyes drooped gradually. Gently he draped a blanket around her because the temperature in the cabin was getting lower. He moved closer to her so that her head rested on his shoulder, her hair brushing his cheek.

As she slept, his mind pondered over the turn of events and how destiny had played an important role in their lives. How was he to know that when he woke up that morning in his hotel room, he would meet Kat on the plane and share the same seats throughout the journey, even holding her as she slept?

He said a silent prayer of thanks as he looked up towards the sky. Unlike Kat, he was not a religious man, but slowly he began to realize that a higher power determined one's life; and if one prayed hard enough, one's prayers would ultimately be answered.

She woke up later to feel a pleasant warmth under her cheek, and her nostrils flared at the feel of body heat that had been familiar a long time ago but was never forgotten. For a delirious moment, she drowned herself in the nostalgia of an unforgotten past, closing her eyes and savouring the calmness and peace that enveloped her being, until complete wakefulness assailed her with a vengeance.

When she opened her eyes, she was shocked to find herself lying in a semi-prone position that placed her head on Josh's chest, his arm around her shoulders in an embrace, her right hand possessively placed on his lap. Her eyes opened wide in horror. Her thoughts immediately gravitated towards the airline staff who must have made their rounds throughout the night. The intimate position she and Josh were in must have shocked them. She would have to be prepared to be the fodder of airline gossip in the future.

She turned to study his now-sleeping face. He looked calm and relaxed. There was even the semblance of a smile on his lips. Gently, so as not to awaken him, she extricated herself, disconnected her seat belt, and cautiously made her way out to the aisle, her eyes searching through the dimness of the cabin for some unoccupied seats so she could be by herself and think things through. When she finally found them in the back row, she lowered her body into the window seat with a sigh and pondered over the circumstance she was in.

It was obvious to her that they were still very much in love with one another. On her part, she had always been sure that her love for Josh had never faded. Her happiness was boundless when she discovered that he still felt the same. Josh was never a consummate actor. His tenderness and his protectiveness were genuine and reminiscent of the younger man who had loved her. She wondered, though, if he had been able to conquer the insecurity and possessiveness that had destroyed their relationship then. Would they face the same hurdles again?

Finally, after much thought, she made up her mind to follow the path that had been thrown open for them. Fate had played a part in throwing them together years ago. Now another chance had been given. She should use the opportunity to try to start a new life with him and help him through whatever fixations that still plagued him. She was certain that he could get professional help if he needed it. Public perception of psychiatric treatment had changed considerably in the years they had been apart, as more studies on domestic violence had been carried out. There would be no stigma attached. Anyway, what did it matter what other people thought, she reasoned, as long as Josh was cured and their relationship was strong.

She was so deep in thought that she failed to see him standing in the aisle looking down at her. He gave her a jolt when he spoke to her at last.

"Kat, is something wrong? Why have you shifted to this seat?" He had accosted her, a note of concern in his voice as he accosted her.

He had woken up to find her seat empty and his body bereft of her warmth. His eyes strayed to the lights indicating the toilets, but they were unoccupied. His search ended four rows behind. He sat down heavily beside her and made sure her seat belt was securely fastened before he clinched his own, his eyes searching her face intimately, trying to decipher what was going on in her mind.

He repeated her name when she didn't reply immediately. "Kat?"

"I needed time to be by myself to think," she replied with a gentle sigh. "We clicked together so well, as if we had never been apart." Her voice was full of wonder. She clenched her fists to stymie the impulse to touch his face. He still had the power to make her tremble. "I never had such rapport with anyone else, not even Jamal."

"Neither did I, Kat," he admitted promptly. "I missed the fun and camaraderie we had together, the discussions and arguments, the fun things we did together, which I couldn't enjoy with anyone else. When I came back after my travels and found out that you had married and had a child, I was happy for you, but I regretted that I had insisted that you marry someone who loved you."

He paused and sighed as if his breath were blocked in his chest. "What misplaced nobility!" He laughed mirthlessly. There was a slight pause before he asked, his heart in his mouth, "Did you love him?"

She took his hands in hers and made him look at her, hoping that he would understand her and accept her answer positively. "Jamal was a good man who was always giving. You can't help but love such a man."

What did she see in Josh's eyes? Hurt? Disappointment?

"But it wasn't like what it was like between us, Josh," she hurriedly explained. "At first, I rejected his proposal, but he persisted. We were good friends who respected one another. After some time, I concluded that a good marriage could be based upon friendship and respect. So I accepted his proposal." She drew a deep, long breath.

He stared at her thoughtfully, trying to process what she had said in his mind.

"There is something else too, Josh. I didn't tell you this before. I wasn't sure how you were going to take it." She became quiet for a long time, wondering whether a declaration of such magnitude should be done where they were—on a plane amid strangers—but if she didn't do it then, when would she be able to tell him?

"What is it, Kat? Please tell me. Don't leave me on tenterhooks," he pleaded, fearing the worst. The longer she paused, the more worried he became. As he was about to plead with her for an answer, she spoke.

"Josh, do you remember my begging you to make love to me before you left me?" she asked, throwing caution to the wind.

"Do I remember?" He laughed harshly. "Oh, Kat, it was all that helped me to retain my sanity in all those hours when life seemed to be hanging on a thread. It was hard for me to endure the pain and devastation of living without you." He shook his head. "It was those last hours with you that kept my hopes alive."

Then, within a second, like a bolt of lightning, realization dawned upon him. His eyes widened in hopeful anticipation. "We have a daughter!" he shouted in unbridled joy, forgetting that he was among strangers.

Other passengers who had woken up for breakfast turned to look at them in surprise and amusement. Josh smiled sheepishly at them but lowered his voice when he turned to her. "Oh, Kat. I thought long and hard about it when George told me you had a beautiful daughter. And then tonight you were so evasive when I asked you about her." He was overjoyed.

"Tell me, tell me, please. What is she like? She must be about seven now, if my calculation is correct. I've often wondered if I had left you with child."

Katarina showed him pictures of their daughter from a small album that she always carried in her purse. Josh was speechless as he cast his eyes on Bella's photos for the first time. She was the embodiment of him as a child, only that she was all girl, from her golden curls to her fancy frocks. He loved her immediately.

"Oh, Kat, she's beautiful!" His eyes clouded for a second. "I missed watching her grow up. I want to see her as soon as possible," he pleaded, an intense longing resonated in his voice.

"That makes two of you." She laughed, seemingly without a care. It reminded him of the carefree Kat of old times. "She's been pestering me to bring back her daddy to her," she informed him.

For the rest of the flight, they talked about Bella, her pet likes and dislikes, her idiosyncrasies and her lovable traits, as well as how much she was loved by her stepfather and her grandparents. Josh was grateful that Jamal had cared for his daughter unconditionally. Kat confessed that she didn't confide in Jamal that she and Bella's father were not married when Bella was conceived. She suspected that he had guessed the truth, but he had never asked her to deny or to confirm it, and for that she was grateful. He treated Bella like his own and was very protective of her.

Josh learned another lesson about love: there was Jamal's kind of love, undemanding, giving, self-sacrificing. He learned to respect the deceased's values, and he was thankful that for the last five years of his life, he was devoted to Kat and his daughter, Bella. He learned not to grudge the years that Kat devoted herself to him.

If they could turn back the plane, he would have begged them to, so excited was he at the prospect of seeing his daughter for the first time. Nevertheless, as it was, he would have to curb his enthusiasm and his desire to catch a glimpse of his daughter for some time yet. It seemed too perfect to be true. Kat still loved him. He was blessed with a daughter, something he had never dreamed of in those years, when he wandered lost and alone, in those foreign lands.

He couldn't bear the thought of parting with Kat again. He said so. She felt the same. So in typical European fashion, he went on his knees and asked her to marry him; and in typical Malay fashion, she pulled him up quickly to sit beside her, embarrassed that others might glimpse a moment that was so private.

"I can't marry you now, Josh, although that is my dearest wish," she replied softly, to his abject misery. "I am in what is called *iddah*, a period of mourning for all Muslim women after the deaths of their husbands, a period of four months and ten days. We're not even supposed to leave our homes, but I've a business to run and I consider it urgent. Dad needs to take a break.". She smiled fondly at him on seeing him frowning. "Don't frown so, darling. I only have fifteen days to complete."

Not wanting to be defeated, he made another proposal, his lips curved in a disarming smile. "What if you stay in my apartment while you're working?"

"Josh!" she protested, staring at him with incredulity. "That means I have to travel hours every day to and from work!"

"In that case, what if I come and stay with you in Reading for that one week? I will be the one to commute daily. Come on, darling. It's only for a couple of weeks before we get married, and we'll plan something that's amenable for our family," he coaxed, feeling as excited as a teenager who was planning his first rendezvous with the girl of his dreams. "I can't wait to meet Bella," he added excitedly. "I'll go home with you to Kuala Lumpur." He spoke tentatively and then thought for a while. "Yeah, that's what we'll do. We are going to meet our Bella next week!" he concluded jubilantly.

***

They hardly slept that night. Kat took him to the family apartment that George had procured years before, when he realized that the cottage was too far from their office or shops. It would be inconvenient for her, as she had been pregnant with Bella. Kat was given a free hand in running the Reading office initially, but when she settled down with Jamal, she moved back to KL. She decided it would be inappropriate for her to live separately, especially after he was diagnosed with leukaemia. The apartment block was situated within walking distance to the River Thames, where they would go for walks or dine by the riverside and enjoy their meals in comfort. There was a wide choice of cuisines, and they were never disappointed.

After dinner, they made themselves comfortable in the sitting room, where they continued to talk. There was so much that each wanted to know about the other. They had been separated from each other for close to eight years, leading separate lives, and both had been devastated by that separation. Katarina especially had been an emotional wreck when she discovered that she was pregnant.

"I cried every night, Josh. I didn't think life was worth living without you, especially after I discovered I was carrying your baby. My parents were supportive. They didn't want me to face the odium and contempt from their friends for having a baby out of wedlock, so Dad took it upon himself to get this apartment and to arrange for Mummy to stay with me until I was ready to return to KL after the baby was born."

Josh, who was sitting on the floor at her feet, experienced a gamut of emotions on hearing the pain in her voice and the difficulties she went through. "I'm sorry I wasn't there for you, Kat." What else could he say? A spasm of guilt and shame overwhelmed him. His jaw tightened, and his eyes closed in contrition.

She shook her head. "It wasn't your fault. I begged you to love me. And I don't regret it now, seeing that we have such a beautiful little darling," she continued, cupping his jaw tenderly with both hands. "I lost several pounds in the first few months, but as the pregnancy advanced, I began to think of the baby more than my own discomfort and unhappiness. I began to take care of myself for the baby's sake. Thankfully, she was healthy when she was born."

He looked at her with pride. He listened to every word, his eyes watching every movement of her lips, a beatific smile on his handsome face. He couldn't remember the last time he had been that happy.

"She weighed eight pounds at birth," she added. It had been traumatic for her then, but with the birth of the baby, things began to look more positive.

"Was it a difficult birth?" he asked, his voice heavy with regret. "I'm so sorry, Kat. I wish I had been there for you."

"The labour pains were bad enough. They lasted for twelve hours," she told him, her face contorting as she recalled those long, horrendous hours.

He took her hands and held them wordlessly, his mind picturing Kat writhing in pain. He grimaced as if he felt her pain too. What could he say that would mitigate the suffering she went through?

"The first time I held her in my arms, she opened her eyes and I saw you looking at me. I was jolted into reality, for she had your eyes. She was the product of our love. Everything became wonderful from then on," she said with a smile. "I lived for her. She is such a lovable little darling." She laughed loudly. "With her endless questions, she opens up a new world for me every day. Do you know she is practising a dance that she choreographs herself in anticipation of meeting up with you?"

Josh couldn't stop laughing as the picture of his beloved daughter, whom he had yet to meet, danced its way into his heart.

As soon as she arrived at the apartment, Katarina had called home to inform everybody that she had arrived safely. She refrained from telling them that Josh was with her. She wanted to savour the time when she could be alone with him. The questions and cross-examinations from her mother and her daughter would take much effort from her to explain in detail. That she left for another day. Her daughter once again reminded her to get in touch with her father. It was bittersweet for the man who was listening to the phone conversation but who had been forbidden to participate.

"I can't wait to talk to her, Kat," he said wistfully. "There's so much about her that I've missed out, all of those years when she learned to smile, to crawl, to walk and then to speak." He inhaled silently. "I can picture you with Bella in your arms and her not knowing who her father is. It could have been a different picture if I had been there by your side." He stared at her, regret written all over his face.

"Don't be so despondent, Josh," she said comfortingly. "I had unstinting support from my family. Dad never said a word of blame, directed to you or to me, nor did he ever show an iota of disappointment. He was supportive all the way. His love for our daughter is beyond definition. She's the proverbial apple of his eye. But Mummy ..." She took his hand and placed it against her cheek as she smiled into his eyes. "Granted, Mummy was very disappointed in me initially." She recalled her mother's first reaction and laughed. "She never doubted who got me in that situation. She wanted to kill you."

"Does she still hate me?" Josh asked. He looked forlorn.

"No, darling. Not anymore. It takes two to tango. She realized that I was not blameless. In fact, it was I who begged you to love me, in case you have forgotten."

"I know we went against all that we agreed upon. Leaving you that night was the most difficult thing I ever did. My spirit was at the lowest ebb. But we have been blessed with Bella, and I could never say that I'm sorry we made love that night." He kissed her forehead chastely. "I hope your mother does not bear grudges against me still."

"She loves Bella to distraction, and because of that, she is prepared to love you too," Kat informed him cheerfully. "Mummy is a very generous person, and she's forgiving. That's one of the reasons Dad thinks she's an angel walking on earth."

The table was turning in their favour. The time was ripe for them to renew their old vows and to forge a new path together, this time with Bella, the product of their love. How poignant were the words of the poet Emily Bronte, and though penned a century ago, they still rang true in the hearts of the two lovers who had found each other again.

*Come, walk with me,*

*There's only thee*

*To bless my spirit now-*

*We used to love on winter nights*

*To wander through the snow;*

*Can we not woo back old delights?*

# CHAPTER 15

"K AT," JOSH SAID, "come sit beside me. We need to talk." He patted the seat beside him.

They had been together for several days. It had been hectic. He would leave early, even before she was awake, and return late at night, by which time both were too exhausted to carry on any serious conversation. They shared a bed together, but he was conscientious in his respect for her need to uphold the sanctity of her belief. They had breached that once and look where it had landed them. That brief ecstatic moment of their union had been a blessing, he secretly thought. Bella was worth any punishment he would go through, despite the fact that he had not seen her in person yet.

Whatever happened, he vowed, Kat would not be deprived of that veneer of respectability that she had acquired back home, and if her friends and family had accepted her story about his relationship with her, he would respect that, but they would have to rectify that as soon as possible and settle down respectably, the way they both wanted. This enforced life of abstinence was driving him crazy.

After the hectic week at the office, he was finally able to get much-needed rest, and he had persuaded Kat to do the same. He looked forward to the time when he would wake up with her in his arms and spend a lazy couple of hours together without having to rush off. He had the persistent need to talk to his daughter, and they spent a few hours planning for that hour when Kat would call home. He couldn't wait for noon, when the time would be appropriate, as the family would have finished dinner by then and would be waiting for her daily call.

Bella picked up the phone at the first ring. Earlier on in the day, when her daughter was at school, Katarina had spoken to her mother about her meeting with Josh, and she in turn had relayed the news to her husband and granddaughter. So it was an excited little girl who answered the phone.

"Mummy, Mummy," she sang, "Grandma said you've found my daddy."

Josh's face lit up with joy. Their faces were so close together that they were breathing into each other's faces, his well-trimmed moustache tickling her nose. As he tried to hear what his daughter was saying, his heart was jumping erratically in his chest.

"Yes, darling," she replied. "Would you like to speak to your daddy now?" She turned to Josh and handed the phone to him with a satisfied smile. This time it was her turn to eavesdrop.

"Hello, Bella." Josh's voice trembled as he tried to control his excitement and happiness. "How are you?" His face was so close to Kat's that he could look deeply into those incredible black pools that were gazing up adoringly at him, a blissful smile on her lips. He caressed them lovingly with his fingers. It was difficult even then to picture his Kat bringing up their baby without him. And she seemed to have done that so well.

"I'm fine, thank you." He heard Bella's polite response. He was impressed by her cool and calm answer, which was quite unusual for girls at such a young age, at least the ones he had come across in his sparse social contacts.

He looked at Kat with new respect. "I love you," he mouthed. Pointing to the phone with his forefinger, he whispered, "She's a delightful gem."

"Are you really my daddy?" Bella asked him pointedly, her high lilting voice filling his ears with indescribable feelings he had never experienced before.

"Yes, I am," Josh replied, adrenalin pounding painfully through his blood at the sound of his daughter's voice. "It's good to hear your sweet voice. Mummy told me a lot about you. I'm hoping to meet up with you soon, darling. Would you like that?"

"I'm looking forward to that, Daddy." It was wonderful that she had warmed up to him immediately. And to hear her address him as "Daddy" uplifted his spirits tremendously. He heard her indrawn breath before she continued. "Is it true I look like you, Daddy? I have blue eyes too. Papa said that's what made me special."

"Yes, Bella. You have inherited my eyes. But that's all. Your papa was right. You're special because you're also a lot like Mummy. You're beautiful, and you have her smile. Did you know that?" Silently he said a prayer of thanks to her late stepfather for his kind and generous heart.

"Daddy, have you and Mummy made up already? You're not going to part with her like you did before?" She questioned him as tactlessly as only the innocent could do. "You won't fight anymore?"

He had not expected that question, for he and Kat had not discussed how they were to explain their separation to their daughter. He turned to Kat with eyebrows raised. *What explanation had she given Bella for their separation?* he wondered silently. Kat, however, only smiled and shook her head.

"No, we'll never, ever be apart again—that's a promise. We'll talk about that when we're together. Would you like that?" he suggested indulgently.

She replied in the affirmative. They continued chatting for a considerable time; she had many questions and answers that sometimes made him roar with laughter. The easy flow of the conversation between them belied the fact that they had yet to meet. She was cheerful, funny and entertaining. From that very moment, he loved her with all his heart and embraced his new role as her father with complete enthusiasm. She was incredibly precious, and he silently made a promise that he would protect and nurture her, come what may. The sheer wonder of it filled him with remorse and humility. For once in his life, he felt totally blessed.

"She's a darling, Kat. I can't wait to see her," he told her as he placed on the table the two mugs of latte he had prepared for them. They enjoyed a light lunch of salad and chicken sandwiches that Kat had prepared. It was exceedingly comforting for him to settle down into a few hours of domestic bliss, an experience that had eluded him for most of his life.

"It won't be long, Josh. Two more days and we'll be home," she stated, sitting down beside him on the sofa, cautiously sipping the hot coffee from her cup.

"How did you explain to her about us?" he asked as he nestled his face in her luxurious hair and inhaled its fragrance.

"I told her that we loved each other but couldn't agree on many things, so we decided to part," she replied quietly as she put her arms around him, her head resting on his chest.

"Fair enough," he responded thoughtfully. "It was true in a way. If we had stayed together, with my crazy moods and attitudes, I would have destroyed whatever feelings you had for me then and our lives would have been in tatters. I guess we could say that our separation was a blessing in disguise. At this juncture, I can safely say that I am cured."

"I'm so happy for us." She smiled tremulously. She turned to him, her eyes lighting up with anticipation. "You haven't told me anything about the years that you were away. What was it like?"

He sipped his coffee quietly. A shadow crossed his face momentarily. When he looked at her, however, his eyes lit up and he smiled benignly. He felt light-hearted and free. No longer was he manacled by his childhood trauma, of that he was certain.

"I haven't been this happy in a long time, Kat. That night when I left you, I was suffocated with misery. For a long time, I didn't really care what happened to me. I thought if I could lose myself somewhere in the jungle or in the desert, it wouldn't have mattered. But as time went by, I began to realize that what I needed was to accept that my behaviour was dominated by my desire for complete control and the overwhelming sense of possessiveness over the woman I loved." He looked at her lovingly. "And that means you!" He kissed her hand with reverence. "I needed to purge that from my system, but I didn't know how."

She looked up at him with great tenderness. "We both didn't understand it then, darling. Maybe if we did, we could have worked it out together," she stated gravely.

"I'm not sure that we could have," he disagreed. "We were young, and our love was new. We wouldn't have been able to handle it then. Now, in hindsight, we assume that we could have done this and should have done that, but I believe that we were meant to travel on a journey that had been mapped out for us. It was very painful for me, but I'm grateful things happened the way they did. Now I can safely say that I'm prepared to take care of you and Bella and not fear that I'll hurt you both with my insane actions," he promised, becoming more convinced as he spoke that he could deliver what he promised her.

She nodded in agreement. "I believe you're right, Josh, and I'm very happy about that. We have to believe in fate and destiny. Sometimes we have to accept what we cannot change. We can only pray for what we need and want, and if we pray hard enough, I believe wholeheartedly that our prayers will be answered." She gave him a brilliant smile. "Just like our prayers to be together right now."

"Yes, I think you're right too," he conceded. "I remember sitting on the solid edge of a gargantuan rock above a monastery in Nepal. This monastery was perched high on a cliff. I looked down into the seemingly cavernous void beyond. It was terrifying. In the deathly silence of the late evening, I could hear the monks chanting their prayers. My heart was heavy. As I stared out into the distant hills and mountains that were partially covered with heavy floating white clouds, I pictured your beautiful face and your sweet smile and your eyes looking at me with great sadness. I missed you so much, but I had already given you up. For one crazy moment, I thought I should maybe jump down from the ledge and put an end to my misery."

"Josh!" she cried, her voice cracking. Her face puckered up in sorrow and commiseration. She hugged him desperately, thankful that he had come home to her finally.

For several seconds, Josh stopped speaking as he returned her caresses and comforted her, once again feeling extremely blessed that he could touch her and hold her, the way he had dreamed of all those lonely years.

He tried to make light of the incident. "As you can see, I'm still in one piece. It was just one crazy moment, darling. In the next instant, I heard the chimes of a bell, which brought me back to the land of the living. An old monk came by and sat down beside me. He was about ninety, I think, for he looked old and frail. He didn't say anything. He just nodded his head at me and smiled."

Josh inhaled sharply. "I heard the flapping of wings, and I turned towards the sky to see a large white-bellied heron flying past until it disappeared from view. The vastness of the space before me unfolded before my eyes as the clouds slowly edged away, and the view of the mountains in the distance took my breath away. I smiled and turned to acknowledge that to the monk, but there was no one beside me."

He shook his head in disbelief. "Until today, I can't figure out whether the old monk was just a figment of my imagination."

"Strange things have been known to happen in the land of the mystics," she agreed. "I've only read of such encounters, of course. No one has confirmed anything. The sceptics would pooh-pooh the whole idea and discredit it as nonsense. Whatever it was, darling, I'm glad that it managed to distract you."

"It certainly did," he concurred. "I stayed on in Nepal for several months," he related to her as he recalled the journey he made. "I trekked across the valleys, climbed the slopes, and made friends with those industrious people who sculpted hill terraces to grow rice, their staple food. I bunked in a yak herder's hut, ate their food, and even learned to enjoy yak meat, which is a delicacy for them and to drink their favourite drink, which is fermented rice with barley."

He laughed aloud when he glanced at her face and saw disbelief written all over it. "What's so unbelievable?" he asked.

"You eating yak meat and living in a hut," she remarked bluntly. "You were fastidious and meticulously tidy. You were not very adventurous where your palate was concerned. You've changed a lot, Josh."

"True. I was, and still am, as you can see, fastidious and meticulous, unlike one lady I know," he teased. He'd made their bed that morning. It was so perfect that she joked about hiring him as the chambermaid for her hotel, should she open one.

"And I'm still crazily in love with her," he asserted, planting a loud kiss on her nose.

"Those people are poor," he continued in a more serious tone. "They lead a very simple life, earning a simple livelihood. They are happy and contented. They are at peace with each other and with themselves. What they exhibited to me was priceless. By living in their midst, I began to ponder about my predilection, to learn to accept what I could not change, but I realized that there were many things that I *could* change. I had plenty of time to think about my life. I learned to forgive my father, for he didn't know any better. I also learned to forgive my mother for submitting to my father's abusive behaviour. Ultimately, I forgave myself for my own failings and earned some peace of mind in the process."

After a pregnant silence, she inquired, "what happened to your father?"

"He died last year. I searched for him immediately after I returned from my travels. He was a shell of his former self. I'm glad I made my peace with him."

It was the moment of truth for her, and she accepted it with a silent prayer of thanks and gratitude. There was nothing in the world that she had dreamed of more than having Josh back in her life, a Josh that had expunged all that was venomous and virulent in his personality.

However, they were getting to be too morbid in an afternoon of tender loving, so she infused some gaiety into their conversation.

"But the yak? Yuck," she said the word in a derogatory way, to his amusement. As she had hoped, he burst out laughing as a picture of the erstwhile animals emerged in his mind.

"The yaks make strange grunting sounds. The first night in the hut, I was awakened by these grunts, which gave me the heebie-jeebies. Until I found out the source. They are very large animals. They look like bovines up to here." He demonstrated by putting his right hand at the top of his neck. "But unlike bovines, yaks have large and sharp horns, small ears, and long shaggy hair to enable them to withstand the cold winters." He grimaced as he recalled an unfortunate incident. "I tried to ride a yak once and fell off. I never tried again."

"You never tried to climb Mount Everest?" she teased.

"And try to beat Sir Edmund Hillary and Tenzig Norgay?" He was amused. "Never. I could never be that adventurous. To climb such a mountain would take a lot of training and preparation, which I was not ready for. The closest I came to climbing a mountain," he recalled, "was when I joined a group of travellers who were led by several *Sherpas* to climb half-mile-high stone steps that led us into the clouds to a wall revered by Hindus and Buddhists alike. From there, we climbed one mountain, the peak of which is thirteen thousand feet high. I can't remember what the mountain is called. Far, far away yonder, hidden among thick white clouds, was the Everest. That was the closest I ever came to the lofty Himalayas."

She woke up the next morning to see him deep in meditation in a perfect yoga pose, legs crossed, eyes closed, oblivious to what was going on around him. She dared not even breathe, afraid that she might distract him. From the bed she quietly and surreptitiously watched him go through the whole routine, with such finesse and grace, until he completed it. He opened his eyes and looked right smack into hers.

He smiled with delight. "Enjoyed the show?" he questioned as he swiftly rolled up the mat and stored it neatly in the corner.

"Perfectly executed," she replied, slowly sitting up in bed, stretching sinuously while continuing to watch him, eyes half-closed, spellbound by his manly beauty, unaware that the blanket had fallen off her shoulders and a tantalizing view of a breast was exposed.

"You'd better remove yourself from that bed," he warned in a strangled voice. "A man can withstand only so much temptation."

He watched her gather her blanket around her and, blushing like an uninitiated maid, rushed to the toilet without further ado. *I must be out of my mind to place myself in this situation*, he thought.

The tough week had put a monumental strain on his self-control. She had suggested that he slept in the guest room, but he desisted, promising her that they would remain celibate until they tied the knot, not ever wanting to let her out of his sight or his arms.

"Look what it's gotten me into," he muttered to himself as he proceeded to the guest bathroom for his morning routine.

Looking into the mirror while brushing his teeth, he was amused to find his lookalike staring back at him. He examined that face with a critical eye. The cold blue eyes that had so characterized him were gone. They now danced with life. The tightly drawn lips were in a relaxed pose.

This face belonged to a man who was at peace with himself and with the world around him.

He was whistling an indefinable tune when he walked into the kitchen minutes later. Katarina was already dressed in tight blue jeans and a loose top that reminded him that they would be travelling in the evening. It was D-day, when they would be flying to Kuala Lumpur. He couldn't wait to see his daughter.

Kat was making scrambled eggs, as fluffy, moist and flavourful as he liked them. Having regained his moral equilibrium, he gave her a chaste kiss on her cheek and proceeded to brew coffee, a job which he volunteered for every morning.

"Josh, about this morning..." she volunteered.

"Shh ... It's okay, sweetheart. It won't be long." He comforted her with a loving hug, although, unbeknown to her, he had been counting the days like a primary school child. The end seemed to be a long way away.

While enjoying his breakfast and in an effort to distract her, he talked about his travels and how he had picked up yoga in the second year of his self-imposed exile when he on a journey to India.

"You wouldn't have recognized me if you had seen me, Kat," he said with humour, grinning from ear to ear. "Due to the hot weather, my skin was extremely tanned and I let my facial hair grow wild. I looked just like any unkempt local person, and people spoke to me in their dialect. Of course, I had no idea what they were saying to me. Just to keep up with my new looks, I began to pick up a word or two here and there and was able to string a few words together that made some sense. Some people even thought that I was loco," he said, his laughter ringing loud and clear.

From across the table, she stared at him incredulously, mouth wide open. It was hard for her to imagine her Josh looking anything but dapper, immaculate and dashing.

"Don't stare so, my love" he objected playfully. "I told you I was going out of my mind. There are many languages spoken in India," he continued chattily, "depending on the region where one comes from. But most people speak or understand Urdu or English. Urdu is a beautiful language which, incidentally, I learned when I was in Northern India. I came across a place in the foothills of the Himalayas, known as Rishikesh. If you remember, the Beatles put it on the world map when they descended on this place several years ago to practise meditation and embrace spirituality."

"I know!" she responded. "They became followers of the yogi Maharishi Mahesh after they visited his ashram in 1968. I remember it well. It received worldwide coverage, like everything else the Beatles did." Her tone became tinged with sadness. "It was also the year we broke up."

"I didn't really know or care then. I was consumed with misery," he responded, shaking his head. "When I was in India, people were talking about it. I wanted to find out how that would help me—or even if it could. I became much saner after Nepal. What if there was more that I could do?

"It wasn't difficult to join an *ashram* by then. In fact, it had become the in thing to experience when you were there. That's what I did." He didn't realize he had been swiftly munching on his breakfast eggs while narrating his activities to her, until he came to the last mouthful. Silently, she scooped another spoonful onto his plate.

"Well, I guess there weren't enough scrambled eggs for you there," she teased.

"Not in the ashram, of course," he retaliated, taking another sip of his coffee and giving her his dazzling smile. "We were put through a stringent regime of meditation classes, where we were taught breathing techniques for stress relief. I survived three hours of *hatha* and *ashtanga* yoga every day during the few months I was there. That really made me stronger. You saw only some of the poses this morning. It was actually extremely strenuous and demanding for the body."

"You can instruct me on some of those moves, can't you?" she asked with enthusiasm.

"When we're legally married, I will teach you anything you want, darling," he replied, tongue-in-cheek, for which he earned a warning glare.

"In hindsight, I think what helped me most were the meditation classes that I joined," he went on in a more serious tone. "They were more than just breathing classes. They helped to maintain calmness of the mind. They were also moments of self-reflection. They taught me to look into myself in order to deal with my problems. I came to grips with the issues that impacted our relationship and realized that I really needed to purge myself of the mental darkness that engulfed me." He paused in order to recoup his thoughts.

"It was like an extension of my first awakening in Nepal, which was, in hindsight, the first lap of my journey of self-discovery," he concluded.

"You did experience some extraordinary events, Josh. I don't think many people would have arrived at the same conclusions, even though they might have undergone similar experiences. I think that you were absolutely focussed on finding a solution, and *voila*, there was your solution," she ventured.

"Well, you won't believe what else I did," he said, teeth gleaming in an impudent smile.

"What? There's more? You really lived it up, didn't you?"

He nodded. "It was sometime in January, a few weeks before I decided to return home and look for you. A few people were talking about jumping into the Ganges and dipping, a ritual following the tradition adopted by the *swamis* for hundreds of years, as a means of expiating their sins. The temperature at this time was around seven degrees. It was a challenge for me to see how far I could go. I was game. What had I to lose? I thought. If I was meant to die in the Ganges, so be it. But to be on the safe side I took special lessons in a proper breathing technique, which enables you to draw warmth into the upper chest."

Slowly he demonstrated it to her and engaged her in the exercise until she was able to do it as well, after which he continued with his story.

"Well, I managed to survive after ten dips while in the water. It was icy cold, but I made it. Some people were able to complete the one hundred and eight dips as required, but I wasn't going to push my luck. As I was concentrating on the dipping, a revelation came to me. I wanted to live. I wanted to find love again. I wanted to find you. Life was precious. So I stopped and climbed onto the banks, shivering like a drowning rat."

"That was an unusual experience. I've never heard of people swimming in such freezing waters. You were crazy, Josh." She shivered in dismay.

"I made a detour to visit the Taj Mal in Agra before I flew home," he said, ignoring her disapproving remarks. "It was a wonderful, wonderful eye-opener for me, as by then my thoughts of you consumed the better part of my waking hours. According to legend, this maharaja who built this absolutely stupendous palace to inter his wife after her death, went into seclusion for one year. When he emerged, he looked old and grey and emaciated. To think that he had been a soldier and a conqueror! Unbelievable! When he died," he resumed after a pause, "his body was buried there too, beside her. If that was not proof of his love, I don't know what is," he concluded.

"Oh, that's a lovely story. I've seen pictures of the Taj Mahal. I read that in the nineteen years of their marriage, the maharani, Mumtaz Mahal, accompanied him to all his battles—and what's more, she bore him thirteen children, seven of whom died at a very young age. I guess in such a marriage, the one who survived the death of the other would be inconsolable and would wish for death himself," she observed thoughtfully.

He chewed on her thought-provoking statement and found that they were of the same mind. At that juncture, he couldn't picture his own life without her.

"Their love and devotion to one another is very inspiring," he remarked. "One day you and I and Bella will make a trip to Agra and pay homage to those royal lovers. I wouldn't want to be in the maharajah's shoes. I don't think I could live without you now, Kat.

"I'm looking forward to our wedding. I promise I've changed for the better," he said after a pregnant silence, during which she expressed her appreciation of him the way only she could, with loving kisses that he responded to enthusiastically.

"I promise I'm totally cured of those maladies you've been exposed to," he continued after a while. "I wanted to be sure that I was completely sane before I contacted you." He paused for a second before he continued. "Immediately after my return, I went through several months of psychotherapy and counselling just to be sure. Presently, I can say with certainty that I've been totally cleansed and we can look forward to a rosy future and building a happy family together. Why are you crying, love?" he asked as tears cascaded down her cheeks.

"For you, darling. For us too." She sobbed, as he took her in his arms and tried to console her. She had cried heartbrokenly, when she was overwhelmed by the loss of her much-beloved father, who had died so abruptly years ago; wept for Jamal, whose life was cut short at such an early age; and sobbed in abject misery when she thought life was meaningless after her breakup with Josh. The prospect of seeing him again had been a seemingly impossible dream.

Now she was shedding tears for that little boy who had been deprived of a happy and normal childhood and who had grown up to become the love of her life. The tears were also tears of purification, of joy and happiness for them both. The grown man had trekked halfway around the world in search of salvation and relentlessly pursued the answer to his inner conflicts and mental imbalance. He had finally emerged unscathed, his soul cleansed, and despite everything, he still loved her!

# CHAPTER 16

THEY HAD TAKEN a direct flight from London, not wanting to delay their arrival in Kuala Lumpur. Josh calculated that they had four hours left, as he couldn't sleep a wink, so excited was he at the prospect of seeing his daughter. He smiled as he turned to look at Kat, who was snoring slightly. Lovingly he adjusted her blanket, planting a kiss on her forehead as he leaned over her. The flight attendant, on seeing that he was awake, stopped by to ask if he needed anything. He declined with a smile. *I don't need anything*, he thought. *All I need is my Kat beside me and I'm the happiest man in the whole wide world.*

He recalled the conversation they had earlier, after about an hour into the flight. She had been browsing through the in-flight magazine. There was an interesting article about an interracial marriage, which gave rise to a question about their own plans. She turned to him and whispered urgently, her voice bordering on panic.

"Josh, we can't get married yet."

He turned to her abruptly, surprised. "Why not, Kat?" he asked, his nerves rattled by her statement.

"You're not a Muslim. Oh, Josh, we never even discussed this. I never asked you if you would convert."

He laughed, a carefree laughter that intensified her concern. He took her hand and made her look at him. "I had no chance to tell you yesterday. We were so busy talking about other things that surprisingly something that important slipped my mind."

"What are you saying?" she insisted.

"Darling," he said, an ecstatic smile curving his lips, "on the last day at the office, the staff were surprised that I had taken a month's leave of absence. I had been cast as a workaholic. Even though I had worked with the company for close to five years, I had never taken much leave before—and what's more, it was for such an extended period of time." He paused to allow her to absorb his information. "I informed them that I was getting married. They wanted to know all about you, and one thing led to another, until another architect, who is a Muslim, asked if I would be interested in becoming one. Within the hour, he brought over the *imam* from the nearby mosque, and there and then I pronounced the *syahadah.*" He added with a laugh, "Not without much prompting, I might add."

She was quiet for a while. It bothered him that she didn't seem happy. "What's on your mind, love?" he asked. "You don't approve of my conversion?" he questioned as he tried to interpret her silence.

"It's not that I don't approve, Josh. I'm elated and honoured that you took that step because of me," she replied. "I'm not overly religious myself, as you know, but changing one's belief is a momentous decision. It takes a lot of self-searching and forethought. It has far-reaching impacts. Have you given it much thought? Besides, you hardly know anything about Islam," she reasoned.

"Kat," he said, his voice thoughtful, "I grew up ostensibly as a Christian, but we never practised or prayed like true Christians. I don't ever remember going to church. We celebrated Christmas, of course, but that was all. Consequently, I have not been properly schooled in Christianity."

"I'm not surprised. I just don't want you to regret later on in life when we are older, when we've been married for ten years or so, and you wake up one morning and realize you've made a rash decision."

"What brought this about, Kat?" he asked, a deep frown marring his forehead. "You're still unsure of my devotion to you?"

She was silent, her mind in turmoil. She pushed up the blinds of the aircraft window that had been drawn down for the night, looked out unseeingly into the darkness and then lowered them again, all the while wondering whether she should continue with her line of thought that had been bugging her ever since she read the article. Puzzled, he watched her movements, his lips compressed into a thin line, silently wondering where the discussion was leading.

She turned towards him, her eyes luminous as she searched his face, now etched with confusion. Gently she caressed his cheek and looked deeply into his eyes. "I'm not saying that you will treat me in the same way, darling, but

I've come across so many cases of foreign men who married Muslim women but who turned their backs on their wives after several years of marriage for women of other faiths."

"And you think I'm that kind of a heel to do that to you?" His voice was firm. "Kat, look at me," he ordered. He held her chin firmly with his right hand so that she could look straight into his eyes and his heart. "Kat," he repeated, "I've loved you from the moment you rushed headlong into my arms ten years ago, and I've never stopped loving you, despite all those years we've been apart. Nothing is going to change my feelings for you. Of that I'm positive."

"It's not that I doubt you or your love, Josh," she replied, her hand clinging firmly to his wrist. "It's just that Islam is such a demanding religion which might be too tough for you to practise. Like all religions, it embraces the good and eschews the bad, but it demands total obedience to the five pillars ..."

"I understand your concern, love," he interrupted. "You should know by now that I do not do anything by halves. I will seriously start studying the religion as soon as you can arrange it, and maybe it would be fun if you could join me too," he added, a smile brightening up his face, his thumb tenderly caressing her cheek. "By the way, if you're interested, my Muslim name is Imran," he said, tongue-in-cheek.

"Love that name," she told him. "There's a whole chapter in the _Qur'an_ dedicated to Ali Imran and his descendants. The Virgin Mary, the mother of Jesus, was his daughter." She leaned away from him to do a mock study of his face and added, "Hmm ... you are one handsome Imran."

"It's the wrong place and time to flirt with me, my Katarina," he murmured seductively, addressing her by her full name, which he did only on special occasions. He pulled her into his arms none too gently, and they continued chatting until her eyes closed in a deep sleep, buoyed by the rhythmic drone of the plane.

Hours later, he was still awake. He was poring over some new designs submitted by one of his junior staff when he heard the captain's announcement urging the passengers to return to their seats and fasten their seat belts. The cabin crew were ordered to take their seats. As he bent to check Katarina's seat belt, he felt the plane plunging downwards violently, as if it was going to land on its belly. While bending over her to wake her up, his head missed colliding against hers by a mere inch due to the violence of the drop.

Katarina suddenly opened her eyes wide in alarm. "What's going on, Josh!" she cried, terrified.

He held her hands tightly. "I guess we've run into some massive air pockets. The turbulence is very bad, darling." He couldn't keep the fear out of his voice.

It was horrendous. People screamed; some muttered incoherent prayers just as loudly; babies wailed; pillows, magazines, and papers flew all over the aircraft. It felt as if a storm was playing havoc with the plane as it bounced up and down and swayed precariously side to side. Katarina clung to Josh in fear.

"I don't want to die, Josh. Please, *ya Allah*, save us!" she cried, clinging to Josh fearfully.

"We won't die, love. It'll be all right soon." He comforted her, although he himself was unsure whether they would pull through. Jumbled thoughts flashed through his mind. If they were to die, who would take care of their daughter? It was not fair to deprive him of happiness which had seemed to be within his reach. He had been ecstatic at the thought of marrying his love and settling down with his family beside him. Silently he closed his eyes and prayed and prayed, his arms tightly bound around Kat.

For what seemed hours, the aircraft waddled through the air like a ship in a stormy sea. Finally, the severe turbulence receded and died down; the plane eventually glided smoothly. Relieved, Josh opened his eyes and checked on Kat. She was pale and shivering in terror, but thankfully she was unhurt. The captain had masterfully manoeuvred the plane and managed to avoid a catastrophe. Someone hailed *"Allahu Akbar"*. Several others joined in, thanking God for a tragedy averted.

The cabin crew, though visibly shaken, behaved in a professional manner. They went round checking on the passengers and began tidying up, collecting objects that were strewn about the cabins and establishing a semblance of order. Fortunately, no one was seriously injured, apart from a cut here and a bruise there.

When Josh checked his watch, he discovered that the entire terrifying episode lasted for only a couple of minutes. "Time seems endless when we are terrified," he said to Kat as he solicitously offered her a few sips of water to calm her nerves. "Everything's going to be fine now," he said gently.

The plane flew along a smooth path thereafter, but the experience left a deep scar in everyone's mind. Kat overheard one woman swear that it was her last flight. "I don't blame her, Josh," she told him. "If there were alternatives, I wouldn't ever fly again."

As they were disembarking, they took the time to commend the pilots for their skill in averting a calamity and to shake their hands in gratitude. The cabin crew had been extremely professional in handling the situation, and though the experience had been extremely terrifying, they were thankful that no one was injured and their lives had been spared.

***

"Your luggage weighs a ton," he complained good-naturedly as he carried her suitcase in one hand and his smaller one in the other. "What have you packed inside this bag, stones? I can't imagine how you managed when you were alone." Although he was grumbling, his smile belied his words.

"Complaining already, Encik Imran?" she teased. "Well, I did some shopping, if you remember. There're lots of knick-knacks for all those waiting for us at home. Among others, there's a doll for Bella, some trinkets for Mummy, and a shirt for Dad. And of course some documents that I need to go over with Dad. As to your other question," she simpered flirtatiously, "why, all I had to do was to smile and to look helpless and some good-looking gentleman would offer his help."

"Well, from now on," he warned, "no more making eyes at anyone. I'm around to do your bidding."

"Thank you, handsome sir," she replied, giggling. "And to be fair, that warning applies to you too. No wandering eyes whether I'm around or not, period!"

Their good-natured banter came to a stop as they spotted their family waiting outside the arrival hall. Josh spied them first: the tall distinguished-looking English man wearing a florid *batik* shirt, laughing helplessly at something the young golden-haired girl was saying; and the elegant woman standing beside him, dressed in the traditional *baju kurung*, smiling affectionately at them both. No one needed to identify his daughter to him. She stood out like a beacon in a dark night.

*This is my family,* Josh thought. A feeling of pride and an overwhelming ocean of love threatened to drown him. He turned to Kat, who was smiling and waving to her daughter as the latter started to run towards them, her grandparents trudging leisurely behind. Bella hurtled herself into her mother's arms and squealed with joy.

"Mummy, Mummy," she cried happily, "you're home!" She turned towards her father, who immediately placed the suitcases on the floor. He was staring at the quintessential picture mother and daughter made as they hugged and kissed one another. In another second, like a ball flying headlong towards the goalpost, his daughter rushed at him, her arms flailing about.

"Daddy! I'm so happy to see you, Daddy," she cried, her face flushed with happiness.

Josh swallowed hard and would have spoken but for the lump in his throat. He returned her embrace silently. He couldn't believe his fortune. This little spitfire was the testimony of Kat's love for him. He would have her no other way. She was beautiful, lively, and intelligent. No superlatives were sufficient to describe his darling. When he found his voice finally, he whispered, "Bella." His voice trembled, his chest bursting with the joy of holding his little girl in his arms for the first time. "Bella," he repeated senselessly.

"Give Daddy a chance to breathe, sweetheart," George's booming voice echoed, accompanied by his buoyant laughter as he gently patted his granddaughter's shoulder. He held out his hand to Josh. "Welcome, Josh," he said, and pulling Suraya to his side, he introduced her. "You remember my wife, Sue?"

Josh gallantly kissed Suraya's proffered hand and politely enquired about her well-being, a little nervous at the prospect of being hounded by her. However, he was mollified when she pulled him into her embrace and kissed him like a long-lost son. He had never forgotten that one splendid Christmas he had celebrated within the bosom of her family in an atmosphere that was abundant with love and cheer many years ago.

***

George had wasted no time in arranging special classes for Josh, conducted by an *ustaz*, a graduate of Al Azhar University, Cairo, who had introduced him to Islam several years before and whose classes he had enjoyed immensely. With the latter's guidance, George had made an intense study of the *Qur'an*. He had acquired sufficient understanding of the words of Allah, which had opened his eyes to the depth and sanctity of the religion that he had embraced and practised with utmost diligence. He fervently hoped the exposure would benefit Josh as well.

As their future son-in-law was going through the two-hour induction for the day, George and Suraya were enjoying their afternoon tea in their sitting room overlooking the South China Sea. Their beach house on the coast of Kuantan was a respite during the weekends from the hustle and bustle of Kuala Lumpur.

At breakfast that morning, Suraya had prepared a special congee for the family. Josh, who had never tasted rice porridge before, thoroughly enjoyed it. He complimented the cook and asked her what the dish was, to which she replied, "It's called *bubur lambuk*, Josh, a special Terengganu rice porridge with *budu*, a special ingredient."

Josh was horrified. "Voodoo?" he said unbelievingly.

A burst of laughter from George, Kat, and his daughter perplexed him. He looked from one to another around the table with a weak smile, his confusion intensified. Saffian, Kat's stepson, smiled quietly as he looked towards their grandmother.

"Daddy," his daughter said, amidst hiccups of laughter, "It's *boo doo*. It's a special fermented sauce made with tiny fishes known as *ikan bilis*."

"How come you know so much about *budu*, sweetie?" her mother asked.

Bella glanced at her grandfather. "While you were away, Gramps took me to the *kampung* where they were preparing it, Mummy. It's a lovely village by the sea, Daddy," she said as turned to her father. "Those village people are very generous. They even presented me with a bottle of *budu*. You would like them, Daddy. You and I and Mummy will visit them one day," she enthused. She turned towards Saffian and asked, *"Abang,* would you like to come too?"

Saffian nodded, smiling as he crammed his mouth with food.

Katarina looked towards Josh, her eyes twinkling with mischief. "See, our daughter has attested that there're no magic potions added."

Not to be outdone and feeling a little foolish, Josh replied good-naturedly, "Well, seeing that I've been chasing you halfway around the world, you can't blame me for assuming that I've been cast under your spell."

For the rest of the breakfast hour, George, who had lived in Malaysia for a long time and who had been made aware of the local culture through his frequent contacts with the Malays, brought to their attention the many practices by which the *pawang* would heal the sick or bring to heel the arrogant, and at times administer love potions, to make a girl fall for the unwanted suitor.

"There's a certain amount of voodoo here too, Josh," he ended with a smile.

"Gramps, you should write a book about it. It would be very interesting," suggested Bella.

"I'll keep that in mind," George replied. "You'd help me with the research, wouldn't you?"

"Certainly, Gramps," she replied. "It would be an exciting adventure. Helping you would be fun."

Dinner was especially delicious as well. Suraya, who was well aware of Josh's taste in food, spared no expense at making his meals as sumptuous as she could. While appreciating Sue's culinary expertise and her thoughtfulness, Josh thought everything would have been ideal if not for the sleeping arrangements. Kat shared a connecting room with their daughter, and he was relegated to one at the opposite end of the bungalow.

"I miss you, darling," he whispered as they were climbing the stairs to their separate rooms.

Bella, who overheard her father's words, chimed in, "Mummy has a large double bed, Daddy. Why don't you share it with her?"

His answer was so garbled that his daughter could hardly understand. He quickly gave her a resounding kiss and hastily bade her good night, before she could utter another word.

Earlier on, after dinner, he had quietly and furtively guided Kat out of the house to stroll along the beach. She took him to her favourite spot, where a large boulder had positioned itself for as long as she could remember. She had been going there whenever she wanted to be by herself or to think. It was déjà vu, she thought, to sit at the same spot in Josh's arms, recalling that the last time she was there several weeks before, she had been thinking of him and calling out to him.

It was a wondrous night, magical almost, as a panoply of stars blanketed the vast open sky. The full moon beamed over them as they sat whispering and renewing their vows to one another. In the background, the waves lapped gently over the beach in a rhythm that echoed hauntingly in the silence of the night. The cool winds that blew across their faces swept her long, heavy hair into total disarray, at times covering Josh's face and mouth as he bent to kiss her. The moonlight cast a mystical glow in their eyes so that each became almost magnetized by the brilliance of the other's.

Suddenly, Josh released her and went on his knees in front of her. It took her by surprise.

"Darling," he said in an unsteady voice. "The last time I knelt in front of you, you denied me. Please let me do it properly this time. Will you please marry me?"

"Oh, Josh, please get up," she replied, pulling him up once again as she did before. "Of course I'll marry you." She had a certain dislike to see him on his knees before her.

Reverently he slid a ring onto her finger, the size and lustre of which shocked her into silence. In the moonlight, it gleamed and blinked as if a thousand stars had been crafted inside.

"Oh, Josh, it's so magnificent!" she cried in wonder, mesmerized by the beauty of his choice. "It's heavy too. Thank you. I love it," she added in a breathless rush of joy as she rewarded him with loving kisses that threatened to devour his sanity.

That splendid five-carat diamond solitaire, a testament to his undying love and devotion, became the subject of family discussion for the next hour as Bella, with her grandmother, pored over and dissected every facet that glimmered and dazzled, while he watched them fondly from his comfortable lazy chair, bathed in a glow of happiness. George had little to say, but he awarded Josh with a benign smile which sealed his approval.

# EPILOGUE

THEY WERE MARRIED at the end of the month. It was the most joyful affair, though small compared to weddings that were customarily arranged in that city, where thousands of guests were often invited. The function was held at their house in Kuala Lumpur, attended only by all their close friends and relatives. Even then, there were whispers regarding the presence of the bright golden-haired young girl, a tall and engaging replica of the groom, who was moving graciously from table to table, her countenance bursting with happiness, impervious to the comments regarding her paternity.

Bella had spent a lot of time with her father, swimming, collecting shells along the beach, and chatting as disjointedly as only she knew how, jumping from one topic to another. She treasured those moments with him, for he treated her with consideration and listened attentively to her grouses while at the same time playing with her like the doting father that he was. He played ball with her and taught her to dive and float as lightly as a leaf. All the while, she was still worried about being left alone with her mother again. Though she adored her mother, she wanted her father to remain, for, to her mind, he was their anchor.

"Daddy," she said while they were sitting on her mother's rock, her elfin face puckered with a tiny frown, "you're not leaving us again after the wedding?"

"What made you say that, Bella? Of course I will not leave you and Mummy. You both are the most precious people in my life. Wherever I go, you two will be with me," he assured her.

She looked at him thoughtfully. "Daddy, I grew up without you for a long time. Why did you leave us? Is it because you didn't love us then?"

Her questions startled him. A puzzled expression flitted across his face. He flushed in confusion, overwhelmed with a spasm of guilt and embarrassment. He had never, beyond any stretch of his imagination, ever considered that his little girl would ponder over his relationship with her mother and query him over that period in their lives. He stared gravely at her for some time with extreme concern, his mind swirling with contradictory thoughts. If he didn't satisfy her with a plausible answer, it would still create doubts in her mind. Yet how was he to explain to her? How did Kat handle that question? Obviously, her answer didn't satisfy their daughter's curiosity.

He racked his brain for a considerable time to find an answer that would make sense to her. He realized that it would be the first of the many questions he would have to answer as her father, as he guided her through the labyrinth of her life.

"Bella, never ever think that I don't love you or Mummy," he began. "I fell in love with Mummy the first time I set eyes on her." With much drama and laughter, he told her about the first time Kat came flying around the corner at campus and careened into his arms.

She giggled uncontrollably as a picture of her mother emerged before her eyes, running in her high-heeled boots, her hair flying wildly in the wind, panting like a prized stallion that had gone astray. Her eyes danced with merriment.

"It's not like Mummy at all, Daddy," she said after her laughter subsided. "Mummy doesn't run around like that. She's sedate and dignified, like a queen," she ventured. "Papa used to call Mummy his queen."

"I see what you mean, darling. She's a true blue lady, the way she walks, the way she talks," he agreed readily, his smile broadening. The unsolicited information regarding her late husband's nickname for Kat almost derailed him with jealousy. He quickly suppressed it. He realized how much more attractive Kat had become since they'd parted ways.

"This was ten years ago, Bella. Mummy was much younger then, and she was full of fun and laughter," he calmly informed his daughter, without referring to her late stepfather.

"We were very happy together, Mummy and I," he recalled, "until I began hurting her with my nasty comments and selfish behaviour. I realized that I needed to find ways to put a stop to what I was doing to Mummy. That's why I let Mummy go." He made no bones about his own part in the unhealthy relationship with Kat and how he decided to leave before the hurt became unbearable for her. "I left without knowing that Mummy was carrying you," he confessed. "I'm sorry, baby."

"I'm sorry too, Daddy," she responded. "Mummy must have been lonely without you."

"Mummy is a very strong woman. She is disciplined too. Make no mistakes about that. Your grandparents took care of you with so much love and devotion, for which I'll always be grateful." He hugged her affectionately.

"One day you and I and Mummy, and maybe Gramps and Grandma, will visit all those places that I visited in the years when I was away, some kind of a family adventure. Would you like that?" he asked.

"Do you think that you'll be angry with me and Mummy ever again?" she questioned him without responding to his offer.

"Of course there'll be times when Daddy gets upset, the way you get unhappy over something." He tried to be realistic. "But I will never hurt you or Mummy, for I have changed. It's like being totally cured of a disease that will never recur. You understand, sweetheart?" He prayed that he had addressed the issue to her satisfaction.

"I think I do, Daddy," she said. She threw her arms around him and hugged him. "I love you," she cried with ebullience, three precious words that he treasured. He fought back tears as he hugged her back.

"There you are, you two." Her mother finally joined them. "What have you been talking about?" she enquired as she sat close to them, a packet of *keropok* in her hand, which she offered to them.

"This and that," Josh offered with a wink. "Are we packed and ready to return to KL, love?"

The wedding had been set for the following Sunday. Suraya and George had left earlier to see to the preparations, leaving the young family together to bond. They would need at least a few days to get the house ready for the function.

"Mummy," Bella intervened, making a grab for several pieces of the crackers, "don't forget my bridesmaid dress! You haven't seen my dress, Daddy." She began devouring the crunchy fish crackers. "Grandma says it makes me look like a princess," she added.

"I'm sure you'll look fabulous, darling," he replied. "Always remember, Bella, you are Daddy's princess, even when you're not dressed like one."

***

The house that George built for his wife was a monument of his love for her and his penchant for gracious living. Set in the midst of an acre of green leafy trees and dappled lawns, it looked spectacular once it was decorated with multicoloured lights that transformed the house into a fairy-tale mansion.

The wedding dinner was held indoors, with soft, dreamy melodies infused with love and romance, playing softly in the background. The main lounge was enlarged, the folding doors opened to unite it with the dining room. Tables for dining were arranged to cater for two hundred guests. The white marble floors gleamed enticingly. A massive dome of stained glass defined the centre of the lounge. Ornate cornices enhanced the edges of the wide ceiling. The grand marble staircase descended into the main lobby, supported on either side by two elegant Roman columns reaching up to the twenty-foot-high ceiling. Its grandeur was enhanced with a tasteful arrangement of fresh roses and ferns. The hall became a veritable Garden of Eden.

The *imam* had married the couple earlier in the day. Josh had even performed the thanksgiving prayer that he elected to carry out, even though it was not compulsory. It made him feel whole and ready to embrace his new role as a family man and a Muslim. He had pronounced the *akad* in the Malay language with such proficiency and enthusiasm that his pronouncements were accepted after his first attempt. He had practised with unending patience with his daughter, who would at times burst into helpless laughter as he tried to pronounce the words in his thick, heavy accent.

At eight o'clock that Sunday night, the newly-weds descended the stairs in their resplendent traditional costumes, accompanied by music of the quartet that played traditional songs celebrating their union. He stole a glance at his bride, who was on his arm. She was a picture of radiance. Bella and her brother followed behind them, each carrying the traditional fans.

When they were seated at the main table, the children took their seats. George started the ball rolling with a speech welcoming the groom into his family. Josh's best friend followed up with the history of the couple's relationship, the parts that were irrelevant duly omitted. Dinner consisted of an array of delicious Malay cuisine that was enjoyed by the guests with gusto. Josh was so keyed up that he ate very little. Kat didn't seem to have much appetite either.

It was a bittersweet experience for Josh. It was a completely alien feeling for him to be feted and entertained on this, the most important day of his life. He had no relatives to speak of, just a group of friends from his office in London, who opted to celebrate the day with him. He looked around him, a fixed smile on his face. The guests were enjoying their dinner, with Brahms's concerto providing an atmosphere of splendour and conviviality. He turned towards Kat, who was speaking quietly to George's VIP guest at the main table. His eyes strayed towards his daughter, who was chatting animatedly with some of their guests, who were probably congratulating her on her splendid performance that she dedicated to her father. A sweet sense of belonging and pride spread through every fibre of his being.

People stayed back to congratulate, to chat, and to get to know the couple, most notably the groom, he being a foreigner to them. He was relieved when the last of the guests left. By then, it was past midnight. George and Suraya bade them good night as they tactfully shepherded their grandchildren off to bed, leaving Kat and Josh for the first time alone together, as husband and wife.

He welcomed the respite because it enabled him to feast his eyes on his wife without intrusion. *How stunning she is,* he thought, *and she is mine.* Without another word, he picked her up easily and carried her up the stairs to the bridal chamber which had been prepared by his mother-in-law and her friends in complete secrecy. Neither he nor his wife had been allowed to enter until then.

They should not have troubled for all the attention paid by the lovers. The cool ambience, the outstanding decor, and the expense thrown into its preparation had no relevance for them. They had eyes for nothing else but each other, as they gave vent to their longing and need for one another, which had been denied for so long. Words were unnecessary, as their passion and yearning for each other, transported them to a world of unbridled sensations and intense capitulation.

Late afternoon the next day, the newly-weds still had not emerged from the bedroom. He woke up first. For a moment, he couldn't figure out where he was. A feeling of deep contentment and well-being flooded him. He stretched languidly. The bed was exceptionally comfortable. The aroma of roses pervaded the room. The air conditioning was droning softly. The curtains were drawn and a thin ray of sunlight filtered through the aperture of the high window, like a shy young virgin. *Kat!* his heart sang.

He turned towards her and lifted himself on an elbow, delighting in the precious minutes of untrammelled pleasure of just looking at her and relishing the sheer perfection of her beauty.

She opened her eyes abruptly and stared directly into those blue eyes that had haunted her for years. She smiled. He smiled back. She stretched seductively and was immediately drawn into his all- encompassing embrace. They remained locked together, like two jungle nymphs, that loathed to let go of each other. When all energy was spent and needs that had been subdued for a long time were momentarily satisfied, words were needed to be said and feelings needed to be expressed.

"I love you, Kat. I could never say it enough." His voice trembled from his chest. "I appreciate everything about you: your beauty, your intelligence, your strength, your gentleness." He grabbed her hand that was gently caressing his cheek. "We've been on a long, long journey together and at times separately." He smiled as he stared deep into her eyes. "If anything, it has made our love stronger." He shook his head as he continued. "I'm never going to blow my chances and lose you again."

"You're never going to lose me, Josh." She nibbled at his ear. "I'll never let you," she vowed. "Whatever problems we encounter, we'll solve them together," she promised.

Ten months later, the stork brought a healthy, happy bouncing Ibrahim "Benny" Reynolds into their lives. The family that Josh had dreamed of all his life finally became complete.

# GLOSSARY

### A

| | |
|---|---|
| **abang (bang)** | Older brother; some wives use the term to address their husbands. |
| **akad** | Marriage declaration by groom. |
| **Allahu Akbar** | Allah is great. |
| **Alhamdulillah** | Thanks to Allah. |

### B

| | |
|---|---|
| **baju** | Dress. B*aju Kedah* or *baju Johor/baju kurung* distinguishes the fashion of each particular state. |
| **batek lepas** | A 1.8-metre piece of batek-designed material fashionable during the period, worn wrapped around the waist. |
| **betul** | True, right. |
| **budu** | Fish sauce made from anchovies, a specialty of the east coast states. |
| **bidan** | Midwife. |
| **bomoh** | Traditional healer. |

### C

| | |
|---|---|
| **cempaka** | Magnolia tree with sweet-smelling flowers of various shades. |
| **cengal** | Heavy hardwood, used for outdoor constructions. |

### D

| | |
|---|---|
| **doa** | Prayers. |

## G

| | |
|---|---|
| **gadis** | Young girl. |
| **gadis pingitan** | Young and virtuous girl, well protected by her family. |
| **gado-gado** | Boiled mixed vegetable salad with peanut sauce. |
| **ganyang** | Destroy. |

## H

| | |
|---|---|
| **habislah** | That's it—we're done for. |
| **hantaran** | Bridal gift. |

## I

| | |
|---|---|
| **iddah** | Stipulated mourning period for widows (four months and ten days). |
| **iftar** | Breaking of fast (at sunset). |
| **Isyak** | Evening prayer, the fifth for the day. |
| **Imam** | The one who leads prayers. |
| **insya Allah** | By the grace of God. |

## J

| | |
|---|---|
| **Jalur Gemilang** | "Stripes of Glory": The National Flag. |
| **jodoh** | Predestined (as in marriage partners). |

## K

| | |
|---|---|
| **kain pelikat** | Cotton sarong made in India. |
| **kampung** | Village. |
| **kan** | Isn't it? |
| **kasihan** | Pity. |
| **kawasan** | Area. |
| **kedondong** | Trees generally found in the wilds or by the riverside, bearing green oval-shaped fruits, sour to the taste. |
| **kueh** | Traditional cakes. |

| | |
|---|---|
| **kenduri** | Feast. |
| **kenanga** | Flowering tree with lime-green sweet-smelling flowers. |
| **kepala** | Leader, head of group. |
| **keropok** | A savoury snack of fish chips. |
| **keruing** | Medium hardwood trees, light red to dark brown in colour, used to make furniture, beams, and rafters. |
| **khat** | Arabic script. |
| **khatam** | Completion of the thirty chapters of the Qur'an. |

**L**

| | |
|---|---|
| **laksa** | White noodles made from rice floor. |
| **lauk pauk** | Dishes served with rice. |

**M**

| | |
|---|---|
| **mak** | Short for emak (mother) \| elderly woman. |
| **mak andam** | The woman who prepares the bride for her wedding. |
| **mak bidan** | The midwife. |
| **mengkuang** | Screw pine. |
| **merdeka** | Independence. |
| **muhrim** | Very close relative, not eligible for marriage. |

**N**

| | |
|---|---|
| **nasi lemak** | Rice cooked in coconut milk. |

**O**

| | |
|---|---|
| **Orang Asli** | Aboriginal tribe. |
| **Orang Bunian** | Invisible community of human look-alikes, believed to inhabit the jungles and hills. |

**P**

| | |
|---|---|
| **padang** | Field. |

| | |
|---|---|
| **Pak Su** | A term of address for the youngest uncle. |
| **pawang** | Medicine man, usually known to have the powers of the occult. |
| **penunggu** | Spirit that's supposed to guard a certain place. |
| **pelita** | Kerosene lamp. |
| **Pondok** | A commune for the elderly who study religion under an imam or religious teacher. |
| **puan** | Ma'am. |
| **pulut udang** | Glutinous rice rolled in banana leaf, with fillings made of coconut and prawn sambal. |

**R**

| | |
|---|---|
| **rakyat** | Citizen. |
| **Ramadhan** | The ninth month in the Muslim calendar—the fasting month. |

**S**

| | |
|---|---|
| **sanggul lintang** | A hairstyle where the hair is folded in the shape of a ribbon on the nape of the neck. |
| **sahur** | The last meal in early morning before fasting starts. |
| **salam** | To offer both hands in greeting. |
| **sambal** | A blended mixture of chillies, onions, and prawn paste. |
| **sayang** | Love. |
| **songket** | Fabric designed with golden threads. |
| **subuh** | First prayer for the day at the first light of dawn. |
| **surah** | Chapter/verse in the Qur'an. |
| **syaer** | Poetry which tells a story, each verse containing four lines. |
| **Syahadah** | The confession of faith. |
| **syariah** | Islamic jurisprudence. |

## T

| | |
|---|---|
| **telekung** | Robe worn by women during prayers. |
| **tepung talam** | Two-layer steamed cake made of rice flour and coconut milk. |
| **tok ayah** | Great-grandfather. |
| **tongkat** | Walking stick. |
| **tongkang** | Barge/vessel to transport heavy goods. |
| **tuan** | Mister, sir. |

## U

| | |
|---|---|
| **umrah** | Short pilgrimage to Mecca. |
| **ustaz** | Mister, a term of address for religious teachers. |

CPSIA information can be obtained
at www.ICGtesting.com
Printed in the USA
BVHW07s2110070818
523863BV00002B/153/P